Shadow of Death

Shadow of Death

ALISON JOSEPH

First published in Great Britain in 2007 by
Allison & Busby Limited
13 Charlotte Mews
London W1T 4EJ
www.allisonandbusby.com

Copyright © 2007 by ALISON JOSEPH

The moral right of the author has been asserted.

A CIP catalogue record for this book is available from the British Library.

10 9 8 7 6 5 4 3 2 1

ISBN 0 7490 8191 0
978-0-7490-8191-1

Typeset in 11/16 pt Sabon by
Terry Shannon

Printed and bound in Wales by
Creative Print and Design, Ebbw Vale

ALISON JOSEPH was born in North London and educated at Leeds University. After graduating she worked as a presenter on a local radio station then, moving back to London, for Channel 4. She later became a partner in an independent production company and one of its commissions was a series presented by Helen Mirren about women and religion. Alison also writes original radio drama and has adapted novels for BBC Radio 4, including the award-winning production of *Captain Corelli's Mandolin*. She has also published various short stories. Alison lives in London with her husband and three children.

For Nat, Wilf and Edie

PROLOGUE

'...For only God can know my heart, my true thoughts, and tho' I, Alice Hawker, commit them to the page, here in this my book, yet without His light they are as nought. The past weighs heavy upon me, yet have I breathed no word of this to a soul, nay not even to my own husband, tho' heaven knows my prattle is of little interest to him. And apart from the Lord himself, 'tis only my little one who shares my prayers, my hopes, my dear Jonjo, for in truth my boy is the light of my life. Since we came here, I have found the burden of being mistress of Collyer to be a dead weight. I know the servants think nothing of my word, the hearths go unpolished, the milk unchurned and yet when Nicolas returns, then they jump to't as if their very lives depend on't...'

The next page was blank. Agnes found she was peering at it under the light from her bedside lamp, as if the paper itself might reveal further secrets. Across the river, she heard a bell toll midnight. She closed the old leather covers and put the book down carefully on the small table by her bed. It would be a shame, she thought, to mislay one of the few truly valuable books in the order's collection at this late stage of the library move.

She wandered down the landing to the bathroom to brush

her teeth. Her reflection stared back at her. She thought she was looking pale, although perhaps that was just the dim light; she ran a comb through her hair, which was short and brown with traces of grey. She hurried back to her room, lay down on her pillows and yawned. Beyond the ill-fitting window the traffic seemed to quieten and slow, and even the rattle of trains from London Bridge was muted with the night.

She wondered if Sister Helena had gone to bed. The thought was irritating. She knew it was her own failing, to resent feeling responsible for anyone, but Sister Helena was a difficult housemate; silent, well-mannered and utterly private. For years Agnes had lived alone, in dread of the privilege being removed, but had felt unable to argue when her superior, Sister Christiane, had said that it would be easier for everyone if she relinquished her own flat and lived in Collyer House with Sister Helena during the moving process, particularly when it was such a complicated sale, and Helena only being a novice, and anyway, a visiting Abbot from Normandy needed the flat for a year.

Agnes hated the house. And it hated her. It seemed to creak and sway; the heating, when it worked, made muffled rhythmic noises. Sometimes she thought she heard footsteps, or a sound like sobbing. Yesterday she'd been on the point of asking Helena if she'd heard it too, but Helena was sitting there, straight-backed and polite, her pale hair scraped back into a thin tail as she picked at a tiny serving of tinned tuna fish, and Agnes had begun to wonder whether, if there was sobbing in the house at night, Helena wasn't the source of it.

Agnes pulled the covers over her against the chill of the room. It wasn't as if the house was even that old. There had been a dwelling on this site in the early seventeenth century, but at some point the property had been donated to a religious order, who had then knocked it down and rebuilt it. The existing building, a shabby and sprawling example of Victorian gothic, had served as an asylum during the nineteenth century. Agnes thought about the waifs and strays, the fallen women and the downright mad, stumbling across the Thames, to be forgotten in the dim marshlands of the south as the rest of London turned its back. Gradually the order had shrunk and the state had expanded, and now most of the building was used by the local NHS Trust as a day-centre for people with mental illness. The sisters kept one wing, where for reasons lost to living memory they housed their library, a sprawling collection of theological texts, mostly using mawkish and sentimental examples from the saints to preach unquestioning obedience, as Agnes had remarked to Shirley the librarian only the other day. Shirley had almost smiled, but had then gone on to point out that the Hawker Bequest was a wonderful collection of rare non-conformist texts and that the order was to be congratulated for handing it over to the nation. After a pause she'd repeated the word 'mawkish', as if to herself, two or three times.

Agnes sighed, rolled over and turned off the lamp. The lights from passing cars flickered on the ceiling.

There was a quiet thump from the corridor, a pad-padding that seemed to pass her room. Agnes lay on her back, staring at the shadows. It must be Helena, she thought.

And then, there it was again, the sound of crying. Agnes heard her heart beat in her ears and began to feel cross. It's thoughtless of her, she thought, all this creeping around at night. It's just as well I don't believe in ghosts, but she could terrify someone of a more nervous disposition.

Again, the sobbing. Agnes tried to match the sound to Helena, a woman of thirty or so, but something didn't quite fit. It sounded more like a child.

Agnes sat up. The floorboards creaked loudly outside her room. She got out of bed, and put on her slippers. Enough is enough, she thought.

She went to the door and opened it, and stared out into the corridor, listening. Now there was a hush; only the cold, damp smell, the dim lightbulb swinging slightly in the draught. Then, a movement at the end of the landing, by the stairs. Agnes took a step towards it. 'Helena?' she called, her voice too loud.

There was something there, and as she approached it gained definition; an animal, she thought, a tail lashing in the darkness, angular ears and jaw. It looked like a dog; a black dog, but as she got nearer there was the crying again, so close that she looked around for its source, expecting to see a child, a baby, perhaps; the cry now a distressed, urgent wail and Agnes wondering what to do with a child in need and a nasty-looking dog and realising that she was in fact scared; very scared indeed.

And then there was silence.

She thought perhaps she'd screamed or cried out.

Downstairs she heard a door open. 'Helena?' she said, and her voice sounded calm and normal, as if there had never been a dog or a baby crying or the lamp swaying on the landing.

'Agnes?' came Helena's voice, as she appeared at the top of the stairs. 'I was just going to bed.'

'Yes,' Agnes said. 'Me too.'

Helena smiled. 'Good night, then.' She turned the handle of her door. 'There's early chapel at the community house tomorrow.'

'So there is,' Agnes said.

'Perhaps I'll see you there.' Helena went into her room and shut the door behind her.

Agnes looked up and down the empty, silent corridor. Then she walked slowly back to her room. She sat on her bed and stared at her shaking legs with interest.

Yes, she thought. It's just as well I don't believe in ghosts.

CHAPTER ONE

'I was supposed to be at early chapel,' Agnes said to Father Julius, accepting the cup of coffee that he handed to her. 'But then they asked me to attend this meeting instead. Apparently you're going too.'

'Yes,' he said. 'It'll be very dull. It's a question of months, if not weeks, before the whole site is sold and both us and the NHS move out altogether.'

He sat down opposite her, a heavy out-breath reminding her that he had become older and more frail. She thought of all the time she'd known him, all the years that she had sat here in this room, the shabby space at the back of his church that passed for his office. The morning sun filtered through the leaded window behind him, brightening the old wood panelling and the worn, red velvet chairs. His head was bent as he leafed through his diary, his white hair so soft that she almost reached out to touch it. She remembered the black dog of the night before, and thought that Julius was so quiet, so peaceful, he would never bring such a creature into being.

He looked up, a smile in his blue eyes. 'What are you thinking about?' he said.

She shook her head.

'More milk? Less milk? Usually when you go all quiet it's

because I've made a mistake with your coffee.'

'I was wondering whether people who see ghosts are somehow responsible for them. I was thinking you were the sort of person who would never see a ghost.'

He frowned. 'Oh, but I have. I think. Once, perhaps. A long time ago. In France.'

'That was years ago. When you were a young priest. When you rescued me.'

'You rescued yourself,' Julius said. 'You'd been sold into slavery, only your parents called it marriage. You'd have run away from your husband's violence even if I hadn't been there to help.'

'If you hadn't been there – I'd have been killed,' Agnes said, and the conversation seemed to be at an end. She sipped her coffee. 'I can't imagine you saw a ghost. Perhaps it was an angel,' she said.

'Assuming that our Lord only sends his messengers when there's something really important to say, I'd rather put that off as long as possible.'

She laughed. 'We ought to go in a minute. Although why you have to be there too, I've no idea.'

'Reasons of history, Agnes. That site of yours, it's still technically part of my parish. It'll be fine, we'll leave it to Philip to do all the talking, he likes that kind of thing.'

'It's easy for him. He's the psychiatrist. He's just got to sort out somewhere else for his patients.'

'And they're easier than books?'

She sighed. 'Oh, the books. I'd like to give them all to a charity shop. But Shirley has to do things properly, write them all down. The decent stuff has been sent to the main house now, it just leaves all the horrible old things about poor young women of great spiritual purity being tested. That and the Bequest, which is under lock and key apart from the odd bits I steal to read.'

Julius looked up. 'The Hawker Bequest?'

She nodded. 'From the original family. The ones who first lived in the house. We're giving it to the nation, but we have to know what's there first.'

Julius picked up a biro and considered it. 'I hope you lot have looked after it.'

'It's in very good nick, actually. But Sister Christiane has had the sense to see that it's more use to a national archive than it is to a small band of nuns. She's got some museum library in Oxford interested.'

'Good for her.' He stood up. 'Come on, let's go and talk about land value and the re-distribution of personnel.'

The glass doors of the clinic swished with sunlight. Inside there was noise, a trolley going past, a buzz of conversation from the tea bar in the foyer, the reception nurse calling for a patient, a porter teasing her – 'Your name means happiness, Beatrice does, so why you frowning, eh?' A woman, shouting.

'—You dare to say that to me? As God is my witness, He sees my suffering. He knows the truth...'

Julius and Agnes walked into the foyer. As the woman's voice gained volume, a hush spread around her. Philip was cornered by his office door, his tall frame in its dark suit backed against the wall. The woman faced him, her long black curls shook as she jabbed her finger towards him. Her other arm was weighed down by a small child, who clung around her neck, pink wellington boots swinging, a teddy bear clutched in the other hand.

'Do you think I need you to tell me what the matter is? You only have the words of a man, but I have the words of the Lord himself, and the Lord sees into my soul. The Lord gives me words of comfort because he knows that it is through my suffering that I will find salvation...'

Julius glanced at Agnes, then took a step towards the woman. 'Tina—' he began, but she was still shouting at Philip.

'...Yea, though I walk through the valley of the shadow of death... Thy rod and Thy staff they comfort me. You think salvation lies in a bottle of medicine? I tell you, our Lord too was tempted by Satan with his false promises. Your pills won't change nothing.'

The child on her hip began to whimper. She wrapped both arms around her, and took a step back from Philip, who stood blinking behind his glasses.

'Tina-Marie—' Julius tried again, and this time she heard him.

'Father.' She managed a weak smile. 'The man calls himself a doctor.' She pointed a thumb behind her as she came towards Julius and Agnes.

'I haven't seen you for a while, Tina-Marie,' Julius said.

'I have been troubled, Father,' she said. She turned her face to him, and the light caught her caramel skin, her sculpted cheekbones.

The hush in the reception area gave way to everyday hubbub as the tension receded. Philip smoothed down his suit, which Agnes noticed was rather expensively cut. He had angular black hair, flecked with grey, which he patted back into place as he addressed Julius.

'You know each other,' he said, then went on, 'She attacked one of the patients.' He had a deep, resonating voice. Some of the people at the tea-bar glanced in his direction.

'Old Francis,' Tina-Marie said to Julius. 'Look, he's still there. And I didn't attack him, I was defending myself.'

In the corner of the foyer a man sat hunched, a rough shock of white hair, uneven stubble on his chin, gaps where his teeth should be as he smiled in greeting, and mumbled something.

'Francis.' Julius turned to the man. 'Still here, then.'

'Aye, Father.' He raised a hand. 'Still here. With Heaven watching over me, and the Black Dog at me feet.'

Tina-Marie uttered a cry, one hand over her mouth. 'See? He's doing it again. I told him to stop, I was begging him, see, and next thing I knew the man there was trying to sedate me.'

'I was not trying to—' Philip began, but Francis was speaking.

'And what is there in Heaven to frighten you?'

Tina-Marie took a step towards him. Her voice was shaking. 'As God is my witness, you bring that Dog in here you never get rid of it.'

The child in her arms began to cry. Julius put his hand on the young woman's elbow and ushered her into a chair and sat down next to her. Her dark eyes softened as she listened to him. Her face relaxed and she gathered the bright fabric of her skirt around her legs. Agnes watched her grow calm, watched her hold her child close. Francis stood up. He looked at Philip for a moment and shook his head, as if he was burdened by a great sorrow too tragic to impart. Then he shuffled away.

Julius was still talking to Tina-Marie, and now he looked

up at Philip. 'Perhaps we could have some tea?' he suggested.

Philip gazed down at him. 'Tea?' he said in surprise. He looked around. 'Perhaps Beatrice...'

Tina-Marie stood up. The child stumbled to her feet. 'No,' she said. 'Not for me. He's waiting for me, he is. There'll be trouble if I ain't there.'

Julius touched his hand briefly on her arm. 'You know where to find me,' he said. Her eyes rested on him for a moment, then she turned to go, clutching the little girl's hand. Her long skirt swung at her legs as the glass doors closed behind her.

'Well, I'd like some tea,' Julius said.

Philip looked around, as if waiting for some to appear.

'Look, there's hardly any queue,' Agnes said, indicating the counter.

'I may not have any...' his hands went to his pockets.

Agnes handed him some coins and patted his elbow. They watched him join the queue.

'I've never seen her at your church,' Agnes said to him.

'She turns up at odd times these days.'

'How come she's here?'

Julius stared at the floor. 'It was the best I could do at the time. She needs to be looked after.' He glanced at Agnes. 'Are you all right?'

'Me? Yes, of course. Just not looking forward to two hours of administration.'

'You seem pale,' Julius began, but then Philip appeared with three mugs of tea balanced on a tray. He put the tray down on the low table, very slowly.

'Sugar?' he asked.

Agnes looked at him. 'No thanks,' she replied.

He sat down next to Julius. 'What was all that about?' he said.

Julius stirred a large spoonful of sugar into his tea. 'She's a very troubled person.'

'I could see that,' Philip said. He looked towards the clinic doors. 'She's very beautiful, isn't she? Extraordinary combination of looks – that dark skin, that long hair...'

'Being beautiful has done her no favours in life,' Julius said.

'She went for poor old Francis,' Philip went on. 'It was lucky I was nearby. And as for accusing me of trying to sedate her... I've only met her once before, she's not a regular. And what was all that about a dog?'

Agnes stood up. 'Hadn't we better go to this meeting?' she said.

'Oh God, the meeting,' Philip said. 'I wish they'd just move us out somewhere, instead of all these bloody meetings. They'll be showing us lovely designs for the expensive flats they're going to build on the site. Again. If they're going to have all this consultation, they could at least have asked us first.'

For the first time, Agnes smiled at him.

'Change management,' Philip boomed, walking down the corridor an hour later. He was wearing a badge which said 'Dr Philip Sayer'. 'Change management indeed. When it's all so bloody simple.' They reached the foyer and he turned to Agnes. 'We're camping out in a crumbling building. The value of the land has shot up, the NHS can sell it for a fortune, everyone gets luxury flats – and me and my poor patients go and camp out in some other crumbling building belonging to the NHS until they sell that off too.'

'My order owns part of this crumbling building,' Agnes said.

'Well, then, they get their share too.' Philip looked down at her. 'I assume they're not too holy for that?'

Agnes met his gaze. 'All holiness is compromised by being in the world,' she said.

'Ah. Yes.' He frowned at her, as if searching for a reply, then glanced along the corridor. 'Here's Julius. Shall we get some lunch? I rather fancy a mozzarella sandwich at that little place across the road.'

They settled in a corner of the cafe. Agnes wrapped her hands around her mug of cappuccino. 'At least the coffee's OK here,' she said. 'Rather than that stuff that English people drink.'

'Are you not English then?' Philip studied her.

'My mother was French,' she replied. 'I spent my childhood in France.'

Julius looked up from stirring sugar into his cup. 'She's just showing off. She's lived here for years.'

She flashed him a look, then concentrated on spooning foam around her coffee. 'I ought to get to the library,' she said. 'I'm playing truant really. This book man is coming in tomorrow and we've got to have everything listed for him.'

'I thought you had a librarian?' Julius cut his remaining sandwich into quarters and began to eat one.

'Oh, Shirley's very sweet, but I've been given the job of helping her.'

Julius smiled at Philip. 'Agnes's order has allowed her to

run amok for years. They've let her work with homeless young people, or addicts, or people like our clients; and now she's taken final vows they think it's time she does as she's told.'

'It's a test of my obedience, to put me in a creepy house and give me boxfuls of books to sort out, most of which are Lives of The Great Saints.' Agnes removed slices of tomato from the last of her sandwich.

'Is it creepy?' Philip considered the tomato slices. 'Our side of the building would be quite pleasant, if anyone had ever looked after it.'

'Well—' Agnes tried a smile. 'Last night I thought I saw a ghost.' She was aware of Julius's questioning glance.

'Really? A ghost?' Philip looked up from his empty plate.

'Some kind of animal…a dog…' Her voice faded. 'It was probably nothing. There's a cat that comes in sometimes, Helena adores it, it might have been her, although she's tabby and this was…' In the bright light and cafe noise, the sensations of the night before seemed far away.

'Surely your tradition doesn't include the possibility of ghosts?' Philip looked from Agnes to Julius.

'Our tradition,' Julius said, 'has many ways of speaking about disturbances of the human soul. It's true that some are more metaphorical than others. Just as in your field.'

Philip gathered his jacket around him. 'When I took this job, with its connections with your church, I was worried that there would be difficulties in the meeting of two such disparate paradigms. I didn't for one moment foresee that we'd be arguing about the existence of ghosts.' Agnes glanced at him as he stood up. He appeared to be serious.

They left the cafe, Philip striding ahead, Agnes and Julius trailing behind.

'Oh dear,' Agnes said, her voice part-drowned by the rumble of traffic. 'Now look what I've done.'

'I mean, at least if he was a Jungian we'd have had some common ground.' Julius took her arm, and once again Agnes was reminded of his frailty.

'It's not as if you really believe in ghosts any more than I do,' Agnes said.

'There have been sightings, in your building.'

Ahead of them, Philip went into the clinic.

Agnes stared at him. 'Tell me,' she said.

'One of my parishioners. Visiting there, when more of your sisters were living there. About ten years ago, maybe twelve... She swore she saw a woman, holding a baby. Seventeenth century dress, her hair pinned up, white puritan collar.'

Agnes unlinked her arm from his. 'But Julius – we don't – we can't possibly believe...'

'As I said, our tradition has various ways of discussing disturbances of the soul. It would be a shame to limit any available metaphors by grasping at certainties, wouldn't it?'

She smiled up at him.

'Look—' he pointed at a low red-brick wall that ran alongside the clinic building. The bricks were small, and many were crumbled and broken. 'That's original, apparently. Seventeenth century. All that's left. And now,' he said, looking towards the clinic, 'I'd better catch up with Philip and try and prove to him that we Jesuits really are God's intellectuals and that you and I are not the superstitious light-weights that he probably takes us for.'

'And how are we going to do that?' They walked together up the clinic drive.

'Oh, I don't know.' Julius glanced down at her. 'Shall we try quoting the medieval mystics? That often works.'

'I'm not sure it'll work on him,' Agnes said, as the clinic doors closed behind them.

Beatrice was at her desk. She beckoned to Julius, then pointed into the corner. Tina-Marie was sitting there, alone. She looked up as Julius and Agnes approached.

'O – Father...' She glanced around, as if looking for someone.

'I thought you had gone home,' Julius said.

'He was there. I didn't go in. I went round to Danielle, she's my mate. I left Leila with her, she's happy there.'

'Who was there?' Julius was frowning with concern.

'Troy. He's not good at the moment, Danielle says I should leave him, but he'd only come for me, I know that.'

'Isn't that more reason to leave him?' Agnes asked.

Tina-Marie looked at her, considered her, then said, 'You're one of them nuns, aren't you? I'm not being funny or anything, but what do you know about it?'

'I was married to a man who nearly killed me. Apart from that, nothing at all.'

Tina-Marie's eyes narrowed. 'Then you'll know how hard it is to leave.' She turned back to Julius. 'It's my little girl I'm scared for. I'm scared he'll go for her too.'

'But a child—' Julius began.

'No.' She shook her head. 'Makes no difference to him. Last night he said, if we could live without that bastard child, that's what he called her, then he and I would be happy.'

'She's not his child, then?' Agnes said.

Tina-Marie shook her head.

'There are refuges,' Agnes said. 'There are places you could go.'

'You don't know Troy. He'd find me.' She gripped Julius's arm. 'Last night, I saw it again, the Black Dog, it was out in the street, just looking up at my window with its yellow eyes. I know that something bad is going to happen, Father.'

A cold draught blew through the reception area as the clinic doors opened and closed again.

'Agnes is right,' Julius said. 'We'll find you somewhere else to live. You can't stay with a man like Troy.'

'When I left that church, when I came back here, I thought he'd look after me.' Tina-Marie pushed black ringlets away from her face. 'I was so wrong. I pray for him, you know, I pray he might change…' Her face tightened, her gaze fixed on something beyond them, her eyes wide with fear. Agnes heard footsteps behind her.

'I thought I'd find you here.' A man approached them and stopped right in front of Tina-Marie. He looked awkward, fresh-faced, shaven-headed, staring down at her with pale narrow-set eyes. He was wearing a sharply cut suit and his thick fingers were encircled with rings.

Beatrice appeared behind him. 'You can't come in here and frighten our patients.' She reached out an arm to his shoulder, but he brushed her away.

Tina-Marie got up from her chair. She stood, hunched, in front of him. He turned and left the clinic, and she followed him.

Julius looked up at Beatrice. 'Can you find me the number

of her social worker? It'll be on her file. We must get her re-housed.'

Agnes patted his arm. 'I'd better go. Shirley's expecting me.'

Shirley thumped a pile of books down on the desk. A cloud of dust rose up towards the high rafters, filtering in gentle stripes through the thin sunlight. 'Sister Lucia wants the Saints all in a pile in case there are any to throw out.' She glanced uncertainly at Agnes, fiddling with a stray wisp of grey hair that had fallen from the tight bun at the back of her head.

'I'm not sure it's up to Lucia to go throwing out Saints,' Agnes said.

Shirley threw her a quick frowning glance. She put her hands into the pockets of her sensible grey cardigan. 'Well, she won't have room to house them in the Hackney house, that's for sure. And I told her, the sooner she can clear this building the better – I'm sure someone tried to break in last night, the lock was all jammed when I tried to get in, I had to get that nice doctor from next door to unjam it.'

'What needs doing?' Agnes settled at the other desk.

'We need to write down all the titles so this book dealer man knows what there is.'

'What about the Hawker Bequest?'

Shirley glanced across at the corner cabinet, at the ancient leather spines stacked inside it. 'Your Sister Christiane said that's all dealt with, although these museum people are rather dragging their feet. But if you ask me, this Mr Harris is after it too. He kept questioning me about it on the phone, did I think it was complete? I said, Mr Harris, how can we know if it's complete, we have nothing to compare it with.'

'When's he coming in?'

'Tomorrow morning. I hope he's not too early, I'm supposed to take Mother to the doctor about her veins, you know what the queues are like these days with the NHS.' She glanced at her watch. 'And I'm going to have to leave early today, Mother said she fancied a bit of fish for supper.'

The windows of the library had deepened to twilight. Agnes sat alone under one of the lamps. She picked up a book and read the spine and put it down again. Then she opened a drawer, took out a key and went over to the glass-fronted cabinet. She scanned the titles, the soft leather spines tooled with gold lettering. Some were blank, and seemed to be hand-written rather than printed. She pulled one out, in the hope of finding more of Alice Hawker's diaries. It seemed to be a list of numbers, prices, sums of money. 'Jan 14th. Saddle, bridle, new bit...' she read. 'Jan 15th. Took delivery of three bags of strong flour...' There were some pages at the end in Alice's handwriting. She put the book on one side.

Another title caught her eye. It was a printed book: 'A treatise on the uses of rods for purposes of divination.' Another book was called 'Discoveries.' A piece of paper marked one page, and Agnes began to read. '...certain words shall be written in a piece of bread which is then given to dogs bitten with a mad dog, thereby to keep them from it...' On the scrap of paper, Agnes saw two words, written in ink. 'Sabaoth Gebella.' It looked like Alice's handwriting. Agnes put the paper back in the book and placed it on the desk. She locked the cabinet, switched off the lights, then put the two books carefully into her bag and left the library.

The hall was dark. She glanced up at the shadows of the staircase, then went down the corridor to the kitchen. The fluorescent light flickered into life. The fridge was empty apart from a half-jar of tomato sauce, a shrivelled lemon and a pint of milk. In the cupboard there was a packet of spaghetti which had spilled open onto the dusty shelf.

In her own flat, she always knew what was in the fridge. Some fresh salad, certainly. Tomatoes, avocados. A paté of some kind, usually. Always, some cheese from the deli at the corner. And proper bread. And olives...

Agnes sat on the peeling plastic of one of the kitchen chairs. There was a thump above her head, then another.

The heating? she wondered. There was no sign of Helena, but then Agnes was used to her absence around meal-times.

Another thump. A growl. No, Agnes said to herself. Not a growl. It'll be the pipes or something.

Then there was a loud musical ringing noise that made Agnes jump to her feet, her heart racing, before she realised it was her mobile phone.

She snatched it out of her bag. 'Hello?' she shouted into it, registering the caller's name with relief.

'Darling, it's me. Athena. Do you fancy supper?'

'You are my guardian angel,' Agnes said.

'Are you all right?'

'No,' Agnes said. 'I'm all alone in a haunted bloody house and there's absolutely nothing to eat.'

'You mean, you could manage the ghosts as long as there was a decent crab paté in the fridge,' Athena said.

Agnes laughed, feeling her breathing return to normal. The room seemed to grow brighter again. 'Where are you?'

'That lovely new Italian place,' Athena said. 'The one on the corner, by the Old Brompton Road.'

'I'll get a taxi,' Agnes said.

'A taxi? You must be scared,' Athena replied. 'Either that or starving.'

'Desperate, actually. See you very soon.'

Out in the hallway, she pulled on her coat. There was an odd smell, a damp, animal scent. As she turned to shut the door behind her, she thought she saw movement on the staircase, a flick of a tail between the banisters.

CHAPTER TWO

Agnes walked into the light and airy space of the restaurant and scanned the noisy crowd. She could see an arm raised in greeting. Charcoal grey wool, she thought. Military, in fact, with brass buttons at the cuff. Athena was wearing bright red lipstick and her dark hair hung in waves, pinned loosely back at her neck.

'Nice jacket,' Agnes said, sitting down opposite her.

Athena picked at a lapel with scarlet-painted fingertips. 'I thought, do I do military this season, or is it what the young people are wearing? And then I thought, even if it is what the young people are wearing, does it matter? Do you remember how I agonised over gypsy skirts last summer, and in the end I bought one and everyone loved it on me?'

'That turquoise one – it was lovely.' Agnes hung her old brown duffle coat on the back of her chair.

'And this was a bargain,' Athena added, smoothing down the collar.

'It's very nice.'

Athena leaned back in her chair. 'You look absolutely ghastly,' she said.

'Yes, well...'

'Have some wine. Chianti OK? They do a nice one here.'

She poured some into Agnes's glass. 'So, did you really see a ghost? I thought you were joking.'

Agnes took a large mouthful of wine. 'I don't know. Last night, some very odd things went on. I thought I heard things – a baby crying, but there was no one there.'

'It's a ghastly house, from what you say. It might just be the atmosphere.'

Agnes looked around, at the candle-lit tables, the bright conversations, the bustle of the waitresses. 'Yes,' she said. 'It might just be the house.'

'Why they can't let you live in your flat—'

'There's an Abbot from Normandy in there at the moment.'

'I mean, sweetie, they've stolen your flat from you and imprisoned you in that place, with all those old books of spells and only a thin wall between you and a load of mad people. And this February weather's been dreadful, and Saturn's retrograde in your sign. It's really not at all surprising if your psyche produces some kind of reaction to it.'

Agnes smiled. 'You sound like your chap.'

'Nic? Me? Oh, nonsense, kitten, he'd be getting you to re-live previous lives to find out what karmic self was returning to haunt you now. Or something. He's much madder than I am. Probably madder than anyone in your asylum.' She smiled, fondly.

'How's his therapy centre going?' Agnes glanced at the menu.

'He loves it. I thought I'd have sea-bream with polenta.'

'Me too. Do you miss him?'

'A bit. It's only Provence, though. And I've got used to living without him. And you know, I love my London life. I love working in the art gallery, and anyway, what would you and I do without each other, eh?'

'Best friends,' Agnes agreed, thinking of Julius.

'Apart from Julius.'

Agnes looked at Athena and they both laughed.

'You've known him longer, that's all,' Athena added.

'But you and Nic—'

'Poppet, it's fine. It's not as if Nic and I have ever lived together. Absence makes the heart, etcetera...'

'You don't sound convinced.'

'Maybe an artichoke salad to start with?' Athena closed the menu and sighed. 'It's lovely, your family house. You were very kind to give it to him.'

'It solved a problem for me too.' Agnes re-filled their glasses as the waitress came and took their order.

'You should see what he's done with the stable block,' Athena said, 'very tasteful, and he's using the hayloft as the computer room.'

The hayloft. That was her father's word for it too. 'Have you been hiding in the hayloft again?' The words uttered with his characteristic English vagueness. 'Your mother's been asking for you,' he'd say. It always sounded like a threat.

'A computer room?' Agnes remembered lying in the bales of hay, reaching up to the sun-baked tiles of the roof, warm to the touch; listening to the scurrying of mice, the breathing of her pony in the stable below.

'Are you all right?' Athena was looking at her oddly.

'I'm fine, really,' Agnes said, and was surprised by the tears which pricked her eyes. She took another gulp of wine. 'Just a bit strung out at the moment,' she said.

'Memories.' Athena shook her head. 'They don't half trip you up.' She picked up her fork as their starters arrived. 'They do this stuff really nicely here,' she said. 'These little hot peppers, and sun-dried tomatoes.'

'It's not as if my childhood was particularly happy, either,' Agnes said.

'That's one of the many reasons why we're friends.' Athena waved her fork at Agnes. 'We both had to run away. My lot, back in the village, wanted me to be a good Greek girl; married to a farmer, loads of kids. Well, I wasn't having that. Mmm, these artichokes are fantastic. My mum used to do them with olive oil and honey...' Her voice shook.

Agnes glanced across at her. 'Not you as well.'

Athena was patting at her eyes with her fingertips. Agnes passed her a handkerchief.

Athena sniffed loudly, and dried her eyes. 'What has got into us?'

'The past seems to be weighing heavily,' Agnes said. In the back of her mind she seemed to hear Alice Hawker's words, a fragment of a voice.

'Saturn can be a dreadful influence,' Athena said. 'And there's Nic researching his family tree, did I tell you? He's on-line the whole time, there's all these sites you can visit.'

'In my old house?'

Athena began to laugh. 'It's really very funny,' she said. 'There's your hayloft, thick with your family history, all those stories layered with the dust – and he's cleaned it all out, painted it all white, installed state-of-the-art computers and is trying to find out who he is. And he's a trained therapist, you'd think he'd know who he is by now.'

Agnes laughed too, feeling her mood grow lighter. She tried to remember the dog, if a dog it was, and was aware that even the attempt to recall what she'd seen drove the phantoms further from her mind.

Their fish arrived, and the conversation turned to the ideal way of preparing polenta, until Agnes said, 'It's funny you said spells.'

'Spells?'

'You said, book of spells.'

'Only because you told me about this bequest, and all these treatises on magic.'

'I think I found one. Today. A real spell.'

'Darling, I do think they should take you off that job and put you back with all those homeless kids or convicts or something safe.'

'It's all right. It's not as if I believe in magic.'

'But you do. Every time you go to church—'

'That's different.' Agnes spoke more harshly than she meant to. 'That's not magic.'

'Well, I don't mean to be rude,' Athena said, 'but if anyone could explain the difference to me, I might still be a believer.'

'But my tradition—'

'I was raised in your tradition,' Athena interrupted. 'The Orthodox version, anyway. When I was growing up, I was surrounded by it. Drowning in it. The women in the village – crossing themselves every five seconds, worrying about evil eyes... And in the end I stopped believing anything at all. There was a black dog that used to wander through our village, poor old thing, a stray, well, the things you had to do to ward off evil when he came by, all sorts of signs of the cross and prayers to the Saints. And then on Sundays, there was the eucharist and then being told at your first communion that you're drinking blood, and not any old blood but the blood of Our Lord who was the son of God who no one's ever seen but he still made a young woman pregnant by an angel – is that any different from burying hair clippings in the garden and walking round them three times or whatever your book says?' She looked across at Agnes, who was gripping the table edge. 'Oh, poppet, I'm so sorry, I didn't mean to upset you, going on about God in that way, it's typical of me, I didn't think—'

'No—' Agnes managed to say. 'It's not that. It's what you just said—'

'I always do it, it's so annoying—'

'The black dog.' Agnes stuttered over the words.

Athena stared at her. 'What about the black dog?'

'That's what I saw. Last night. A dog. And then it disappeared, and all I could hear was a baby crying, so loud it could have been next to me.' Agnes felt her voice was shaking. 'And then, one of the patients in the centre today said something about a black dog. And then I found a book of spells, and the woman who first lived in the house, Alice, she'd written down the words you say against mad dogs...' Her words tailed off.

Athena reached across the table and took her hand. 'It's serious, then,' she said.

Agnes met her gaze. 'It can't be. I don't believe in all that.'

Athena relinquished her hand and poured them both some more wine. After a while she said, 'Perhaps it's not a matter of believing in it. Perhaps there's something in the house, and you're just a witness to it.'

'How very comforting.' Agnes managed a smile.

'It's funny,' Athena looked up at her, 'last time Nic and I went out to dinner he was saying that people have more choice than they realise. He said that when someone is in crisis they choose the form it takes. And I disagreed with him – I always do, he never seems to mind. He's such a love. But now I'm thinking, perhaps that's what this is. You've taken final vows, and they've shut you away in a house that's wrong for you, and your sense of wrongness is represented by the dog.' She broke off and giggled. 'Listen to me, Nic would be proud of me.'

'So, what should I do?'

'Easy. Get those nuns to give you back your old job doing something normal with murderers or drug addicts. And get that horrible old Abbot or Bishop or whatever he is out of your flat.'

Agnes had seen Athena into a taxi, and waited for a bus, assuring Athena that she was OK, after most of a bottle of wine (and yes, how did they get on to a second bottle?) she was feeling perfectly brave – and now she was walking up the drive to the door of the old house. She found herself hoping, fervently, that Helena was in, and wondered what had happened to the old self that relished solitude.

Her key clicked in the lock. Helena's shoes were in the hall. She must have gone to bed, but that was better than not being there at all, Agnes thought.

She crept through the quietness of the house to her room. She switched on the bedside lamp and the bright Anglepoise at the desk, and breathed again. She got out her prayer book, lit a candle, keeping all the other lights on, and turned to a page.

'…Yea, though I walk through the valley of the shadow of death, yet will I fear nothing. Thy rod and thy staff they comfort me…'

She remembered Tina-Marie, challenging Philip. She remembered the poor woman's visible terror. She turned the page.

'…The Lord is my light and my salvation, whom then shall I fear? The Lord is the stronghold of my life, of whom shall I be afraid?'

There was a step outside her room. Then another. An animal pad-padding.

She waited, waited for another sound. There was silence.

Agnes jumped up from her prayers and went to her desk. She took out the books from the library and turned to Alice's notebook.

She could hear a gurgling noise.

The pipes, Agnes thought, flicking through the pages. After lists of housekeeping, there was a passage of writing.

'Nicolas thinks that there is an evil spirit upon me. I pray to the Lord to release me from it, but all I see is the black dog. If I cannot be cleansed, then they will take away my baby boy, my dear one…'

Agnes shut the book and slapped it down on the desk.

'The Lord is the stronghold of my life, of whom shall I be afraid…'

She remembered what Athena had said, about casting spells. The old women in her village, using the liturgy as a form of words to ward off evil spirits.

The Lord is my light and my salvation...

Then, there it was. That sound again. The sound she realised she feared more than the growling.

The child crying.

Yea, though I walk through the valley of the shadow of death...

Agnes took a deep breath and flung open the door. The corridor was deserted, but the sound persisted. She followed its direction. It seemed to be coming, not from the staircase this time, but from the hall.

She hurried softly down the stairs. There it was again, louder now, a mewling cry, right at the front door.

Agnes stood in the darkness, her hand on the old brass handle, hearing the echo of centuries in a baby's cry. Then she flung the door open.

The sound continued from somewhere at her feet.

She looked down. There, on the step, was a child. A red-faced, angry-eyed, open-mouthed toddler.

She stood there, staring at it. The girl was clutching a pink blanket around her face, from which peeped soft dark curls. The other hand hung on to the ear of a teddy bear. The crying faltered as the child stared back at her.

Agnes gazed out into the night. There was no one to be seen. Aware of the gathering cold, she looked down at the girl. She bent down and picked her up. Then, hugging the child to her, she stepped back inside and closed the door behind her.

CHAPTER THREE

'It's Leila,' Agnes said into the phone. 'It's Tina-Marie's child. We have to find her mother.' Agnes tried to keep her irritation out of her voice, as Sister Lucia, on the other end of the phone, argued with her.

'No, she hasn't said her name,' Agnes argued back, 'she's probably in shock. She hasn't said a word. But I know who she is.' She tucked the phone under her chin, yawning. Morning sunlight streamed into the room they used as an office, brightening the heavy oak panelling. Lucia was promising to talk to the provincial later that day, and suggesting that Agnes contact Social Services.

'I have,' Agnes said, her irritation turning into blind fury. 'And the police, and the hospitals.' What do you think I've been doing? she wanted to say. We've had the police here, we've been up all night with a distraught little girl, and if it hadn't been for Sister Helena having the sense to find an all-night store to re-stock their larder, the child would have starved to death by now. 'Yes, Sister,' she said. 'Thank you. Yes, we'll hear from you later today.'

She rang off.

Agnes dialled another number. 'Julius,' she said, as he answered. 'Have you found her?'

'Are you sure it's her child?' He sounded tired. 'You only caught a glimpse of her at the clinic.'

'It's Leila. Of course it is. I'd recognise those wellingtons anywhere. And I've got Sister Lucia being as uncharitable as only a religious person can be, desperate for us to get rid of the poor wee thing, she doesn't want the press to get hold of the story when we're trying to sell the building. But how can I hand her over to the authorities when I saw her with her mother only yesterday? Have you asked at the clinic?'

Julius sighed. 'There's no sign of her. The thing is, Agnes, I didn't want to say all this in front of Philip, but Tina-Marie's in a terrible way. She's been asking me about evil spirits, and whether the church could exorcise her. She thought there was a black dog who followed her around, and that if she was cleansed, as she put it, the dog would leave her alone. She used to be a member of some kind of sect, out in Essex, and it's done her a lot of harm.' Julius listened to Agnes's silence, then said, 'Are you there?'

'Mmm? Yes.' Agnes leaned heavily against the desk. Outside the sun went in behind some clouds.

'And that boyfriend of hers is dangerous. And I'd ask Philip, only he didn't come to work today. Apparently his wife's ill.'

'Oh.' Agnes rubbed the back of her neck. 'Julius, can you keep looking for her?'

'Yes,' he said. 'I will.'

Agnes hung up. She flopped into a chair and stared at her feet for a while. Then she went to find Shirley.

* * *

'I suppose there's a tradition of it.' Shirley looked up from a list she was writing.

Agnes frowned at her. 'Of what?'

'You know. Church doors. Women who can't cope, handing over their off-spring to become holy sisters.'

'Oh.'

'Is it against the law now, though?' Shirley brushed dust from a book which lay on top of the pile in front of her.

'That's what Lucia seems to think.'

'You could raise her. She could become one of the community here. It's charity, isn't it?'

'Mmm.' Agnes was imagining her fellow sisters trying to cope with a child novice, as the door opened. Sister Helena was standing in the doorway, holding a large, soft bundle. 'She's asleep,' she whispered. The child was dressed in clean clothes, wrapped in a new blanket. Helena's hair hung in pale tendrils, and her face looked pink and young. 'I went up to the High Street for some clothes – I took some of the housekeeping money, no one will mind, will they?' She looked at Agnes, uncertainly.

'No,' Agnes said. 'Of course they won't.' She nodded towards the child. 'She looks very sweet,' she said.

Helena gazed down at her. 'I'll pop her in her bed for now.'

The door closed softly. Shirley looked up from her pile of lists. 'There's some,' she began, 'who maybe weren't cut out for the monastic life.' She glanced at Agnes. 'Not that it's for me to say.'

'Oh, you can say it,' Agnes said. 'We just have to think it. In fact, if you'll excuse me, I need to have a word with her.'

Agnes found her upstairs in her room. Helena had arranged

a mattress on the floor, edged it round with pillows, and the child nestled there, fast asleep. Helena was sitting next to her, a book on her lap, untouched.

Agnes knocked on the open door. 'Helena—'

She looked up. A flicker of anxiety crossed her face. 'What?'

'We know this child. We know the mother.'

'So you keep saying. I've never seen her before. But then I don't have much to do with the day centre.' Helena placed the book on her table. Next to her the child stirred in her sleep, settled again.

'But she answered to Leila. Last night.'

'She's only three. She'd probably answer to anything.'

A sudden ring at the front door interrupted them. Agnes closed Helena's door behind her and went downstairs.

A man stood in the doorway, peering apologetically from under a shock of gingery hair, his shoulders hunched under a tweed jacket.

'Jonathan Harris,' he said, waving a crumpled business card at her.

Agnes stared at him.

'B-book dealer,' he added.

'Oh. Yes. Of course.' She managed a smile. 'Come in. I'll take you through to the library.'

'Y —you were expecting me, weren't you?' He half-turned back towards the front door, as if about to flee.

'Yes, of course. Here we are.' Agnes opened the library door. 'Shirley – this is Mr Harris.'

Shirley looked up from her desk. 'Ah. Oh. Lovely.' She stood up. 'Goodness, there's a lot for you to be getting on with here. Well, um—' She stood, her hands in mid-flap.

'My interests are quite specific,' he said. 'Nothing too recent. Unless it's a special edition. But anything about magic, I'll have a look at that.' He glanced around him. 'I'm not just a removal man, you know.' He gave a brief bark of laughter.

'Well,' Shirley said. 'You'd better help yourself.'

He began to scan the shelves, running his finger along some of the spines. 'It's quite a collection,' he said. 'And of course, you have the Hawker collection too.' He turned, suddenly, and fixed his gaze on Shirley.

She was stacking books on her desk. 'Yes,' she said, not looking up. 'That's all signed away now. It's going up to Oxford.'

He continued to stare at her. 'I heard there was a gap,' he said.

'A gap?' She smiled at Agnes, as if she and Agnes were both indulging a small child.

'Yes,' he said. His hands were thrust into his pockets, his elbows locked to his sides. 'I'd have thought you'd have known.'

'What kind of gap?' Shirley turned to face him.

He hesitated, frowning at her. Then he shrugged. 'Perhaps I'm wrong,' he said. 'It's a family collection, isn't it? All sorts of rumours circulate about those kinds of things.' He turned back to the shelves and continued to study the spines.

Agnes touched Shirley's sleeve. 'I've got to go,' she said, quietly. 'Another stupid meeting at the day centre. Will you be all right?' She tilted her head towards the book dealer.

'Of course,' Shirley whispered. 'Why ever not?'

* * *

The dull, beige room was full of people. Agnes sat with an untouched sandwich in front of her, two curling slices of white bread from which peeped a pale sliver of cheese. A man in a shiny navy blue suit was talking.

'...Enormous gratitude, both to the church and to the funding bodies, for enabling this project to grow and develop. The disposal of the building, therefore, will allow us to take our vision of community mental health provision forward into the future.'

He finished and sat down. Various people nodded. Philip was there, sitting across the room from her. He looked tired. Then another man stood up and began to explain that as a member of the site development team, he was there to make the transition to the new building as easy as possible. Agnes glanced at her sandwich, then at her watch, then at the door. Through the glass frame she could see two people, deep in conversation.

Two women. One was Helena. The other was Tina-Marie. There was no sign of Leila.

Agnes looked around the meeting. She was hedged into the corner, between two polo-necked men from the architects. She stumbled to her feet, apologising as she picked her way through several pairs of legs, people's briefcases on the floor, aware of Philip darting questions at her.

She pushed open the glass door. The corridor was empty. She ran into the foyer. Old Francis sat in the corner. He raised a paper cup to her. Beatrice was there, shouting into a telephone. She hung up as Agnes approached.

'Was Tina-Marie here?' Agnes was breathless.

'Yes. I just saw her.'

'Where did she go?'

Beatrice screwed up her eyes, staring down the corridors. 'They went outside, I think. She was here just a minute ago. With one of your lot, I think.'

'Did she have her little girl with her?'

Beatrice frowned. 'No, Sister, she didn't. I thought it was odd.'

'Did they leave together?'

'Yes. They went out them doors, then one went one way and one went the other. I remember seeing it that way.'

'Thank you.'

Agnes left the building. She stood in the street, blinking in the traffic's roar. The sun was obscured now by heavy clouds, and the air was damp. People waited at the lights to cross. There was no sign of Tina-Marie, or Helena.

She ran round to the convent entrance, let herself in and stood in the hall. 'Helena?' she called. There was silence. She ran up the stairs and knocked at her door. 'Helena?' The door was locked.

The house was quiet. No Helena. No Leila.

She went back downstairs, down the corridor and into the library. Shirley was there, writing titles on small squares of card.

'Have you seen Helena? Or the child?' Agnes tried not to sound breathless.

Shirley shook her head. 'No, dear. I've been here all the time, that Mr Harris has only just gone. Odd chap,' she added. 'Asked me very strange questions. He said the Hawker family were involved with magic, back when the first house was built here. He said there was a crystal, you know, for telling the future, wondered whether I'd seen it. He said there was a book that went with it. Worth a fortune if it's ever found, he said.'

Agnes half-listened, aware of another sound, a growling coming from the hallway.

'Sshh—' she interrupted Shirley. 'Can you hear that?'

'Hear what?'

They stood in silence for a moment.

'Nothing,' Agnes said.

'An odd little man, Mr Harris,' Shirley said. She looked up at Agnes. 'I was rather hoping,' she said, 'that you might be free this afternoon.' She gestured to the heaps of books, the card-index boxes.

'Yes,' Agnes said. 'Of course. Be back in a moment.'

She opened the door out into the hall. She stood, alone, listening. Nothing. She called Helena's name, again. There was no reply.

She went into the office and dialled Julius's number. 'I saw her,' she said, as he answered. 'Tina-Marie. She was talking to Helena, then they both disappeared. No Leila now either.'

'I've been looking for Tina-Marie all day,' he said.

'She was in the clinic,' she said. 'Then they all vanished.'

She heard him breathing. Then he said, 'I didn't think Helena was involved with the day centre?'

'She isn't,' Agnes said. 'She claimed not to know her, or Leila either.'

'Are you sure it was her?'

'Positive.'

'Why would she want to get involved?'

Agnes thought about the transformation in Sister Helena. 'I've no idea,' she said.

'I'll keep trying,' Julius promised.

For the rest of the day, Agnes sat in the library with Shirley, writing lists. Shirley continued to chat, about her elderly mother, about the varicose veins, 'she won't have them removed, but they're causing her such trouble—' and speculating on what she might do once the library was moved to the convent. 'I can't imagine they'll have a use for me there...' Agnes was aware of a nervousness, a sense of expectation at the pit of her stomach.

It was twilight when she left the library. She went over to the day centre, and rang the bell. Philip answered the door.

'There's no one here,' he said. He stood with his back against the door, as if he was guarding it.

'Can I come in?'

He considered her, looking down at her, as if it took some effort. 'I suppose so,' he said.

'Tina-Marie's vanished,' Agnes said.

'I heard,' he said.

She walked ahead of him, into his office. 'And Leila, her little girl, has gone too. She was with us last night, someone left her on the doorstep.'

Philip followed her into his office. 'I'm not sure I can be responsible for my patients if they disappear,' he said.

Agnes sat down. 'Do you have an address for her?'

'Julius asked me that too. I do, but I'm so short staffed, I can't send people knocking on doors. We've been phoning her mobile all day as it is, but we got no answer.' He sank into a chair opposite her.

'Are you all right?' Agnes took in his pallor, the dark shadows around his eyes.

He passed a hand across his forehead. 'Yes. No. Not really.'

'Julius said your wife was ill.'

'Yes.' He met her eyes. 'She seems to be sinking into depression.'

'Oh.'

'It's a case of "Physician heal thyself". Or in this case, Thy Wife, I suppose.' He tried to smile.

'Is there any reason for it?'

He shook his head. 'Not that I can see. She's started going to church – ' he blurted the words out.

'Oh.'

Philip shook his head. 'You're not the person to say this to, for obvious reasons, but it is part of her illness.'

'Those of us who believe—' Agnes began.

'I'm not suggesting you're ill,' Philip said, 'or Julius. But when an otherwise sane and rational woman starts to talk about what God wants her to do, and this is coupled with exhaustion, despair, inability to carry out even the smallest tasks at home...' He looked up at her. 'Surely even you will accept that it might be a symptom?'

'Yes,' Agnes said. 'I can see that.'

'I work in a world of evidence, you see. It's at the heart of my work. I'm a scientist. I'm part of a long and admirable tradition, a painstaking process, to which many brilliant minds have contributed, to find out what works. It's all about proof.'

'But faith—' Agnes said.

'Faith is believing in something you know can't possibly be

true.' Philip picked up a pen from his desk and placed it in a plastic tray. 'Forgive my bluntness.'

'So – your wife...' Agnes could hear shouting outside the building.

'My wife is unwell. She seems to think there's an old man in the sky who has plans for her. She prays to him. I can't begin to see that this is anything other than magical thinking, like casting spells—' The shouting was now much nearer. Agnes looked through the open door of Philip's office to see Troy and another young man march through the glass doors. They stood in the foyer and looked around them.

Philip jumped to his feet. 'Bloody security in this place. How did that bloody door open like that? The sooner we move to some kind of fortress the better—' He strode into the foyer. 'Can I help you, gentlemen?'

Troy faced him, his fists clenched at his side. 'Where is she?' His fingers looked swollen between their thick bands of metal. His face emerged pale and taut from a crisply cut shirt.

'I assume you mean Tina-Marie?'

'Don't mess with me,' Troy said.

'We've been looking for her all day ourselves.'

'She owes us. Me and Ryan here.' The young man behind him nodded. He had cropped red hair, a blank look in his eyes. He slouched, and his baggy top and jeans slouched too. 'She fucking owes us,' Troy went on.

'If I see her,' Philip said, 'I'll tell her you're looking for her.'

Troy took a step towards him. He was standing very close. 'You laughing at me?'

Philip didn't move. 'No,' he said.

'Because if you are, I'll slice you.'

'I'm sure you would,' Philip said. 'I have no doubt of that.'
Philip had Troy by the elbow and was now propelling him
towards the door. Ryan followed, edging towards Philip's
other side. The glass doors opened, and the two young men
were on the other side as they swished shut again.

Philip leaned on a panel, and the doors locked.

Through the glass Agnes could see Troy, rigid with rage,
aiming a kick at the door, which thudded but remained
unharmed. Then the two men sloped off into the night.

Philip was rubbing his knuckles.

'How did you do that?' Agnes smiled at him.

'Training.' Philip glanced at his watch. 'I should get home.'

His watch hand was shaking. Agnes said, 'Will you be all
right?'

He shrugged. 'Sure. Why not?' He went to his office and
picked up his briefcase. 'I'd offer you a lift, but you only have
about three yards to go.' He locked the clinic doors behind them.

They stood outside. The clouds had cleared and the nearly
full moon was rising above the roofs. Philip looked down at
her. 'What I said about God – please don't take it personally.
I was talking about mental illness. Whereas, in your case, I'm
not saying I understand it myself, but...'

'You mean, I may be wrong but I'm not mad.'

He smiled. 'Something like that. See you tomorrow.' He
touched her arm.

She watched him walk round to his car, heard the beep as it
unlocked. She remembered the empty fridge and realised she
was extremely hungry. She turned and went down the main
road to the supermarket.

* * *

Half an hour later, it came on to rain, drizzle giving way to a heavy downpour. Approaching Collyer House, carrying several dripping wet carrier bags, she thought she saw a figure standing by the rhododendron bush on the drive. She went up to the front door, then looked back, scanning the darkness. She called out from the doorway. 'Hello?' There was no answer, and when she looked more closely, there was no one there.

Once inside, she switched on all the lights. The house seemed to ooze emptiness. She went into the office and dialled the main convent house in Hackney. Agnes heard it ring and ring, and remembered that the ringing of the phone was often ignored, and even if answered, it would be in frosty hostility.

She heard a soft female voice give the number.

'Oh, Madeleine – oh, thank goodness,' Agnes said, glad to hear a friend.

'Agnes? Hello. What—?'

'I mean, thank goodness it's a friend at the end of the phone,' she said. 'I was imagining—'

'It's all right. I'm on phone duty. What's the matter?'

'Have you seen Helena?' Agnes steadied her voice.

'Us? No, not for days. She was here on Sunday, not since then. Is there a problem?'

Agnes wondered how to explain. Outside, the branches of the rhododendron bush shivered in the light from the windows. 'No,' she said. 'Probably not.'

'I can't imagine you're lonely,' Madeleine said.

'Me?' Agnes tried to laugh. 'No. Of course not.'

After exchanges of gossip – old Sister Phyllida had broken her leg trying to prune the big apple tree, when Sister Lucia had expressly told her not to, and on Phyllida's birthday, of all days; Sister Martha had got a bit sharp with Sister Felicité because she thought she'd criticised her shepherd's pie – Madeleine said she'd better go as the bell was ringing for compline.

Agnes stood in the office. The silence echoed around her. Compline, she thought. She saw the sisters gathering in the chapel, the candles, the warmth.

She went down the corridor to the kitchen. She unpacked her shopping – fresh tagliatelle, garlic, sour cream, Normandy butter, herbs, salami, parmesan cheese. Cat food, which she'd bought just in case, and which she put away in the larder cupboard. The cat clearly adored Helena, but for now she'd just have to manage with Agnes.

She settled to cooking, soothed by the steam and the stirring and the grating. She opened a bottle of Chianti and set it down near the cooker. She thought about Philip. I suppose I should be flattered that he thinks I'm sane, she thought. Although, then that makes my beliefs even more wrong in his eyes.

She wondered what it would be like in his world. A world of evidence. A world without God.

She opened a drawer and took out a damask table cloth, laid the table for one, poured some wine. She took a silver candlestick down from the mantelpiece and lit the candle and murmured the words of the grace. She looked at the candle-light refracted through the glass of wine and wondered what Philip did in moments of gratitude. Perhaps he thanked existence, or science, or evolution. Perhaps he didn't need to be grateful.

There was a loud scream outside. A male voice, shouting, another scream, a heavy thump. Silence.

Agnes ran into the hall, flung open the door, staring out into the pouring rain.

Tina-Marie was lying on the steps. Her eyes were wide open. Her skin looked strange and creased. From her mouth came a rattling, rasping sound – an endless rhythm, filling the night with horror.

Then it stopped.

CHAPTER FOUR

The policewoman clicked off her phone and crossed the hallway to where Agnes sat on the stairs. She sat down next to her. 'That was the hospital. She was DOA. Knife wound. Several, in fact. He meant business.' She was thin and wiry in her uniform and had cropped blond hair.

Agnes put her hand across her eyes. 'What about her child?' she said. Her voice didn't seem to work properly.

'We don't know yet.'

'One of the sisters here knew her,' Agnes said. 'They were talking, today. Yesterday…' Agnes ran her fingers through her hair.

The policewoman put her hand on Agnes's arm. 'We can talk about all this later. You've had a shock.'

Yes, Agnes thought. A shock. A dying woman on my doorstep. I suppose I am. In shock. She looked up to see Philip standing over her, offering his hand to the policewoman, introducing himself.

The policewoman shook his hand. 'WPC Yvette Newland,' she said.

'What time is it?' Agnes asked him.

He checked his watch. 'Half past two. Just after.'

'She's dead,' Agnes said. 'I found her. On the steps.'

He put his hand on her shoulder. 'Yes,' he said, 'I know.'

* * *

Later, when everyone else had gone, Philip and Agnes sat at the kitchen table. Agnes handed him the bottle of Chianti and a corkscrew. 'I had a glass earlier,' she said. 'I put the cork back in.'

'I wish I could do that,' he said. 'Just one drink, I mean.'

She took the glass he handed her. She held it between her fingers, gazing into it. Philip was staring at the table. After some minutes he said, 'Shock, I suppose. Does peculiar things.'

Agnes took a large mouthful of wine. 'Yes,' she said. 'Shock.'

'I mean,' he went on, 'finding her. Can't have been nice.'

'No.' She took another mouthful of wine. 'No, it wasn't.' She held out her glass and he refilled it.

'I was thinking about you,' she said. 'Earlier, when I was having supper, and saying grace, I wondered what you do when you feel grateful. I mean, if there's no God to thank.'

He looked at the glass of wine in his hand. 'I can be grateful to the universe, can't I?'

'On what evidence, though? I mean, why should you see it as benign?'

'Oh, I don't see it as benign. As far as I'm concerned, it just is. It's enough for me that the universe is here; that we exist.'

'But how does that give your life meaning?' Agnes asked.

He frowned at her. 'I'm not sure I need to have meaning.'

'But if you're just a random bit of dust hurtling through space – what's the point?'

'There may not be one. At least I'm not telling myself fairy tales.'

'But if the fairy tales make us aspire to something more, allow us to be greater than we are—'

'You're kidding yourself. What about suicide bombers?

Look at what they learn from their fairy tales. Or poor Tina-Marie, for that matter. She was in terror of some kind of vengeful God. I think that's why she took up with Troy, she thought he'd protect her.'

Agnes remembered the woman dying outside her door and shivered. 'What are we going to do?'

'Do? Us?' He looked at her. 'There's nothing we can do.'

'But Helena's vanished. And Leila.'

'Leila.' He frowned.

'Troy hated Leila,' Agnes said.

'The police are on to him. We've done what we can.' He poured another glass of wine. Agnes was aware of deliberately drinking, drinking fast, trying not to think about Tina-Marie lying there on the step...

'How's your wife?' she said.

'Serena? Not good.'

'Why is she depressed?'

He sighed. 'It's about children, really. We weren't that bothered, we thought. We met quite late. She had some fertility problems too...' He sipped his wine. 'And then she found she was pregnant, last year. Only, it turned out it was ectopic. Surgery, horrible business. Chances of conceiving even less now. It's been very bad for her.'

'Poor her.'

He drained his glass. 'I suppose that's one issue you people don't have.'

Agnes remembered how Leila had nestled, fast asleep, in Helena's room.

'You can just leave all that to other people,' Philip was saying.

Behind him the kitchen window was growing pale with the dawn. Agnes yawned. 'Perhaps I'll go to sleep after all,' she said. He stood up.

'Thank you for sitting with me,' she said, leading the way back out into the hallway.

He glanced up the stairs. 'You're right about this being creepy, this place.'

'You mean, you might allow for ghosts after all?'

He looked down at her. 'And you do?'

'No,' she said.

He gathered his coat around him. 'Well, at least that's where our belief-systems meet. On the absence of ghosts.' He opened the front door. Agnes saw him staring straight ahead, not wanting to look at the steps. He hesitated, turned back to her. 'Good night,' he said. 'Try and sleep.'

She shut the door behind him. She switched off all the lights and went up to her room. The rain had stopped, at last. Around her, in the early daylight, the house seemed to settle and grow calm. She fell fast asleep.

Julius sat at his desk in the late morning sunlight. He took off his glasses and began to polish them.

'One can't help but feel culpable,' he said. 'I knew she was in trouble. I knew we should find her a safer place to live.' He sighed. 'We were too late.'

Agnes carried a mug of tea over to him. She rested her hand briefly on his shoulder. 'Black dog,' she said. 'What did she mean?'

Julius put his glasses on. 'She was very troubled. I told you about how, when she came to us, she'd fled some kind of community. A cult of some kind. I tried to show her a different God, a kinder one. I'm not sure I ever succeeded.'

'And no one knows where Leila's gone. And Helena.' Agnes picked up her mug of tea and went and sat opposite him. 'Philip says all faith is dangerous. He was talking about suicide bombers last night.'

Julius glanced at her. 'When?'

'He appeared at some point. I think the police must have called him. He was very sweet.'

'Ah.' Julius nodded. 'At least he talks to us.'

She smiled. 'Why shouldn't he?'

'We must seem so strange to him. Clinging to our medieval world view in the face of scientific progress. Still, I suppose he's used to working with people more crazy than us.'

Agnes heard the clock strike the half hour. 'I'd better go.' She stood up. 'Sister Lucia's meeting us in the library to discuss what to do. And then, after that, I'm meeting Athena for lunch. What about you?'

'Oh, I'm just here. The police want to ask me about Tina-Marie, who she knew, who she went around with. She had a sister, apparently; they're trying to trace her.'

Shirley led Sister Lucia to a chair, then sat down at her desk. She crossed her legs, uncrossed them, and waited. Lucia settled stiffly into her chair, smoothing her plain grey skirt. Agnes sat down next to her.

'Well,' Lucia said. She looked from one to the other. 'A most unfortunate business.' Her hands went to her hair, tucking a few stray wisps behind her ears.

'We still have our job to do.' Shirley sat, straight-backed, thin-lipped.

'Yes, yes, of course. Our concern is your safety, that's all.'

'I can hardly think that little thug is going to come back for either Agnes or me.'

'The question remains,' Lucia said, 'as to whether Agnes continues to live here. Helena has solved the problem herself.' Again, the hiding away of her hair, as if in memory of the wimple she must once have worn.

'Helena?' Agnes turned to Lucia.

'I thought you knew,' Lucia said to her. 'About her mother. She's gone to visit her. She phoned us yesterday.'

'Where did she phone from?'

Lucia frowned at her. 'I assumed she was here. Wasn't she?'

'No,' Agnes said. 'She wasn't.'

'Well, anyway, she appeared this morning, they called her in, she had a meeting.'

'And have they granted permission?'

'Apparently they have. She's there now.'

'Where?'

Lucia shrugged. 'How should I know where Helena's mother lives? Somewhere in the country, I think. All I know is that she's gone there.' She turned back to Shirley. 'I appreciate your commitment to the task. And Agnes, if you'd rather live in the community house—'

Agnes smiled at Lucia. 'I agree with Shirley. We might as well carry on as we are.'

* * *

Agnes allowed Athena to fill her glass with Pinot Grigio. Around the circles of white tablecloths there was soft hubbub. Beyond the sunny windows, high heels and tailored jackets passed by.

'But sweetie, really,' Athena was saying, 'you're clearly in danger. They can't keep you there.'

'It's better than moving in with all the others.'

Athena poured wine into her own glass. 'Mmm. Perhaps.'

'And the police reckon they're closing in on Troy. He's been sighted once today already, they told Julius. Nice coat.'

Athena blushed, and stroked the fake fur collar as it hung on the back of her chair.

'It looks like Nicole Farhi,' Agnes said.

Athena went even pinker. 'You know that discount warehouse place? I got it there. Complete bargain, you know. I haven't told Nic yet.'

'Does he have to know?'

Athena pursed her lips. 'No. I don't suppose he does. He was going to come home this weekend, he'd have seen it then, I'd have had to tell him, he notices these things. But as he's not coming back after all, I don't suppose I need to tell him. Ever.'

Agnes caught her expression. 'You're cross with him,' she said.

'No. Not cross. I just can't see why his family tree is more important than me. He said something on the phone last night about being descended from Basque nobility, I didn't even know a Basque was a person, anyway, there's some library you can visit to find out, across the border in Spain, so he's doing that instead of coming to London.'

'Oh.'

'And his therapy centre's really busy. Did I tell you, he's found a housekeeper?'

'A housekeeper?'

Athena broke off a piece of bread. 'She's called Chantal. Her family goes back years in the area, he said.'

'I must know them, then,' Agnes said. 'She's probably descended from Marie, our old housekeeper.'

'Anyway, she's wonderful, apparently.'

'If she's related to Marie, all the gossip will be round the village in seconds.'

'Well, God knows what she'll make of his clients.' Athena picked up the menu. 'So, what's happened to that poor little girl?'

'Leila? I think Helena's taken her away. I hope she has, they've both disappeared anyway.'

'So you're completely alone in that spooky house?' Athena shook her head. 'They can't let you stay there, really, kitten.'

'Tina-Marie and Helena knew each other, and they pretended not to. Helena came to us from a cult, and Julius said that Tina-Marie was involved in a cult too, and I think it was the same one, which was why afterwards they pretended to have no connection.'

'Oh dear.' Athena was scanning the menu. 'I want everything. Shall we have a starter and a pudding, that way I can have this passion fruit meringue thing they do, it's fab.'

'You see, it makes sense.' Agnes opened her menu. 'Helena was very odd. Very secretive. She hardly ate, you know. She had all these ideas about relinquishment. She said it was about obedience.'

'Oh, honestly, how stupid. To starve yourself just out of obedience to God? I mean, if she was doing it to fit into a size ten I'd be more sympathetic. I'm going to have the artichoke starter and then pudding. What about you?'

'I'll have mussels, I think.'

Athena refilled their glasses. 'Silly old Nic. I'm just going to have a great time this weekend without him. We've got a drinks do at the gallery tonight, and then tomorrow we're meeting this new artist, Simon wants to show him. He does these metal sculpture things like birds, you hang them from the ceiling. I just hope they don't land on someone's head, the insurance will be astronomical. Or perhaps it will count as an Act of God, what do you think? What's so funny?' Athena added, as Agnes began to laugh.

Agnes approached Collyer House feeling light-headed from white wine and lack of sleep. She wondered why there were people on the doorstep, men, mostly, carrying cameras, then realised too late that they were journalists.

'Miss, can you tell us—'

'Did you know the dead girl—'

'I gather you're all nuns who live here—'

She ran round to the clinic entrance and through the glass doors.

Beatrice raised a hand to say hello. Philip was in the foyer, and came over to her. 'Troy's on the run,' he said.

'How do you know?' Agnes felt suddenly exhausted.

'That little tyke he goes around with was lurking outside.

I pinned him up against the wall and asked him some questions. He said Troy was at his place this afternoon when he heard the news; he didn't even know Tina-Marie was dead, according to Ryan. He's in hiding now, and he swears blind he never did it. Then I phoned the police, who'd only just missed him. But they think he's staying local.'

'There are loads of newspaper people outside my front door,' Agnes said.

'Shall I walk you round there?'

It had started to rain. Philip, abstracted, offered her his arm. The doorway was deserted.

'Oh,' Agnes said. 'They've gone.'

'Off to another murder, perhaps,' Philip said. He paused at the foot of the stairs. 'Will you be all right?'

'I'll be fine,' she said. 'After all, we don't believe in ghosts.'

He smiled at her, made as if to tip a non-existent hat, turned back to the clinic.

That night, Agnes fell into deep sleep. She woke early, to a grey, rainy dawn. She lay in bed, aware that something had woken her. Some noise, some disturbance. She had a memory, a dream perhaps, of hearing a baby's cry. She went out on to the landing, down the stairs. The hallway was deserted, the front door firmly locked. She opened the library door.

The first thing she saw was the jagged hole in the window. Then, the glass shards scattered across the floor, the upturned piles of books, the trail of paper across the carpet. A door to the cabinet of the Hawker Bequest had been flung open and still swung slightly, a rhythmic glint in the soft light.

She picked her way to Shirley's desk phone and called the police.

CHAPTER FIVE

'So the police don't think the two things are connected?' Shirley picked up an overturned chair and sat down on it. 'It seems odd to me. That poor young woman and now this.'

Agnes yawned. 'They were very helpful. But, no, they don't. They think Tina-Marie was a victim of domestic violence, and they think this is a burglary gone wrong.'

Shirley surveyed the broken glass, the books strewn across the floor. 'An odd kind of burglary if you ask me,' she said. She looked at Agnes. 'Are you all right?'

'Hungry, actually,' Agnes said. She wondered if there was anything for breakfast. 'The police said we could start to tidy up.'

'Good.' Shirley went over to the Hawker cabinet and closed the door. 'Of course, they can't let you stay here now.'

Agnes frowned at her. 'But if no one's here at night—'

'We'll just have to get the collection out of here ASAP. I do wish those museum people would get a move on.'

'I've no idea if anything was taken,' Agnes said.

'Well, that's today's job,' Shirley said. 'At least there's all the cards I've written, they don't seem to have touched the index.'

'It's Saturday,' Agnes said. 'You shouldn't be at work.'

Shirley shrugged. 'I'll just tidy up for a bit. Mother's

expecting me for lunch.' She surveyed the bits of paper on the floor, the slivers of glass. 'Who would do a thing like this? It's as if they were looking for something. I wonder if they found it. It's like that Mr Harris yesterday, saying there was a gap in the Hawker collection. I did press him some more, but he wouldn't be drawn.'

'Perhaps he did this.' Agnes managed to smile.

Shirley looked at her in surprise. 'Oh no,' she said. She looked all around her, then back at Agnes. 'No one who cares about books would do this.'

Some hours later, Agnes walked through the glass doors of the day centre. The rain had eased, and there was a chill in the air.

The foyer was deserted, apart from Beatrice, who was at the counter, pouring tea from a large enamelled teapot into a tray-full of polystyrene cups. She nodded in greeting, then picked up her tray and glided slowly down the corridor, out of sight.

'Af'noon, Sister.' The rough voice came from behind her.

'Francis,' she said, turning round. He was in the far corner of the lounge area. 'No one else here?'

'Only me,' he said, and gave his smoky laugh. He looked slightly neater, and his hair stuck up from his head in short grey chunks.

'Have you had a haircut?' Agnes sat down next to him.

He pulled at a tuft of hair. 'Did it meself, didn't I?' He turned his soulful eyes on her. 'Felt bad, t'other day. With Father J. here an' all. And now she's gone, eh?'

Agnes nodded at him, wondering how much he knew.

'It's a bad world, eh? As God's my witness,' he said. 'No one deserves that. I told her, whenever it was. I says to her, that man's no good for you. He'll see you dead as soon as let you out of his sight.'

'The police seem to think they'll catch him,' Agnes said.

Francis turned to look at her again, levering himself stiffly round in his chair. 'Police? Pah! Them coppers. Take no notice of the living, then go tut-tutting over the corpse. Someone should have taken care of that girl when she was alive, her and her wee girl. She had a good heart. A temper fit for the devil, but a good heart.'

'Francis—' Agnes met his rheumy gaze. 'What did you mean by the black dog?'

'Ach—' he shook his head. 'That's what upset her.'

'Did you mean—' she hesitated. 'Did you mean a real dog?'

He shifted on his chair, his red lips working. Then he said, 'The way I see it, you can go one way – ' he pointed to the ceiling, ' – or you can go the other way.' He pointed to the floor. 'And me, see – I gave up my place up there a long time ago. And when I says about the dog, that's what I meant. My familiar, see? If I get too la-di-da about myself, he drags me down.'

'But do you – do you actually see him?'

Francis shook his head slowly. 'But it was the wrong thing to say to her, and I admit it now. 'Cos that girl, she was frightened of something. Scared half to death, she was.'

'What was she scared of?'

Francis smiled his crooked smile. 'They say this building's haunted,' he said. 'In the old bit. A ghost of a black dog.' He considered Agnes. 'Maybe you've seen it?'

Agnes inclined her head, and Francis went on, 'Tina-Marie, see, she said she'd seen it. And other ghosts, too. She said she'd seen the woman there, who walks the corridor with her wee child. You could hear the bairn crying, she told me.'

'Who says this?' Agnes tried to sound calm.

He pursed his lips. 'Tina said there's a way through from this building to the old house next door. She said the ghost had showed her.' He grinned at her. 'Stories, you know. Living as I do round here... I been sleeping on the stones out there, on and off for years. The past, you see, it lies beneath the streets, it seeps out through the cracks and whispers in me ears...' He broke into a laugh, which ended in a fit of coughing. 'Still,' he went on when his breath returned to him, 'it's all right for you lot, isn't it. When it comes to ghosts – your God will keep you safe, eh? All you have to do is say the holy words. Me too, I pray to him to keep it all at bay.' He leaned towards her and grasped her hand with his rough fingers. 'I still believe, Sister. I still have me faith. But him...' he gestured with his head towards the ceiling... 'Him, he gave up on me years ago.' He let go of her hand, and smiled at her. 'Don't blame him though,' he added. 'How many chances are you going to give a man, eh?' He put his head on one side. 'Any chance of a cup of tea, Sister?'

She brought him his tea, heavily sugared, and then left the centre. It had come on to rain again. She walked down the road towards the shops, her feet splashing on the pavement. She thought about the history beneath, seeping through the cracks.

When she got back, Shirley had gone. On the convent answering machine, there was a message for her to phone Sister Lucia at the main house.

'Ah, yes, Agnes. We've been discussing you.' Her voice was

brisk, and Agnes felt a sense of dread. 'Can't really stay there. With Helena gone you're the only one there at night, clearly isn't safe. Thought you could have Sister Brigitte's room here as she's in France for a few days.'

Agnes sighed. 'Thank you, Sister.'

'You'll be here for the service tomorrow?'

Agnes remembered it was Sunday tomorrow. 'Yes, Sister,' she said.

'Well, that's fixed then. We'll find you something useful to do. See you in the morning.'

Agnes hung up. She stared at the phone, listening to the rain against the window. Then she left the room. She went out to the hall, hesitated with her hand on the library door handle, then opened it.

The room was in near-darkness. She switched on the lamp at Shirley's desk and sat down.

I don't have to be here any more, she thought.

In her mind she saw the community house; the bright kitchen, the comfortable lounge, the quiet of the chapel. She thought about how it would be, to be given 'something useful to do.'

I have something to do, she thought.

Beyond the high windows, she could hear a rumble of thunder.

If I leave this building...

She thought about the night ahead of her. She recalled Francis's words, that God would keep her safe. She envied him his faith.

She stood up and went over to the Hawker cabinet and unlocked it. All the leather volumes seemed to be there, intact.

Whatever the burglar was searching for, he hadn't found it. She picked up one of the books, checking for Alice's handwriting. It was a printed Latin text. Next to it there was a small wooden box. She replaced the book, but picked up the box. She opened it. It seemed to hold some kind of wooden necklace. She put the box in her pocket.

She left the room, locking it behind her. In the kitchen, she turned on all the lights, unpacked her bag of vegetables and began to chop them for soup. In the light and warmth of the kitchen, grating carrots, slicing fresh bread, tasting a very nice sheep's cheese that she'd found in the deli, she found herself rehearsing tomorrow's argument.

'But I need to stay in the house,' she would say. 'Someone has to be there. Someone has to find out what happened. Helena has disappeared. So has Leila.'

They'll ask me why, she thought to herself. 'Why you?' they'll say. This thought silenced her for a while, as she stirred the soup, dipping in a spoon from time to time to taste it.

She pulled a stool up to the kitchen table and sat down. They'll ask me what makes me so special, she thought. What makes me so sure that it's up to me to find the answers?

She had a sensation of the room growing smaller, the ceiling getting nearer. Why me? The thought repeated itself.

She remembered Athena's words, that taking her final vows had triggered a crisis, a sense of wrongness.

Why me, she thought again. Because I care, she thought. I have to find out more about Tina-Marie. I have to find out what her connection was with Helena. I have to find Leila. And, I have to find out who was responsible for the break-in.

She stood up, tasted the soup, added a splash of cream and brought it to the table.

By the end of her supper, she was firm in her conviction that she would stay in the house until it was sold. The police are on to Troy, she thought, running washing-up water.

She remembered that Tina-Marie had mentioned a friend, Danielle. She wondered where she lived.

Why would Troy and his friends break in to the convent, she wondered, drying up the saucepan. She put her plates away in the cupboard, thinking to herself that she needed to find out more about Jonathan Harris.

She switched everything off and went out to the stairs. The landing light cast long shadows through the banisters.

She started up the stairs.

I will stay here, she told herself, trying not to see movement in the dim shifting patterns of light.

She sat on her bed and opened the little box, and took out the necklace. It was a string of wooden beads, arranged in groups of ten, with a small cross hanging from the end.

A rosary, Agnes thought. Alice's rosary?

It looked very well made, and polished with age.

Was Alice a Catholic, then? Agnes wondered. But Nicolas was Protestant, we know that.

It might explain some more of their difficulties, she thought.

She put the rosary back in the box and began to read Alice's diary again.

'...I set the crystal on the table, with the light behind it as the woman had instructed me. As God is my witness, my heart did cry out to see him, my dear boy, my baby. I gazed into the glow of the crystal's light, and with all my will did urge him to appear. And then, just when my heart was failing, my faith waning, there he was; my baby boy, so bonny and pink-cheeked; and it didst warm my heart so that I did give myself to weeping, but they were tears of joy. E'en though my husband does conspire to have me forget, God has granted me the consolation of this vision.'

Agnes turned a page. 'I have been obliged to hide the crystal. My husband, so sure in his beliefs, talks of spells and magick, and I am in terror lest he say I am a witch and then all will be lost. Elizabeth counsels me to keep my silence, and this I shall do.' There was a gap, then she had written, 'The proud have digged pits for me, which are not after Thy law. They persecute me wrongly, help Thou me.'

Agnes stared at the words for a while. She closed the books and tucked them away into a drawer, with the rosary box. Then she turned out the light.

For a while she lay awake, listening to the sounds of the house, the creakings and the shiftings.

It is time to be brave, she thought.

'Into your hands O Lord I commend my spirit...'

The women's voices rose up to the rafters of the convent chapel. Agnes glanced around, at the familiar faces, the stained glass, the polished wood of the pews flecked with rainbow colours. The priest was raising the host, the silver chalice in his hands glinting in the sunlight.

'This is my blood, which is given for you...'

Casting spells, Philip had said. Invoking holy words, as Francis had called it.

She joined the line of worshippers to take communion. She thought about Alice Hawker, doing the same thing. She thought about the past, buried beneath the streets.

Afterwards everyone gathered in the kitchen. Madeleine fought through the crowd with a mug of tea which she handed to Agnes. They settled on a bench in the hall, the hubbub of voices murmuring in the background.

'How nice to see you,' she said. Agnes smiled at her, at her spiky brown hair, her warm hazel eyes behind their rimless glasses.

'You make it seem so easy,' Agnes said.

'What?' Madeleine brushed biscuit crumbs from her stripey mohair sweater.

'Oh, I don't know. Faith. Community. Living here.'

Madeleine laughed. 'I'm out a lot,' she said.

'They want me to move back,' Agnes said.

Madeleine glanced at her. 'Well,' she said, 'I hear it's all got a bit hairy where you live.'

'Yes. You might say that.' Agnes wondered how to explain.

'You mean, having murders on doorsteps and break-ins is still better than this lot.' Madeleine pointed a thumb towards the kitchen.

Agnes laughed. 'No, it's not that.' She thought about Tina-Marie, about Alice Hawker.

'You're feeling responsible again,' Madeleine said.

Agnes sighed. 'Yes,' she said. 'That's what it is.'

'And you feel they've already taken away your flat, the least they can do is leave you alone. I bet that house is haunted too.'

Agnes was about to reply, but Madeleine went on, 'I'm not surprised Helena needed a break.'

'That's just it,' Agnes said. 'I don't believe Helena's at her mother's at all.'

Madeleine gave Agnes a questioning look. 'In fact,' Agnes went on, 'I was going to ask you a favour.'

Madeleine feigned a heavy sigh. 'Agnes's favours,' she said. 'They usually involve trouble.'

'No, no,' Agnes said. 'It's just a matter of finding Helena's mother's address in the files. I thought you'd probably have access to the office.'

'So, just a little breaking and entering, then.'

'You don't have to—' Agnes began, but Madeleine rested her hand on her arm. 'Tomorrow,' she said. 'I'm on filing duty in any case. And if I can do anything to help after that poor woman was found—' she was interrupted by the sound of footsteps behind them, and Sister Lucia appeared on the stairs. 'Ah. Agnes. Shall we have this meeting? I suggest the library.'

Sister Lucia pulled up a chair. It was a large, high-ceilinged room, with white-painted shelves. Agnes sat down opposite her.

'You can see we're getting organised.' Lucia waved vaguely at the stacks of books. 'Shirley is a godsend, we could never have moved the library without her.'

'There's lots still to do,' Agnes said.

Lucia looked at her. There was a slight pucker of her eyebrows. 'That house is unsafe,' she said. 'You must move here.'

Agnes leaned back slightly in her chair. 'Someone's been killed,' she said.

'The day centre is no longer our responsibility.' Lucia sat straight-backed, her lips pursed.

'It's not about the day centre,' Agnes said.

'That poor girl was nothing to do with us. I appreciate your concern, Agnes, but we can't have you being at risk of random acts of violence.'

'Not random,' Agnes said. 'It's about the house,' she said, aware that she wasn't making sense. 'Whatever happened to Tina-Marie is connected to the sale of the house.'

'The house,' echoed a voice behind them. They both swivelled in their chairs. The door had opened silently, and Sister Phyllida stood there, leaning on a stick, her leg in a plaster cast. She was diminutive, dressed in black, round-faced; Agnes was reminded of a photograph that had stood on the mantelpiece in the high-ceilinged living room of her father's flat near the Parc Monceau in Paris: her English grandmother, he'd told her, but in her child's mind the image was always confused with that of Queen Victoria.

'That house,' Phyllida said, shuffling into the room. She went over to the shelves and began to scan them. 'Just looking for an old friend,' she said. 'Nice to have them back.' She pulled a book from the shelf and leafed through it, resting it on the stick handle. 'Julian of Norwich,' she said. 'Haven't set eyes on her since I lived there,' she said.

'When did you live there?' Agnes got up and pulled out a chair for her, and she lowered herself into the seat, breathing hard, her leg stuck out in front of her.

'There were lots of us in those days,' Phyllida said. 'Every room upstairs, the chapel packed. We all worked in the clinic with those poor young mothers. But it was the library I loved. They'd find me in there in the small hours, chase me off to bed.'

'Did you read the Hawker collection?' Agnes sat down next to her.

'Oh no.' Phyllida shook her head. 'Under lock and key that was, all the time. Said it was bad for us. Rumour was there was spells and all kinds of things in those books.' She reached across and patted Agnes's hand. 'Just as well you're in the house to look after it,' she said. 'All sorts of mischief lurking in those corridors.' She laughed.

'Do you mean ghosts?'

Phyllida rubbed the plaster on her leg. 'This thing does itch so,' she said. 'Ghosts?' she added. 'We heard all sorts of stories. When the house was first built, three hundred odd years ago, there was a mother and her baby son living there, and the boy died. People said she walked the corridors. And there was a story about a dog, growling in the night.' She smiled at Agnes. 'I didn't see anything myself. But then, ghosts are for the faithless, aren't they?' She stood up, clutching her book.

'Did you get your birthday parcel?' Lucia asked.

'Yes. From my nephew. It's an ashtray. Can't think why. Perhaps he stole it from one of the many pubs he frequents.' She turned to Agnes. 'You look after that house,' she said, hobbling towards the door. 'I have happy memories of my time there.'

The door closed behind her.

Agnes faced Lucia.

'Just because—' Lucia began.

'Someone has to look after it.'

'Phyllida has no authority to say so.'

'She's right, though,' Agnes said.

'I can't believe you want to stay there. We'll have to ask the police to keep a watch on the house—'

'They are anyway.'

Lucia stood up. 'I knew it would be like this. I told them, don't make me responsible for Agnes.'

Agnes stood up too. 'You don't have to be.'

'Do your vows mean nothing to you?' Lucia's eyes were dark with rage.

They had reached the door, and Agnes held it open for her. She had an image of Tina-Marie, lying wide-eyed on the stone steps. She thought about Leila and wondered, again, where she was. 'My vows mean everything to me,' she said. 'That's why I have to stay in the house.'

Lucia swept through the door. Agnes heard her heavy shoes loud on the staircase. She gathered up her bag and left the convent. Outside it had come on to rain.

CHAPTER SIX

Beatrice stood outside the day centre and waved her fist. Two men, laden with cameras, ducked. 'We've got our job to do here, and we don't need you people taking photos,' she shouted, above the roar of the morning rush-hour. 'If folks had taken more notice of the poor girl when she was alive, she'd still be with us now.'

She turned on her heel and went back inside. One of the nurses clapped.

'I mean it,' Beatrice said.

Julius took two mugs of tea from the counter and carried them over to the corner of the foyer where Agnes was sitting.

'You survived the night, then?' he asked her.

'Absolutely fine,' she said. She'd read more of Alice's diary, a passage about a battle having taken place near her home when she was a child. Agnes had put the book down and settled into deep sleep. 'Perhaps it was Helena making all the growling and weeping noises after all.'

'Do you think your order will ever speak to you again?'

Agnes sipped her tea. 'I've always been a disappointment to them. I think they hoped that I'd magically change.'

'They should know better than to believe in magic.'

Agnes smiled at him.

'Anyway,' he said. 'I've got Danielle's address.'

'How did you get that?'

'It came up on the parish roll, which is odd because I don't think they're Catholic. I think Tina-Marie lodged there for a bit. They're old friends. As long as she's still where she said she was. The Walworth Green Estate. Near Elephant. Block E11, it says here.' He handed her a slip of paper.

'Are you condoning my rebellion?'

He rubbed his forehead. 'Agnes, all I know is, that a vulnerable person for whom I might have been considered responsible has been killed, and that her child is missing. Of course I'll do what I can to help.' He stood up. 'I only popped in to catch Philip, but he's not here. I'd better get back to church.'

Agnes checked her watch. 'And I said I'd help Shirley this morning. That book dealer is coming in again at ten.'

Jonathan Harris shuffled into the library, hugging his coat around him.

'I heard about the terrible incident to befall this place.' He looked from side to side. 'But you ladies have made an excellent job of tidying up, I see.'

Agnes and Shirley exchanged a glance.

'Let me take your coat.' Shirley took a step towards him.

He held out his coat, still surveying the room. 'So – was anything taken, do you think?'

'We don't know yet,' Shirley said.

'The Hawker collection —?' He looked over to the cabinet.

'It seems not.' Shirley crossed the room and hung up his coat next to hers.

'If I might have a look, perhaps...' He went towards the

cabinet, his arm outstretched towards the door.

'Whatever for?' Shirley said. Again, she glanced at Agnes.

'I might be able to see what's missing.' He stopped, mid-step, and looked at them.

'What do you think might be missing, Mr Harris?' Agnes waited as he looked at the floor, his cheeks flushed. 'This crystal you mentioned,' she went on. 'Is it that that you're interested in?'

He stared at her. 'Have you got it – the crystal?'

'No,' Agnes said. 'We haven't.'

'Oh.'

'How do you know about it?'

'Oh, I – um—' He fished in his pocket and brought out a large white handkerchief. 'It's one of the things I specialise in. Magic, you see. And the seventeenth century, when the Hawker family settled in this house, well, it was a time when magical beliefs rather took hold, after the civil war, the king had been beheaded, people's certainties were shaken, things were rather opened up...' He looked from Agnes to Shirley, wringing his handkerchief in his hands. 'There was talk of a crystal belonging to Nicolas Hawker, that's all. When I heard the collection was leaving this house and going to Oxford...' He looked at his handkerchief in his hands, and put it back in his pocket.

'Perhaps that's what the burglars were after,' Shirley said. She crossed to a pile of books that were sitting on her desk. 'Mr Harris, these are the ones we thought would interest you. Nineteenth-century first editions, most of them. Perhaps we could get on?'

He blinked, appeared to shake himself. 'Yes, yes, of course,' he muttered.

* * *

Late that afternoon, after boxfuls of books had been listed and packed, Agnes checked her phone and found a text from Madeleine.

'Here's Helena's mother's number. Nothing to do with me. Please eat this message.'

She smiled, and stored the number in her phone. She left the convent and caught a bus to Elephant and Castle.

The sun had barely penetrated the clouds all day, and now was giving way to a misty twilight. Agnes made her way past dingy tower blocks, round scrubby patches of grass, until she found block E. The lift door was jammed open. She walked up two flights of stairs to Flat 11 and knocked on the door.

The door opened an inch. A woman's voice said, 'Who are you?'

'I've come about Tina-Marie. I'm a friend of Father Julius.'

The door slammed shut. After a moment it opened again, a tiny crack. 'You know Father Julius?'

'I work with him. I'm Sister Agnes.'

The door opened just wide enough to let Agnes in. The young woman locked it behind her, the bolts jammed hard across. She was wearing a short denim skirt pale against her dark legs, and her hair was extended into long black corkscrew curls.

'Sister?' she said.

'I'm a nun.'

'Oh. I'm Danielle,' she said, extending a hand. 'Don't they lock you up?' she added, as Agnes shook her hand.

'It depends.' Agnes followed her along the threadbare carpet into the living room. Yellowing net curtains were roughly draped across the windows.

'Here, sit down.' Danielle gathered an armful of magazines from a leather-look armchair and put them on the floor.

'Is this your flat?' Agnes sat in the chair.

Danielle laughed. 'I wish. I'm stuck here with Mum and my sister. She's a pain, my sister.' She flopped down on the sofa.

'How did you know Tina-Marie?'

'She came to my school. We were about twelve. I think it was after her dad left, they were rehoused.' She giggled. 'She was a laugh, Tina was. On her first day she nicked a packet of fags. There was this PE teacher we couldn't bear. Anyway, she was sitting near us in the canteen, and her ciggies were just on the table in front of her, and Tina-Marie managed to nick them from right under her nose. And then this teacher, she was like looking for them, under the table. We laughed... We were mates after that.' Her gaze went to the faded curtains, seeing beyond them. 'Will there be a funeral? I don't like to think of her, lying in that bleedin' fridge.'

'Yes. At some point they'll release the body for burial. They're contacting the family.'

'Her sister must know.'

'Where's her sister?

'Dunno. Up north, maybe.'

'We didn't know any of her family,' Agnes said.

'Her mum's died. And her dad probably doesn't care. He went back to Ireland, everyone said.'

'Anyone else?'

'Only bloody Troy.' A loose thread curled from the arm of the chair, and Danielle pulled at it. 'I knew he'd kill her. He hated that baby—'

'Whose was the baby?'

'She had him with Jared. He was sweet, lovely bloke he was. A bit different, you know, I always thought he was gay. I only met him once, maybe twice.'

'Where is he?'

'I don't know. Someone said he went to America after they split up.'

'Does he know she's dead?'

'Dunno.' She frowned. 'Doubt it. It's not like it'll be on the news over there.'

'Why did they split up?' Agnes shifted in her chair.

Danielle shrugged. 'I don't know. They were good together, I always thought. But then he started going to this church thing, and she went with him a few times. And after that we didn't see her no more. Maybe a year or so, we didn't see her.' Danielle looked at Agnes. 'Don't you wear them things, you nuns?'

'Not any more.'

The loose thread had grown in length, and she began to twist it into a neat coil. 'And then, after all that time, she turned up here, one night. And she just came in, all normal, she had baby Leila with her, and a couple of the girls were round, and we all made a big fuss of her. But she was different. Kind of nervous. Kept checking her phone, you know. And we said, what you scared of girl? And she said, no one. Anyway, after that we started seeing more of her, and she became a bit more like normal again, she came out clubbing with us lot again, things like that. And that's how she met Troy. But I wish she hadn't.' Her hand went to her eyes, and she dabbed at a tear. 'I so wish she hadn't.'

'When she was scared—' Agnes began. 'When she first came back, with the baby – who was she scared of?'

Danielle picked up a bottle of sugar-pink nail varnish and shook it. 'Dunno.'

'Was she scared of Leila's father?'

Danielle put down the nail varnish. 'No, not him. He weren't never that kind of bloke. I don't think he'd lay a finger on her. I never heard her say nothing about that.' She leaned back in the chair. 'I think it was that church they went to. I think she was scared of them. I think that's why she liked your priest friend, 'cos you weren't like them.'

'Do you know where it was, this church?'

Danielle shook her head. 'Out Essex way, maybe. I think she said that.'

'When Jared hears about her death – will he come here, do you think?'

Danielle frowned. 'If he's in America – I doubt it. They split up, you know, they didn't see each other. I think he was really upset.'

'And Leila?'

Danielle shrugged. 'He's probably got a whole other family out there. You know what guys are like—' She stopped, then added, 'Or maybe you don't…'

'I know enough,' Agnes said, and Danielle smiled.

'He might come back if he hears Leila's missing,' Danielle said. 'He weren't a bad bloke, and he's all she's got now.' Her eyes filled with tears. 'I keep thinking, maybe I could have done something, I knew Troy was trouble, I could have warned her…'

'You mustn't blame yourself,' Agnes said.

'Do you think Leila's all right?' Danielle blinked back more tears.

Agnes thought about Helena and Tina-Marie, their urgent conversation seen through the glass door. She stood up. 'Yes,' she said. 'I have to think that.'

Danielle led the way to the front door and unbolted it.

'Thanks for seeing me,' Agnes said.

'It's nice to talk about her,' she said. She stood, hunched in the narrow doorway. 'Do you believe in ghosts?' she said.

'Well, I—'

'Sometimes I think I see her,' Danielle went on. 'Down there—' she pointed outside. 'Down in the stairwell where the kids hang out. I think I see her, walking up the stairs, carrying little Leila. And then it's not her. It makes me cry, you know.'

Agnes reached out and touched her arm.

'When you find out where baby Leila is – will you tell me?' Danielle turned tearful eyes to her.

'Yes,' Agnes said. 'I will. Will I find you here?'

'Me?' She managed a thin smile. 'Me, I'm not going nowhere. Even if I wanted to.'

Agnes said goodbye, and heard the heavy bolts slam shut behind her. She walked down the stairwell, amid shouts, angry noises, a bottle thrown somewhere behind her, the smash of glass against the concrete.

As she searched for her keys on the doorstep of Collyer House, she heard her name. She turned round. Philip was standing at the foot of the steps.

'Agnes – have you got a moment?'

'Philip,' she said. His jacket was crumpled, his hair awry. 'You look dreadful,' she said.

'I'm not...not at my best,' he said.

She descended the stairs. 'Yes,' she said. 'I've got more than a moment. I've disobeyed orders again, and I'm rather on my own now.'

'Do you want a drink? Do they let you drink?' He looked down at her, distracted.

She smiled. 'Yes.'

'From the sound of it,' he began to walk down the drive, 'whether they let you or not has nothing to do with it.'

'Would that it were otherwise,' Agnes said, falling into step next to him.

He pushed open the heavy glass door and held it for her. Agnes saw oak panels and frosted glass. 'This seems to have become my local in the last few weeks,' he said, as she passed through ahead of him. She was aware of warmth and noise, and Philip beside her, his glasses steaming up. 'What'll you have?' he said. 'I imagine vows of poverty prevent you buying a round.'

'It's slightly more complicated than that, but I'll have a whisky please. Single malt with ice.'

He raised an eyebrow. 'That's poverty for you.'

She found a table in a corner while he queued at the bar. A series of prints hung on the wall; there was the old London Bridge; there was a wide muddy thoroughfare, busy with horses and carts and coaches, all passing a version of the pub she was now sitting in, she realised.

'Yours is the one with ice.' Philip put two large whiskies down on the table.

'Look,' she said. 'History. Is that really this pub in that picture?'

'Could be.' Philip sat down on the bench opposite. 'It's quite old. At least, its foundations are.'

'Like Collyer House, then.' Agnes sipped her drink.

'How are the ghosts?' He swirled his whisky round in his glass.

'Oh, quiet. At the moment.'

'You're there on your own now?'

She nodded, and he went on, 'I don't get it. Giving up your life like that, making vows...' He studied her, briefly. 'I've looked at the Bible, once or twice. There's no way you can tell me that a work like that carries any kind of universal truth. It's a bundle of documents, put together over centuries, mostly for political reasons...'

She put her glass down. 'You'd be surprised to find I agree with you. At least, in part.'

'So, why sign up to it then?'

'Sometimes, I suppose...' She stared at the table, tracing the grain of the wood with a finger. 'Sometimes you just have to say Yes. Perhaps it's like getting married.'

'Getting married? It's nothing like getting married. I married Serena because I love her. You can't tell me your relationship with your God is in any way like that. For a start, I know my wife exists.'

She glanced up at him. 'You weren't at work today.'

'No.' He took a sip of whisky. 'Serena...I'd arranged an appointment for her – with a colleague, good man, I've known him for years. Psychiatrist, one of the best. So, we drove up to the hospital, in Hertfordshire. And she refused to get out of the car. Just – refused. I didn't know what to do. I couldn't carry her into the hospital, could I? So, we sat there for a while. I tried everything. At one point, I remember shouting at her, trying to tell her that it was for her own good...' He passed a hand across his forehead. 'And then we went home. That's how I spent today.'

'And how is she now?'

'She seems to blame me. She – she's not saying much, really. I tried to get her to eat, she's not really doing that either.' He drained his glass. 'Thing is – all she'll talk about – is Heaven.'

'Heaven?'

'I blame this priest she's started seeing. It's the local church, near us. Catholic, I think it is. Serena was raised a Catholic, it came from her mother's side. It's had no great significance, she's barely mentioned it up till now. Anyway she seems to think that this baby who died – well, it wasn't even a baby, was it – she seems to think it's gone somewhere. She's got out some old Bible, sits there with it, turning the pages. It's as if she's looking for clues...' His voice shook.

Agnes finished her whisky. 'How awful,' she said.

He looked up. 'For her, or for me?'

'For both of you.'

'The thing is,' he said, 'She's the person I love most in the whole world, and I don't know how to help her.' He stood up. He picked up Agnes's coat and held it for her to put on.

The pavements were wet, splashed yellow with the streetlights. They walked in silence to Agnes's door. He nodded at her, then went to his car.

* * *

Agnes sat at her desk with Alice's notebook in front of her. She began to leaf through it, finding recipes, housekeeping, worries about various horses and servants. She turned a series of blank pages. The end of the book was filled with writing.

'My mother did bring to me her rosary, a simple wooden string it is but to me it is as gold. I shall keep it in its box away from Nicolas's eyes, for he holds such things to be as magick charms and not of God at all. Lord but it is hard to breathe here. I dream of being back at Cranfield. I spoke of these things to my husband. I told him of the life we had as children there, roaming with my brothers, the trees we climbed, my brothers fishing in the Welland. All Nicolas did say was that I was free to go back to my father's house, and take my father's name once more, but that my son would stay here at Collyer. He has hardened his face to me, and his heart is of stone. This is my fear, that I will die here. I will die. God keep my child.'

Agnes closed the book. She wrapped her cardigan around her, although the room was warm. She checked her watch – it was not yet ten. She took out her phone, found Madeleine's text, clicked on the number she'd stored and pressed *Call*.

'Sedmore nine five double eight.' The voice was crystal English.

'Am I speaking to Mrs Padgett?'

'Who is this?'

'This is Sister Agnes. From Helena's order. I'm sorry to phone so late.'

'She's out.' The words were a bark. Agnes expected her to ring off, but the line remained open.

'When will she be back?'

'Soon, I expect.' The voice softened again. 'Can I take a message?'

'Actually—' Agnes thought fast. 'It was you I was hoping to see. I'll be in the area tomorrow, and I wondered whether I could pop in.'

'Whatever for? Who did you say you were?'

'Sister Agnes.' She took a chance. 'We're worried about her.'

'You're not the only ones,' came the reply, followed by a silence.

'Would you be able to see me?' Agnes waited.

There was a small sigh, then Mrs Padgett said, 'Yes. If you must. I'll be here at lunchtime, don't expect anything special.'

'Of course not.'

'I hold you people responsible, if you must know.'

'That's perfectly understandable,' Agnes said.

'We lunch at one.' The line went dead.

Agnes rang off. Lunch in Buckinghamshire, she thought. She imagined tea-plates with pink roses on them.

I just hope she doesn't throw them at me.

CHAPTER SEVEN

Athena wrapped her hands around her wide white cup and stared out of the steamed-up windows. 'They're not all like that in Buckinghamshire,' she said. 'She might be perfectly sweet.'

Outside, people hurried to work. Agnes watched the sea of legs, the umbrellas tilting above them. 'She's very cross with us,' Agnes said. 'And I don't blame her.'

'But if this woman you're looking for is there, this fellow nun—'

'I don't believe she is.' Agnes broke off a piece of croissant and spread it with butter. 'It all sounded completely unconvincing.' She gazed out at the rain. 'And as for taking the order's dreadful old car up the M40 in this, I can't imagine I'll even get there. And they're so cross with me, I'm going to have to steal the keys.'

Athena stirred milky foam around in her cup. 'I know where this is leading,' she said.

'No, really. I couldn't possibly ask you.'

'The silly old thing has been sitting out in my residents' parking space for weeks, I bet people think it's abandoned, I never use it, I don't understand the congestion charge as it is, if they bring it in for Kensington and Chelsea, which of course they're bound to do, I'm never going to drive again...where was I? Oh, yes, of course you can borrow my car. It'll prevent anyone towing it away.'

'You're a true friend,' Agnes said.

'I might get another croissant,' Athena said. She broke off a piece of Agnes's and chewed it.

'How was your weekend?'

Athena's face brightened. 'It was fab, thank you. The drinks do in the gallery went really well, Simon was delighted, everyone loves the birds, I told you about them, didn't I? Metal sculpture things, huge, this bloke called Justin does them, he's quite well known, apparently, and some of the people who turned up were quite famous, like that bloke from that band, oh, you know the one, long hair, shouts a lot...Anyway, where was I? Oh, yes, the weirdest thing about it all was that Justin brought his brother along, he's called Jake, he does the heavy stuff, they have a foundry somewhere, can you imagine? But the weird thing was, I knew Jake. I'd met him, years ago, I started a fashion course at college, didn't finish it of course, but there was a friend of mine, Anita, on the course, and Jake used to go around with her. He was doing photography, I think, or maybe sculpture...Anyway, we ended up sitting in a corner catching up. It was great. He lost touch with Anita. He thinks she got married and ended up selling holiday flats in Cyprus or somewhere.' She stopped, breathless, pink-cheeked.

'So, this Jake—'

'What?' Athena met her eyes.

'Oh, nothing.'

'I mean, after all these years...' Athena spooned the last of her coffee out of her cup. 'He was always a good-looking man, I suppose.'

'And now?'

Her face clouded. 'To be honest, sweetie, things would be a lot easier if Nic could be bothered to remember that we're in a relationship. Do you know, it's Valentine's day today?'

Agnes smiled. 'I think for us nuns the story of St. Valentine is all about self-renunciation leading to some ghastly painful death. Most saints' days are.'

'Oh, darling, you nuns don't half make life difficult for yourselves. You see, for us lesser mortals, St. Valentine's Day just means that gorgeous men send you cards and flowers and chocolate and things.' She pulled a sulky face. 'Unless you're me, of course, when nothing happens at all. Come on, let's go to my place and I'll give you my car keys.'

Agnes pulled in to check the map. The rain had eased as she left London, and a watery sunlight was breaking through the clouds. Away from the motorway, stalled by the side of the road, she could even hear birdsong.

She started the engine again and pulled out into the main road. A left turning, then a right, and there it was: a tidy drive, at the end of which stood a house. Agnes drove up the gravel and parked. The house was neatly square, made of scrubbed-looking red brick, with a shiny new garage extension. Around the door there was a spindly climbing rose, its few remaining leaves spotted brown.

The door was glossy green, and as Agnes got out of the car, it opened. A woman was standing there. Agnes saw an elegant sweep of blonde hair, patent court shoes. Even her apron seemed tailored.

'You came, then,' she said. Her eyes scanned the scratched paintwork of Athena's Polo.

'I had to,' Agnes said, glancing at the BMW which sat sleekly in the garage.

'She's not here.' She spoke with a tilt of her chin, the words a challenge.

'I know,' Agnes said.

'Well, I just want to know where you people have sent her.'

'Us?' Agnes tried to look tall. She wished she'd hired a car, something brand-new and fast. She wished she wasn't standing on the lower steps.

'Helena told me her order were sending her away, but I was to pretend she was living here.'

'Mrs Padgett,' Agnes began. 'Helena's in danger. One of the patients at our day centre is dead, as I'm sure you heard. She had a small child. The last time I saw the child, she was with Helena. Then they both vanished.'

Mrs Padgett looked down at her. 'I read about it in the paper, the dead girl. Well, all I can say is, Helena didn't mix with people like that.'

'They were part of some church together,' Agnes said. 'In Essex.'

Mrs Padgett opened her mouth. She put out one hand to the doorframe, to steady herself. 'Oh,' she said. 'Were they both in it? Are you sure?'

'Tina entrusted Helena with her little girl when she knew she was in danger. They must go back a long way. And I knew from Helena's background that she'd been in a cult.'

'Yes.' Mrs Padgett breathed out. 'That man—' she spat the words. 'The Reverend,' she said, as if the sound itself tasted bitter. 'He was never going to leave her alone.' She appeared diminished, defeated, her hands pulling at the fabric of her apron. 'Well,' she said, 'you'd better come in.' Her heels clicked across the parquet floor as she led Agnes into a wide living room.

'My husband isn't here.' She gestured to one of the chintz sofas, and Agnes sat down. 'He has Alzheimer's, you see. I rather rely on the respite care these days.' She spoke briskly. Agnes sensed an habitual deflection of sympathy. 'I did set lunch for two, I wasn't sure if you'd come.' She squeezed her hands together in the pocket of her apron.

Two places were set at one end of a long mahogany dining table.

'Do you have other children?' Agnes asked.

'No.' Mrs Padgett fetched paper serviettes, folding them carefully in half. 'We're not a religious family.' She stood back and surveyed the table. 'We were surprised when Helena expressed an interest in all that.' She turned to Agnes. 'We're just ordinary people, you see. I'm not the sort of person whose daughter decides to be a nun.' Her voice choked on the last word. She wiped her hands on her apron and went out to the kitchen. Agnes heard plates being arranged. 'It's nothing special,' Mrs Padgett said, re-appearing with two plates of sandwiches. 'Do sit down.'

Agnes came to the table. Mrs Padgett took off her apron, folding it neatly over the back of one of the chairs, and sat down opposite her. She passed her a plate of sandwiches. Agnes saw the neat, crust-less triangles; the tremor in her hands as she put the plate back down again. She didn't take any food herself. Instead, she put her hands to her face and breathed out. 'I need her back,' she said. 'If she's in danger, I hold you people responsible.'

'Tell me about this church in Essex,' Agnes said.

Helena's mother took her hands away from her face. She picked up a small cheese sandwich and placed it on her plate.

'She was such a promising child,' she said, and her voice grew level again. 'She played the violin, did ice-skating. We were always very close. She went to college, she was training to be a physiotherapist. She got a placement in Southend, at the hospital there. She always used to phone, or write, lovely chatty letters. I still read them sometimes.' She stopped, biting her lip. 'Then the letters changed.' Absently, she picked up the plate and offered it to her again. Agnes took a ham sandwich and waited. 'She mentioned a friend, a girl. She'd go on about a church they went to. We didn't think much of it at the time. When someone says church, you think of one like the one in the village here, don't you. Flower arrangements. Coffee mornings. You don't expect to be asked to give up your life.' She looked at Agnes. 'She'd come home and try and convert us, and each time she was thinner. I think he took their money, I think she couldn't afford to eat. We didn't understand what she was saying, she'd get very upset, I think she really believed that we would go to hell. It became quite apparent that she wasn't going to work any more, she'd given up her studies. In the end, my husband, Donald, said we must go there. We must find out what's happening to our daughter.'

She stood up and fetched a jug of water from the sideboard, and filled both their glasses. 'We met him, the Reverend

Malcolm Noble.' She shook her head. 'He looked like an ordinary vicar. We were surprised. We didn't know what to expect, I suppose.' She took a sip of water. 'He was very friendly. Very charming. My husband thought he was American, a slight accent he had, though he seems to have been here for years. He said he was very pleased to meet us. He said he didn't like to drive families apart. I told him, but that's exactly what you are doing. Then he sent for Helena and she came in, and she was very pleased to see us too. At the time we were reassured, you see, but we were wrong. It was awful, to see her hanging on his every word like that.'

'What happened then?'

'We came home without her. The months passed. And then one day she came home. She wouldn't say what had happened, but it was quite clear that it was all over with the Reverend Malcolm Noble. We'd try to draw her out, but she wouldn't say much. She began to eat, she put on weight, she began to smile again. We were delighted to have our daughter back. We suggested she return to her course, but she said that everything was different. She was still religious, you see. She said that God would make it clear what she had to do next. And so the weeks went by, and then she got a job in London, didn't she, and that was when she encountered your lot.' She stopped, overwhelmed by the effort of so many words.

Agnes was gathering crumbs with a fingertip. 'Mrs Padgett,' she said, 'how did Helena know Tina-Marie?'

'It's not a name I've ever heard,' she replied.

'They were both in this Essex church,' Agnes said. 'They must have met there. She had troubles of her own, Tina did.

And when she knew she was in danger, she gave baby Leila over to Helena to keep her safe. And now they're both in danger,' she finished.

'As I said before—' Mrs Padgett met her gaze, her blue eyes steely. 'I hold you people responsible.'

'But if someone chooses to run away—'

'It's your God, isn't it,' she interrupted. 'Without your God, everything would have been all right. My godson lives in the next village. A lovely boy. Works in the city now, one of those banks, they look after him, they do. They used to spend a lot of time together, Helena and Richard. Why she couldn't have just...' She broke off, turned her head away. 'Some idea of another life, a life after this one.' She stood up, and began to gather up the plates. 'I didn't do anything wrong,' she went on. 'This life is enough for me. I raised my daughter. I nursed my husband. If there is a God, surely that's enough for him?'

Agnes got up from the table. 'Yes,' she said. 'Of course that's enough for him.'

'So why did you people tell my daughter to give everything up? Why have *you* given everything up?' Her voice was louder now, and a spot of pink appeared on each cheek.

They stood either side of the table. Agnes hesitated. 'I suppose everyone has to choose their own path,' she said, hearing as she uttered them how empty her words sounded.

'And my daughter, you say, has rescued some baby belonging to a drug addict, and is now in danger herself. What kind of choice is that?' She glanced around the room, as if the polished mahogany, the silver picture frames, the antique vase, were all somehow in agreement with her.

Agnes reached for her coat and began to put it on. 'Mrs Padgett,' she said. 'I can't begin to know how you must feel. But I give you my word, that I intend to find Helena and bring her safely back.'

'They sent you, didn't they? Your order. To try to appease me.' She took her hands from the table and stood, weakly, in the room. Outside the sun came out, and the dark polish of the table rippled purple in the sudden light.

Agnes looked at her. If only they had, she thought. Wouldn't it be nice, to be here on behalf of Sister Lucia, rather than expressly against her wishes.

'But then obedience is what it's all about, isn't it.' Mrs Padgett's expression had hardened again. 'That's all you people know. That's how you made Helena do what you wanted, rather than what anyone else might have wanted for her.'

Obedience, Agnes thought. It would be so restful, to obey. To let the police sort it all out. To do as the order wishes, and leave Helena to her own fate. 'I think I'd better go,' Agnes said.

At the door, Agnes offered her hand, and Mrs Padgett took it briefly, good manners prevailing. 'I'll keep in touch,' Agnes said. 'Please trust me.'

There was a distance in Mrs Padgett's eyes.

Agnes pulled out her notebook and scribbled down a number. She tore out the page and handed it to her. 'This is my mobile number. Just in case,' she said.

Mrs Padgett held the piece of paper between her fingers. 'Thank you,' she said.

Agnes got into the car. The tall trees behind the house

swayed in the breeze, the afternoon sun flickering through their branches. She started the engine and pulled away. In the mirror she could still see her, standing immobile on the gravel drive.

If it wasn't for God, she thought, stuck in the nose-to-tail traffic of the M40. If it wasn't for God...

Without God, Helena would have married her nice stockbroker. Tina-Marie wouldn't have been in fear of her life. Francis at the day centre wouldn't believe that he's been rejected by Heaven. Alice Hawker's husband wouldn't have accused her of witchcraft. Philip's wife wouldn't be retreating from him, looking for clues in the Bible.

Without God I wouldn't be a nun.

Isn't that enough for God, Mrs Padgett had asked. Raising your children, nursing your husband, doing the flowers and the coffee mornings in the church hall. A polite, restrained, English God, who means no harm.

But what happens when we find a God that asks for more, a vicious God who asks for our obedience and then demands a sacrifice: that we starve ourselves, that we give away all our money; that we kill, ourselves or others?

Better no God, Agnes thought, than one who asks for blood.

She tucked the car into a space in the day centre car park. Philip was in his office, and he looked up as she came in.

'I'm becoming an atheist,' she said.

'Glad to hear it,' he answered. 'An intelligent woman like you, bound to see sense some time.' He continued to write some notes.

'I thought you might have left.' She glanced at the clock on his wall. 'Everyone else has.'

'Catching up on paperwork. Also,' he said, 'they've arrested Troy. I texted you.'

She took her phone from her bag and looked at it. 'So you did.'

'A young woman came here. Pretty thing. Long legs.'

'Danielle,' Agnes said.

'She said could I let you know that he's behind bars where he belongs. Words to that effect.'

'Good.' She sat down on the shabby armchair. 'Now all we have to do is let Helena know, wherever she is, so that she can bring Leila back.'

'Also, that little girl needs her father, the young lady said. And she was going to try to find someone who knew him, some chap in America.'

'Oh.'

'I'm glad it makes sense to you. I hadn't a clue what she was on about.' He leaned over his papers, the scratch of his cheap pen the only sound in the room.

'Philip,' she said. 'How is it, then, in your world with no God?'

'Oh,' he said. 'It's a peaceful place. No religious wars. No sectarian violence. No suicide bombers.' She noticed how he didn't smile. 'Everything is rational, you see. In my world, our beliefs are governed by evidence. No ghosts, no magic.'

'Is no one wrong about anything, then, in your world?'

He put down his pen and rubbed his chin. 'There's debate, because, of course, the evidence is open to interpretation. But you see, even if two people disagree about what they see under a microscope, neither of them will start a war as a result.'

'But—' she felt tears well in her eyes, for a reason she couldn't explain. 'In your world,' she went on, 'what would Julius do?'

He frowned at her. 'Ah, yes. Julius,' he said. 'The place of moral goodness in a scientific universe. Open to debate, of course. Do we act well as human beings because of evolutionary programming? Does, in fact, a belief in God, such as Julius's, confer some kind of heritable advantage?'

'We're supposed to be celibate,' Agnes said, 'so it wouldn't be much use.'

He smiled.

'You see, everything Julius does,' Agnes went on, 'relates to a higher order.'

'Does he think he'll be rewarded in heaven?'

Agnes shook her head. 'He's wiser than that. It's about this life, now. It's about discerning God's will in everyday life.'

'And if I live with no sense of God's will,' Philip said, 'am I incapable of doing good?'

'No,' Agnes said. 'Of course not. Some of the best Christians I've ever met have been atheists.'

'So your view is, if someone like me is a good human being, that's your God working within me whether I like it or not?'

Agnes was silent. They were sitting in the twilight, in near darkness. 'I couldn't presume to say that,' she said, after a while.

'My wife,' he said, suddenly, 'my wife lives in your world. A world of sin and suffering and punishment. A world where wine turns into blood – where the ghosts of dead babies whisper in the night...'

In the dim light she thought perhaps he was crying.

'Agnes,' he said, and his hand reached out for hers. 'She has left me behind.'

They sat in silence. Outside the rush-hour traffic hurried and hooted and squealed. Agnes thought about Alice Hawker, about the old red bricks beneath them. 'All I can say,' she said, 'is that perhaps God – whatever it is, this God – perhaps it's what Serena needs.'

'How can this God help her?' He spoke sharply. 'She needs real help, medical help. She's in pain.'

'All I know is what I believe,' Agnes began, but he interrupted.

'You can't tell me your God is the solution to the madness. As far as I'm concerned, your God is the madness.' He stood up, and reached for his jacket. 'I'm going home,' he said. 'Whatever home is these days.'

Outside he wished her goodnight, distant, his eyes already on his Peugeot where it sat in the car park. Agnes went round to her door and let herself in. The silence was familiar now, and soothing.

That night she lit her candles, settled on her cushion, picked up her prayer book. She leafed through the pages until she found the liturgy for that day.

'The proud have dug pitfalls for me in defiance of your law; All your commandments are true; but they persecute me with lies, O come to my help; They have almost made an end of me on the earth...'

Her hand went to Alice's rosary.

The proud have digged pits for me... The words circled in her mind.

Outside her room, the landing creaked. She thought about the woman in a white collar who had been seen, walking the corridor.

They persecute me wrongfully, help Thou me.

An image came to her of the stones beneath the house, the foundations of the past leaching out into the present.

She thought about Alice's fear of death, her terror of her husband. She remembered how Tina had frozen in fear when Troy came to find her in the clinic.

She watched her candle flicker in the darkness. Help Thou me, she thought, addressing not the war-like God of her imaginings, but a God beyond words; beyond ghosts and magic, beyond obedience and sin.

Tomorrow I will go to Julius's mass, she thought.

CHAPTER EIGHT

'And afterwards, he went throughout every city and village, preaching the good news of God's kingdom; and the twelve were with him, and certain women, who had been healed of evil spirits, Mary called Magdalene, out of whom went seven demons...'

Agnes looked up to the pulpit as Julius read the lesson. Behind him, the sun went in, and the stained glass window faded into thick strokes of lead.

Afterwards she cupped her hands around the tea that Julius passed her, as if to warm her fingers.

'Julius,' she said. 'These spirits that had to be driven out of the women...'

'Oh,' he said. 'Today's reading. Always a tricky one.'

'What do we think about it?'

He glanced across at her and smiled. 'We?' he said.

'Philip's wife, Serena, she's seeing ghosts and things. She's also seeing a Catholic priest.'

'Often to be confused with spirits from the other side.' Julius settled in his chair by the window.

'Please be serious.' Agnes flashed him a look. 'Philip says she's in pain and needs medical help. Anti-depressants sort of help. He and I were in the clinic last night. I wanted to be an atheist like him, and he wanted to have some sense of what his wife is going through. Neither of us managed it.'

Julius got up and added some more milk to his mug, then sat down again. 'Why did you want to be an atheist?' His voice was edged with concern.

'Because of Alice. And Helena. And little Leila. Because sometimes people's idea of God drives them to behave very badly.'

'But that's not true belief.' Julius stirred his spoon round in his mug. 'If we create God in our own image, then we create a false god. All the wisdom of our tradition warns against it. God doesn't want us to be unquestioning.'

'But what if people aren't wise? And what if a religion takes advantage of that lack of wisdom? Philip says it's better to have no religion at all.'

The morning sun crept through the leaded window. Julius smoothed a wisp of white hair from his forehead. 'And what do you say?'

Agnes took a sip of tea. 'In Collyer House,' she began, 'something very bad happened. Alice was living in fear, and then either she died or her child died, or both.'

'Is she the lady with the white collar, then?' His eyes met hers.

'We don't believe in ghosts, Julius,' she said.

'Nor we do.'

'We don't believe in demons being cast out of women either, do we?'

'You mean this morning's reading?'

She sighed. 'I just think Philip's right, about Serena. She's not well. We don't really believe that God is speaking to her, do we?'

Julius picked up the old brown teapot and refilled their cups. 'Of course, one does have to be careful.' He sat down again. 'It's all about discerning the will of God.'

'Tina was worried about devils and black dogs, and then she died.'

Julius reached across and laid his hand briefly across hers, then withdrew it. 'Your order can't want you to continue living there.'

'No,' Agnes said. 'They don't.'

'Should you be disobeying them?'

'It's discernment. As you said, God doesn't ask us for unquestioning obedience.'

He leaned back in his chair. 'It often happens,' he said, 'with final vows...a kind of crisis. A reaction against the very finality of it all...'

'Julius, someone has died. Her child is in danger. This isn't me having a crisis, this is real.'

'You could just leave it to the police.'

'But how do I explain it all to them? How do I explain Alice and her fears?' Agnes looked at her watch. 'I'd better go. There are still lots of Saints to be packed into boxes.'

He stood up and opened the door for her. As she went out to the stairs, he put his hand on her arm. 'Take care of yourself,' he said.

'Mr Harris will be here in a moment, he's going to take the first few boxfuls away.' Shirley smoothed the dust from a book cover and placed it on a pile. 'I must say, I'll be glad when this is over.'

'What will you do?' Agnes added another book to the same pile.

'Well, Mother needs me,' Shirley said. 'It's probably best if I spend some time at home with her before I think what to do next. I've put Mr Harris's boxes over by the door there.'

'I'm sure the order can find you something else to do.' Agnes picked up a book and frowned at the spine. 'Does Jonathan want *Helpful Tips for the Rose Grower?*'

'Put it on the Maybe pile,' Shirley said. 'The order have been very kind, but it's probably time to move on. And Mother is getting more and more frail.' She glanced up at the boarded-up window. 'I'll be glad to leave this house, I must say.' She pulled her cardigan sleeves down to her wrists, as the doorbell rang. 'That'll be Mr Harris,' she said.

Jonathan bustled into the room, with a young man behind him. Agnes saw the same gingery hair, the same uncertain expression. 'This is M-Matthew, he's come to help me. I brought my old Volvo, you see.'

Shirley indicated the boxes by the door.

'Good,' Jonathan said. 'Good. Well, let's get going.'

Agnes looked up at the library clock. 'Talking of cars,' she said, 'I promised to return one to someone.'

Athena and Agnes carried trays of salad to a corner table and sat down. 'Oh dear, it's all a bit crummy.' Athena looked around, at the high stools and chrome tables. 'But I haven't got long, Simon needs me back at the gallery. And it's just as well you brought the car back, too, Jake wants me to give him a lift later on.'

'Jake?' Agnes scratched her head.

'Oh, you know, I told you. Justin's brother. Justin's the one doing the big bird sculptures, and Jake's the boy I knew all those years ago from college, well, obviously, not a boy now, more of a man...' Athena stopped, pink-cheeked.

'Doesn't he have a car?'

Athena speared a circle of cucumber with a plastic fork. 'Oh, he has a van thing, but Justin's got it at the moment at the foundry, and I said I'd help Jake move the first pieces over to the gallery from the studio in Hoxton.'

'That's very nice of you.' Agnes put a straw into a carton of pomegranate juice and tasted it. 'Are you sure this is good for you?'

'Sweetie, it turns out it's miracle stuff, the seeds are really difficult to eat but as juice it's just brilliant, really. Did I tell you I lost two pounds last week, without even trying?'

'What's brought all this on, then?'

'All what?' Athena glanced out of the window. 'I like that woman's jacket,' she said, 'look, that tweed one just passing.'

'Mmm,' Agnes agreed, following her line of vision.

Athena turned back to her. 'When Nic was here, I used to have facials. Not often, but just from time to time. And I'd have my nails done, properly. And I was thinking about it, on Sunday evening. I looked at my nails, and they were just, you know, normal. Plain.'

'Like mine—' Agnes offered her hands for inspection.

'You're a nun, it's different.'

'Well—' Agnes surveyed Athena, her hair pinned back in loose curls, her crisp white shirt and black jacket, diamond studs at her ears, scarlet nails. 'You look great today.'

'This is me, you see, sweetie. This is how I am. On Sunday

I thought, because Nic's not here, I'm losing all sense of what I'm like. And then yesterday, Jake told me I looked nice, I was wearing that cashmere jumper of mine, you know that lilac one that hangs really well? Well, he said something nice about it, and I felt – I felt like a plant that's been neglected and then someone waters it. Don't laugh—' Athena looked across at Agnes. 'Just because you've relinquished all that, doesn't mean I don't need it. And then over dinner Jake said that he'd had this feeling, as soon as he'd seen me at that gallery on Saturday, that something had happened.'

'Happened? What, between you two?'

'He's very perceptive, he's got Moon in Pisces it turns out.' Athena ate her last leaf of lettuce.

'Did he tell you that? Do men know such things?'

'No, kitten, don't be silly, I looked it up in my charts.'

'So when did you have dinner with him?'

'Last night. There's a fish restaurant, Spanish sort of place, near the gallery, I've always meant to try it. We had a lovely evening, we always used to get on really well, he said he'd always fancied me, I laughed it off of course, but...' Athena closed her plastic tray, suddenly serious. 'I ought to get back,' she said.

'So what happened?'

Athena twiddled her fingers through a lock of hair. 'When I got home I phoned Nic. We had a chat, you know. And he was very jolly, and he told me all about the weekend and how he'd gone off to some archive just near Barcelona, and how he'd seen some bit of paper, a marriage certificate from 1879 or somewhere, which proved something about his great-grandmother possibly being Jewish, I'm afraid I lost track.

And I listened to him going on about the past, and after a while I said, but what about Now? I said, I need you here, now. I don't want you to be in 1879.'

'What did he say?'

'He said, he's more fully Here, Now, if he learns about Then. He says, it's about looking for clues, finding out who he is.' Athena tucked the lock of hair behind her ear.

'What did you say?'

'What I wanted to say was, Jake is lovely and attentive and he makes me laugh, and last night, as you know, was Valentine's night, and during dinner he produced a single red rose, you know, one of those really special expensive ones, and I wanted to say to Nic, the day has come and gone and I've heard nothing from you, not a card, nothing—'

'And what did you really say?'

'I said, "Fine, be like that then". And then I hung up.'

'Oh dear.' Outside the wind chased circles of litter across the street. 'Perhaps Jake is wrong,' Agnes said. 'Perhaps nothing has happened between you.'

'Sweetie, even if it hasn't happened yet, it's bloody well likely to happen soon—'

Agnes's phone made a loud musical noise. Athena screwed up her nose and shook her head.

'Hello?'

'This is Mrs Padgett. Helena's mother.' Her tone was clipped, polite.

'How nice of you to ring,' Agnes said.

'I thought I'd give you the address, in case you want to go and see him.'

'Who?'

'Malcolm Noble and his horrible church, of course.'

'Oh.' Agnes fished one-handed in her bag for a pen and paper.

'After you'd gone, I thought things over. And I thought, the important thing is that, even if they've arrested the boy who did it, Helena might still be in danger. With that little girl you told me about. And...' Her voice faded, then came back. 'Don't think this means I have any sympathy with you people, because I don't. I'm just trying to do what's right. Now, do you have a pen to hand?'

Agnes wrote down the address as she dictated it. 'Thank you, Mrs Padgett,' she said. 'I'll keep in touch.'

'Yes. Good.' She rang off.

Agnes put her phone away.

'Well?' Athena had put her coat on and was standing, waiting.

'I've got to go and talk to a false prophet,' Agnes said.

'I don't know how you can tell the difference.' Athena turned and headed for the door.

'That's just the problem,' Agnes said. 'It does make atheism seem more sensible.'

Athena turned to her, her hand on the door handle. 'Oh, sweetie, no, not you. If you give up your belief in God, what hope is there for the rest of us?' She swept out into the street, Agnes close behind.

'You mean, someone has to believe?'

'Of course, kitten. If I was a better person it would be me. As it is...'

Agnes met her eyes. 'As it is, what?'

Athena sighed. 'As it is, I'm about to help a gorgeous man

drive a giant iron pigeon across London. It can only lead to trouble.'

Agnes laughed. 'Talking of driving – you wouldn't be able to spare your car tomorrow morning?'

Athena frowned. 'Simon claims to need my driving skills this week. And if that's not an act of faith, I don't know what is. I mean, with all these secret cameras everywhere, you can't even do your lipstick at the traffic lights without being arrested these days. Tell you what, though, there's a Mercedes dealership with very good car hire offers down the Kings Road, I passed it the other day. We could go and play there tomorrow if you like.'

'But—' Agnes stared at her. 'I can't afford—'

'Look, sweetie, I owe you. All that work you're putting in on behalf of my soul, I can at least hire you a nice car for the day. I'll meet you first thing before work.' She kissed her on both cheeks and turned to go. Agnes watched her stride out to the main road towards the gallery, clutching her fur collar around her cheeks against the sharp wind.

She let herself into Collyer House and went straight to the library, which was empty. There was a note in Shirley's neat handwriting left on the desk. 'Have had to pop home, Mother's had a fall, nothing serious I think but needs sorting out. S.'

Agnes stared around her at the half-empty shelves. She looked at the Hawker cabinet and thought about how soon they'd be parting with it. She supposed she'd have to replace Alice's diary before the museum people came and took it away. Even though...

She thought about Nic tracing his ancestry. Looking for clues, he'd called it. She thought about the bits of spells written out in Alice's hand on the thin, faded pages.

There was a knock at the door, then it opened and Jonathan Harris came in. 'Oh—' he took a step back. 'I was expecting…I didn't think…'

'Shirley's had to pop out for a bit,' Agnes said.

'Ah, yes, Shirley.' He ventured further into the room. His assistant appeared behind him. 'We – um – we thought we might…' He turned to Matthew, who nodded in apparent agreement but said nothing.

'Did you get the boxes removed all right?' Agnes tried.

'Yes. Yes, all done.' He stood on one foot, leaning on Shirley's desk. The other foot rubbed against his ankle.

Agnes waited. Jonathan exchanged glances with Matthew, then said, 'We wanted to have a look at – would you mind if we—' His gaze went to the Hawker cabinet.

'I suppose not,' Agnes said. 'I'm sure I can trust you of all people to be careful with it.'

'Precisely.' He nodded at her, then hurried to the archive and opened the doors, Matthew at his heels. Agnes saw how Matthew even walked like Jonathan, the same uneven gait, as if one leg was shorter than the other.

She sat at her desk with a list of books, but mostly watched Jonathan. He had put on a pair of white gloves, and was now taking the books in turn from the shelves, leafing through them with great care, then replacing them. From time to time he'd show Matthew a page, and Matthew would nod, then the book would be replaced. As he worked his way through the shelves, the search seemed to become more hurried; as he replaced the last book, holding it as if it might break, it was with an air of acute disappointment.

'It's not here,' Jonathan murmured to Matthew. 'I was so sure it would be.'

Agnes broke the silence. 'Are you looking for something?'

Jonathan turned away from the shelves, and stood, hunched and guilty-looking. 'I thought...it was just I'd heard...'

'Is it about the crystal?' Agnes tried.

He nodded. 'There was supposed to be a book that went with it. I thought if the book was here, it would be a guide, perhaps, as to the whereabouts of the crystal.'

'What book?' Agnes thought of Alice's diary, sitting on her table upstairs.

'I don't know what it would be,' he said. 'A book of spells, or magic, I assume. That's the problem, you see—' He clutched his tweed jacket around him, turning one of the buttons in his fingers. 'If I knew what I was looking for, it would all be so much easier.'

'Do you think,' Agnes looked from one man to the other, 'do you think that our burglar was after the same thing?'

Matthew's pale face blushed pink and he stared at the floor. Jonathan shook his head. 'You'd have to know it was here.'

'But people do, don't they? Now the museum have announced that they're taking it—'

'But without knowing the Hawker family history, you'd have no sense of the value of it. And anyway,' he went on, 'the c-collection was hardly touched.'

'Unless,' Agnes went on, 'someone put it all back afterwards.'

Matthew was standing on one foot, the other foot rubbing his ankle. He touched Jonathan's sleeve, then indicated his watch.

'Oh, yes.' Jonathan fastened up his jacket. 'We have to go. The boy's just reminded me...'

'Are you related?' Agnes heard herself ask.

'Us —?' Jonathan looked at her. He made a chuckling noise. 'Oh, no,' he said, shaking his head. 'Not us. Come on, Matthew.' He headed for the door, Matthew ambling after him. Agnes heard the front door close behind them.

She sat at her desk. Perhaps genetic similarity attracts, she thought. Perhaps Jonathan just chose to employ Matthew because they look alike. Perhaps he didn't even notice how alike they are.

If they are related, why would he lie about it?

She remembered his certainty, that the burglar didn't know about the Hawker family. Which implies that he, Jonathan does.

He might be lying about the burglary too.

I should have told him about Alice's diary, she thought. But then, if it is a clue, I need to find out too.

CHAPTER NINE

A thin rain softened the concrete slash of the A13. The windscreen wipers on the CLS 500 sprang smoothly to life. She pressed a button to her left, and music filled the car.

"…Living my life in sunshine," someone was singing on the radio.

Agnes smiled. Sometimes Athena is just the person you need, she thought, remembering the conversation in the Mercedes car-hire centre earlier that morning. A narrow young man in a suit too large for him was standing at the counter, waiting, while Agnes tried to fill in the form.

'What's the matter?' Athena had peered over her shoulder.

'It says Occupation,' Agnes had said.

'Well, write it down, then,' Athena had said. 'Nun. What's the problem?'

'OK,' Agnes had said. 'Nun.'

They'd both looked at the man's expression.

'Don't worry,' Athena had said to him. 'I know they have vows of poverty, but it's on my credit card, OK?'

"…Living my life in the sunshine of your love…" The road widened to dual carriageway, and Agnes pulled out to overtake, then braked as she saw a speed camera. She remembered driving in Provence with her husband, Hugo taking the bends on the country roads at top speed, both of them laughing. But of course, she'd been laughing with fear, and Hugo had been laughing at her fear.

Then again, Hugo was at his least frightening when about to crash an Aston Martin on a French mountain road. It was when they got home that the danger would begin.

Agnes pulled clear of the speed camera and put her foot down. She felt the quiet power of the engine, its smooth acceleration.

But I've taken my vows, she thought.

Now I've taken my vows, ought this to be different?

Does God have a view on speed cameras? Would Jesus slow down in a thirty-mile-per-hour area?

She thought about Athena's cheerful hedonism, her uncomplicated glee over a new lipstick or a pair of shoes. As the road rose to a flyover, the sky filled with watery sunlight, and a rainbow cut through the clouds in a burst of colour.

God's promise, she thought. Or, a physical effect produced by light refracting through water. She wondered what it would be like to see the rainbow simply as the workings of the laws of physics rather than the workings of the Lord, and concluded that it would be no less true or beautiful.

So, where does that leave God? she began to wonder, but was interrupted by the well-brought-up female voice of the car's Sat Nav issuing a sudden instruction to turn off at the next junction.

She found herself on the road that Mrs Padgett had described in her detailed instructions. She took a left turn down the lane to the village. The sun had gone in. The fields were flattened under the silvery sky, as if all trace of life had been washed away. Then, there it was, the white house, as Mrs Padgett had described it, with several outbuildings. Agnes could see a huge, thatched barn. There was a wide, newly varnished gate, fastened back, with no visible name. She went up the drive and parked outside.

She got out of the car. Somewhere in the distance, a dog was barking. She pressed the key lock, and the car responded with clicks and flashes of lights. She took a few steps up the drive.

The house seemed deserted. It was a generously proportioned old farm house, beautifully restored. The well-kept garden hinted at money. Down a neat path, a side door led to the kitchen. The front door was broad, with a bell pull. She pulled the cord and heard it ring in the house. She could hear hesitant footsteps, and then the door opened. A pale young woman stood there, wispy and uncertain. In one hand she clutched a bright yellow duster. 'Yes?' she said.

'I'm looking for Pastor Malcolm,' Agnes said.

'They're all in the church,' the woman said, as if Agnes must know this already. 'I should be there too, but I'm on house duty.'

'And where is the church?'

'There. In the barn.' She waved the duster towards it.

'Thank you,' said Agnes, turning away. She heard the door shut behind her, heard the sound of a hoover starting up.

Agnes's feet crunched on the path. Voices rose up faintly to meet her, growing louder as she approached. She caught something about God's promise in the rainbow.

She pushed the door open and slipped inside.

There were bright spotlights, people playing guitars, a

keyboard, other people clapping. On the stage, a fresh-faced young man was singing into a microphone. In front of Agnes a curly haired woman swayed and clapped. She turned, still singing, smiling, and thrust a hymn sheet into her hands. Agnes tried mouthing the words.

'He lifts me up, when I'm down, he fills me with his love...' Agnes looked at the words on the page. '...He gives me everlasting life.' Agnes was still wondering whether to join in when the song was over, and the fresh-faced young man said something about peace, and everyone had to greet one another. There were beaming faces, a sea of hands reaching out, the keyboard playing sentimental chords. It seemed to mark the end of the service, and a chattering tide of conversations started up around her.

Someone turned to her. 'You're new, aren't you?' It was the curly haired woman. Agnes saw her dazzling smile of perfect teeth. She had grey eyes, and her hair was a gingery gold. 'Come and have some tea.'

Agnes followed her through the crowd to a large table. The woman thrust a polystyrene cup into her hand. 'There are biscuits sometimes,' she said. 'It depends who's come to offer...' Her voice tailed off as her gaze was caught, her eyes following someone through the crowd. Agnes looked up and saw a broad-shouldered man in a cream jacket, a lined, tanned face, neat, receding brown hair; he was shaking hands, laughing, a hug for someone here, a kiss on the cheek for someone there.

'That's Pastor Malcolm,' the woman said, breathless, her eyes still fixed on him.

'He didn't lead the service, then,' Agnes said.

'No,' the woman said. 'He likes us to do it. He only does the healing these days. Look, he's coming this way.' Her voice was frayed with expectation.

'I'd like to meet him,' Agnes said, moving towards the excited hubbub that now surrounded him.

'Come on, then,' her new friend said.

As they approached the group, he glanced up from the centre of it. 'Lizzie,' he said, to the curly haired woman. 'How's things?'

'Much better thanks,' she said.

'Thank Him, not me,' the Pastor said, tilting his head to the ceiling, and Lizzie giggled. 'This is someone who wants to meet you,' she said, launching herself towards him, as if Agnes was the trick by which she'd keep his warmth, his light upon her just that bit longer.

Agnes felt the Pastor's attention switch to her. He took a step towards her. 'And you are—'

'Sister Agnes,' she said. There was a questioning shifting amongst the group.

'Sister?' His arm was outstretched, and she offered him her hand. His grip was warm, insistent.

'I'm a nun,' she said.

'It's all the same Lord,' he said, and smiled. Two or three onlookers laughed.

'I think you know one of my fellow sisters,' she went on. 'Helena Padgett.'

The smile didn't falter. He still gripped her hand. 'Helena. Of course. How is she?'

'Fine,' Agnes lied, and smiled back at him.

His gaze was benevolent and radiant. He relinquished her

hand, and said, 'Stay around, Sister, if you can. I'd love to talk to you.' Agnes noticed the trace of American in his accent.

Curious glances were flicked towards her. Then the Pastor moved away, and the crowd went too, lapping against him.

Lizzie watched them go. 'I knew Helena,' she said, quietly.

Agnes sipped at her plastic tea and waited.

'I didn't think she meant it,' Lizzie said. 'About being a nun.' She turned to Agnes. 'Is she happier now?'

'Was she unhappy here?' Agnes deflected the question.

Lizzie stared at the rough wooden floor. 'We had to energise lots for her.'

'Energise?'

Lizzie smiled at her. 'It's what we do. It's like praying, only more powerful. Pastor says, ordinary prayer is like whispering to God. This is like shouting to him.'

Agnes felt momentarily sorry for God. 'And did it work, this energising?'

Lizzie smoothed the sleeves of her striped jumper. 'Sometimes people are deaf to the word of the Lord,' she said.

'And Tina-Marie?' Agnes tried.

Lizzie lifted her head and stared at her. 'I heard,' she began, then lowered her voice. 'I heard she was dead.'

'Yes,' Agnes said. 'She is.'

'She told me once she was in danger. She asked me to pray for her. I said, we must tell the group, we must energise, but she said, no, she didn't want to tell them, she wanted me to pray for her alone, as a friend...' Her words breathed themselves out.

'Did she say what danger?'

Lizzie shook her head. 'She was often frightened. She was scared for her little girl...' She stopped.

'Why?' Agnes could hear the rain pattering on the thatch of the roof.

Lizzie glanced at her. 'Pastor says, God made us in the image of Adam and Eve. And that's the true way to be. "Male and Female, created He Them." Pastor says, you should get married, and that's how you must have family life. Not on your own, not like Tina-Marie.'

'Did he tell her this himself?'

'Oh yes, he did. We believe in honesty, our church does.'

'But just because she had a child on her own, that doesn't mean it's dangerous, does it?' The barn doors had been flung open, and a grey, damp light spilled through the gap. People were beginning to leave, and there were clusters of farewell hugs and the Pastor shaking hands.

Lizzie shrugged. 'If you put your soul in danger, then maybe the Lord signals to you.'

'But just because she'd had a child on her own—' Agnes began, aware of Pastor Malcolm watching her as the crowd dispersed.

'You're a Christian,' Lizzie said. 'You must know it's wrong.' She fixed her with a warm, open gaze. Agnes wondered what to say.

'Ladies—' The deep gravelly voice cut in, and the Pastor stood beside them. 'I'm sorry to interrupt, but I would love to talk further to our visiting Sister.' He took hold of her hand again. 'Come to the house, if you like.'

She looked up at him, and caught the piercing blankness of his stare.

'Thank you,' Agnes said. 'I'd like to.'

Lizzie watched them go from the church doorway. She gave a wistful little wave.

Once inside the house they were alone, although Agnes thought she could hear movement upstairs, above the thick beams of the kitchen ceiling. The old brickwork was painted white, and condensation settled on the newly restored window frames. Rain swished against the glass.

'What can I get you?' Pastor Malcolm stood in the middle of the room. He glanced uncertainly at the kettle. 'There must be some coffee somewhere,' he said.

'Isn't this your house?' she asked.

'I – um...' He began to open cupboards. 'There are always people staying,' he said in answer. 'Here we are.' He produced a jar of instant coffee, switched on the kettle, placed mugs firmly on the tiled work-surface as if to assert some kind of ownership.

The kettle whispered into life.

'So,' he said. 'What brings a nun to a church like ours?' He sat opposite her at the table, resting his chin on his hands. Again, that smile that didn't reach his eyes.

'I'll be honest,' Agnes said. 'Helena joined us, as you know, and has now disappeared. And Tina-Marie, whom you also know, is dead.'

He shook his head. 'We'd heard. The police came and asked us about her. We couldn't give much information, of course. We loved her, as we love all our church. And poor little Leila. How we cherished that child.' He stared at the expensive wooden table top.

Agnes watched him, then said, 'Of course, in our teachings, it's frowned upon to have a child outside marriage.'

'Oh, no, Sister, surely. The Lord's message of charity outweighs such considerations. We welcomed that young woman as our own daughter.'

'She never felt worried, then, or threatened, while she was here?'

'Absolutely not.'

The kettle clicked off, and he got up from the table. 'I fear,' he said, as he busied himself with spoons and mugs, 'that our influence was not enough to keep her safe. She had other friends, other people in her life...' He poured boiling water into the mugs. 'Sometimes you can't protect a person from their own desires, can you, Sister?'

He brought the mugs to the table, opened the fridge, took out a bottle of milk. From somewhere in the house, Agnes heard a hoover starting up.

'Sugar?' he said. She shook her head, and he sat down again. 'I hadn't heard about Helena,' he said. He stirred his spoon around in his mug, but his attention was on Agnes. 'Where might she have gone?'

'We don't know.'

'She was...' He cupped his mug in his hands. 'She was never the most stable of women,' he said. He raised his eyes to Agnes. 'Did she fare better in holy orders?'

Agnes wondered what to say. 'It's a hard path for most of us,' she replied.

'Well, of course, shut up in a convent, removing yourself from real life,' he began. 'That deliberate narrowing of your interests. Here, you see, we turn ourselves outward to the world.' He looked at her, lizard-like, unblinking. 'I tried to tell her, when she was so troubled with desire, that if only she could offer it up to the Lord she would be able to live in peace.'

Desire. Agnes heard the word as it rested on the air between them, but Malcolm was still speaking. 'We are so frail, so mortal. And yet, the Lord is always there for us. Sometimes, Sister, I think our only sin is in trusting our humanity, when if we only listened, we would hear the call of the Lord.'

Agnes met the lucid brilliance of his gaze. She nodded. He went on, 'But of course, you know all this. You hold the Good News in your heart, as we do.' He glanced at her mug which was three-quarters full of instant coffee. The hum of the hoover dissolved into a rumble of thunder, and he looked up at the window. 'I'm sorry not to be able to help you further,' he said.

Agnes stood up. 'Thank you for your time,' she said.

'Do visit us again.' He joined her as she went to the kitchen door, and opened it for her, peering out at the rain. 'Helena said,' he began, as he took her hand to say goodbye, 'that you have a wonderful library.'

Agnes smiled up at him. 'It depends on your interests,' she said.

'She said it went back centuries.'

Agnes took a step outside. 'You know what convents are like,' she said. 'Narrow in their outlook. I'm afraid our library is the same.'

'Don't you have a seventeenth-century collection?'

She glanced up at him. 'Yes,' she said. 'We do.'

A frown briefly creased his smooth features. 'You see, I'd

heard...' he began, then seemed to change his mind. 'Well, perhaps it's worth a visit one of these days.' The hoover was growing louder along the corridor.

'You'd be most welcome,' Agnes said. 'But we're moving the library. And the Hawker Bequest is going to Oxford for the nation.'

He blinked at her. 'What, no longer at Collyer House?'

Agnes was about to reply, when the hoover crashed into the kitchen, followed by the wispy woman. 'Sorry, Pastor,' she said, in a pale voice. 'I tripped—'

'No,' he said. 'Not now, Marina. Not here.' He spat the words through thin lips.

'Sorry,' she said again, gathering up the hose and hurrying from the room.

Agnes had taken another step outside, into the rain. 'I must go,' she said.

'Yes, of course.' The smile had returned, the easy cadences of speech. He shook her hand. 'Thanks for coming, Sister—' and his glance fell on the car. 'Is that your car?'

'Well, it's hired—' she began, anticipating his surprise, but all he said was, 'I've got my eye on the SL when I next upgrade. My Saab's all very well, but... Anyway, it's been great. You're always welcome.'

As she got into her car she heard the kitchen door slam shut.

The traffic was heavy on the A13, the oncoming headlights blotted with rain. Agnes drove slowly, muted fields on each side. In her mind she could still hear the rhythms of the service, the clapping and the chords. 'He gives me everlasting life...'

Everlasting life, she wondered. What kind of promise is it? She wondered what Malcolm believed, whether he thought it was angels and harps, or white light, or perhaps just more of the same, more guitars and clapping and adoring smiles from the crowd and a Mercedes SL.

She reminded herself to ask Julius what he thought about the promise of everlasting life. The drizzle had turned to rain, and Agnes was transfixed by the sensor-driven rhythm of the windscreen wipers. She wondered whether Athena's credit card would stretch to a whole week of car hire, and concluded, thinking about the Nicole Farhi coat and the new urgency for facials and red nails, that it almost certainly would not.

She parked outside the clinic. Through the twilight, the glass doors welcomed her into their bright space. Beatrice was on the phone in reception. There was no one in the waiting area, and Agnes was about to go back to the house, when she heard someone call her name. She turned to see a woman in crisp trousers and high heeled boots walking towards her along the corridor, her well-cut hair swaying at her collar.

'Yes?' Agnes said, as the woman caught up with her. 'That's me.'

'I'm Serena Sayer,' the woman said.

'Of course,' Agnes said. Of course she would be like this, Philip's wife. Cool and blonde and straight-backed like this.

'I was looking for Philip,' she was saying, 'but he doesn't seem to be here.'

'He's probably at the hospital,' Agnes said.

'Oh.' She seemed to shrink, and her clear gaze clouded over.

'Yes,' she said. 'The hospital.' She stood in the corridor, her hand at her neck, fingering one of a string of pearls.

'Can I help?' Agnes said.

Serena looked at her, frowning. 'You're the nun, aren't you. That's how I recognised you. From what Philip said about you.'

Agnes wondered at Philip's accurate description, but Serena went on, 'He says you talk the same rubbish that I do.'

'How very helpful—' Agnes began, but Serena interrupted.

'If you can see the dead behind the living, then it's true, isn't it? Just because other people can't see it, they shouldn't call it rubbish.' The effort of speaking appeared suddenly too much for her, and she stumbled. Agnes caught her arm and led her to a chair in the waiting area.

'No,' Agnes said. 'It's not rubbish.'

'I can see,' Serena said, as if in explanation. She leaned against the chair back, her hands in her lap. There was a false stillness about her, betrayed by the constant flutter of her fingers, fiddling with the cuffs of her suit, tweaking at the dulled brass buttons.

'Since my baby died, I can look at people and see how they really are. I can walk along the street and I can see it like mist, like a dream, and I know that I could just wake up, I could just choose to wake up from this life, because it's only sleeping, this life, there's another life that's about being truly awake...'

Agnes still had her hand on Serena's arm. 'And where is that life?' she asked.

'It's where my baby is,' Serena said, and smiled at her. 'It's with God.'

'But—' Agnes spoke softly. 'But Serena – you're here. You're not with your baby.'

'You sound like Philip.' Serena's eyes lit up with sudden fire as she met her gaze. 'That's what I'm trying to tell you. I'm with my baby because I can see the life beyond this one. It's like a veil, I can see behind it. I can see how easy it would be to just reach out and cross to the other side.'

'And die, you mean?' Agnes softened her grip on Serena's arm.

Again, the empty smile. 'If you want to call it that.'

Agnes took a breath, then said, 'Why do you want to die?'

'Oh, I'm not saying that. I'm just saying it would be easy.'

'How does Philip react when you say things like this to him?'

'He doesn't understand.' Serena pouted, as if her husband was refusing her a new pair of Jimmy Choos. 'But I thought you would,' she went on. 'When I'm in church, the words speak so clearly to me. "Lead me in the way of the life everlasting". That bit.'

Agnes felt suddenly cold. '...The life everlasting,' she echoed.

'Exactly.'

'Serena—' Agnes tried to keep her voice calm. 'God wants you to live this life. He doesn't want you to die—'

'But of course he does. He wants us all to join him. That's what all the teachings say. "Your sins are forgiven..." That's how we can be with him.'

'What if it was a sin to kill yourself?' Agnes tried.

Serena was silent. She stared at the floor, tapping at a scuff mark with her pointed toe. 'I'm already partly there,' she murmured. 'When they said my baby had died…' Her hair fell forward like a curtain across her face.

In the silence they could hear the hum of the fluorescent lights above them. Then the glass doors swished open and they both looked up.

'Serena—' Philip stopped in the entrance as the doors closed behind him. 'What are you doing here?'

Serena smoothed her hair, straightened her shoulders, managed a smile. 'I was looking for you,' she said.

He was about to speak, but then took a step towards her and reached out his hand. 'I'm here now,' he said.

She got to her feet and put her hand in his. 'We've been having such a lovely chat, me and Agnes,' she said, turning back to her. 'I'll come another time if you don't mind.'

'Any time,' Agnes said.

'I only came back to lock up,' Philip said, gesturing vaguely at the empty space.

'I'll do it,' Agnes said.

'Yes. Good. Thanks.' He still had Serena's hand in his, and now he led her to the door, murmuring goodbyes. Serena turned and waved at her, and they vanished into the darkness.

Agnes unlocked her front door and stood in the hall. There was a heavy silence in the house, and she went into the kitchen and put on a saucepan to boil for pasta, again. But then the weariness lifted, as she put on more lights, and chopped some fresh basil leaves, and opened a packet of organically grown pine-nuts, and found there was a nice bottle of 2003 Côtes du Rhône which she must have bought only the other day.

She poured some wine and sat down and watched the light

glint ruby red through the glass, and thought – does this count as rebellion, as the self choosing the world, a rejection of my vows? Or is this a celebration of them, this gratitude for God's creation?

She thought about what Serena had said, about the thin veil between this life and the next. Surely, Agnes thought, it's better to sit here, now, and be glad of this life, than try to —

She jumped, aware of a sudden movement, but it was only the tabby cat, slinking through the narrow gap of the doorway. It watched her, and she stared back, meeting its yellow gaze. She found the cat food in the cupboard and spooned some into a bowl, wrinkling her nose against the offal odour.

The cat finished eating. It wandered over to an old newspaper in the corner of the kitchen and settled down to wash itself. When Agnes looked again it had gone.

The landing light cast deep shadows, the rain beat against the windows. In her room she turned on all the lights and took out her Bible.

'...The Earth shook, the heavens poured down water, before the God of Sinai, before God the God of Israel...'

Agnes closed the Bible. She went to her desk to get Alice's rosary, and her eye was caught by the diary. She picked it up and turned a page at random.

'They will kill me,' she read. 'For their God is not my God, my faith is false in their eyes...' The rest of the page was blank. She turned to the next page:

'Save me, O God, for the waters are come in unto my soul; I sink in deep mire, where there is no standing; I am come into deep waters, where the floods overflow me. O God, thou knowest my foolishness, and my sins are not hid from thee...'

After this a page was torn out. Then Agnes read, 'God did send the flood waters to wash clean His creation. But now His people turn from Him to wickedness once more. He will wash clean his world and wash my sins from me. He will flood the earth, and this house will be purified, and the stains of death washed clean...'

Agnes closed the book and listened to the rain outside. She heard creaking on the landing, and wondered if the cat had come upstairs. The house felt hostile, and she wondered whether to take up Athena's offer of her spare bedroom. She looked at her mobile phone, and thought about Athena's bright kitchen, her pale wood table, bowls of salad and glasses of wine...then jumped as the phone rang.

It was a number she didn't recognise. 'Hello?'

A man's voice, well-spoken and polite. 'Is that Sister Agnes? I'm Jared, I – knew Tina. I'm Leila's father.'

'Oh. But you were—'

'—in the States, yes. I've just got back. Can we meet? Tomorrow?'

'Yes, of course. Tomorrow.'

'I'm sorry to sound so desperate—' his voice became thin.

'Don't be sorry,' Agnes said.

'Where shall I find you?'

'Do you know the clinic – no, of course you don't. Tell you what, meet me at the house I'm staying in, it'll be quiet there.' She gave him the address. 'It's the door up the steps, with the peeling paint. Ten-thirty?'

'Ten-thirty. Thank you. See you then.'

The rain sounded heavier in the silence. Agnes opened her Bible again. 'For anyone who wants to save his life will lose it; but anyone who loses his life for my sake will find it.'

She sat with the book open on her lap, thinking about Serena treading so lightly between this life and the next. No wonder Philip is frightened.

And, she thought, getting up to close her curtains, he'll accuse me of making it worse.

CHAPTER TEN

'You should have kept away from her.' Philip towered over
her, a mug of cold coffee in one hand, a bundle of files tucked
under his other arm. Behind him the clinic reception area
bustled with noise in the morning sunlight.

'She was here. She wanted to talk to me—' Agnes felt at a loss.

'Presumably because she knew you'd indulge her nonsense.'

'Philip, you can't expect me to change my beliefs just
because your wife is ill—'

'I can expect you to keep your so-called beliefs to yourself.'
His voice was raised, and people glanced towards them.

Agnes saw the colour rising in his face, the anger beneath
the surface. She wondered if this was how Serena saw him. 'If
I was Serena I'd hide from you too,' she heard herself say.

'What do you mean?'

'What I said.' Agnes stood up. 'Your wife is in a fragile
state. You can't bully her out of it, just because you wish she
agreed with you.'

'How dare you?' The mug in Philip's hand was shaking.
'You're the one talking to a suicidal person about ever-bloody-
lasting life. If I was guilty of such professional misconduct I
could be sued. But you people, because you can call it God—'

'Oh for heaven's sake, Philip.' Now Agnes was shouting.

'God is a sideshow in all this. Your wife feels she's been touched by death, because of the baby. She's in crisis. She's using a particular language to describe it, that's all. The problem isn't God. It's about you, and your wife, and whether you can start to listen to what she's saying.'

Philip stared at her. Agnes turned back to him. 'I only called in this morning because I thought I'd see Julius. I've got a meeting next door. Do excuse me.'

She was aware of the glances as she passed through the reception area to the doors.

The library was deserted. Agnes remembered, with relief, that Shirley had to take her mother for a hospital appointment this morning. At exactly ten-thirty, the convent doorbell rang.

A man stood on the doorstep. He had short black hair in tight curls, olive skin, dark brown eyes. He offered her his hand. 'Hi, I'm Jared,' he said.

She led him into the library. He stood nervously in the dusty light, looking around him, his hands in tight fists. 'I got a flight back as soon as I could,' he said. 'The police have already questioned me, over there. I don't know how they found me, most people who knew Tina had given up on me.'

Agnes gestured to a chair and he sat down. 'But, you see...' he went on. 'But I hadn't given up on her. I never gave up on them, Tina and our little girl. And now she's dead, and our baby has disappeared...' He stared at the table in front of him, his knuckles against his lips.

'Can I get you anything?' Agnes asked. 'Tea – coffee?' She noticed his well-cut jeans, the cuff-links at the wrists of his shirt.

Jared shook his head. 'I keep asking myself,' he went on, 'why would Troy wish that little girl harm?'

'I was going to ask you the same question.' Agnes pulled up a chair and sat down opposite him.

'From what I can work out,' he said, 'Tina arranged for Leila to go into hiding. Tina must have known she was in danger. And she was proved right.'

'I went to see Malcolm Noble,' Agnes said.

He seemed to catch his breath at the name. 'Did you meet him?' He leaned forward. 'How is he these days?'

'He seemed very successful,' she said. 'At least financially, and for all I know, spiritually too.'

'Spiritually,' he repeated. 'I don't call that spiritual.'

'How well do you know him?'

Jared pushed a paperclip around on the desk. 'I used to know him quite well.'

'You were part of the church?'

He nodded. 'For a while, yes. I haven't seen Malcolm for a long time. I hope I never see him again.'

'Did you hear from the police about Tina-Marie?'

'I already knew. Do you know Danielle?' He looked up from the paperclip.

'Yes,' Agnes said. 'That pretty girl who lives in those flats—'

'At Elephant.' He nodded at her. 'She got in touch with a mate of mine, didn't she? He told me,' Jared went on. 'He phoned me. Anyway—' he sighed, looked up at her '—At least Troy's behind bars. Remanded in custody, Ahmed said.'

'Yes. Apparently a witness has come forward to say that they were seen in the street, Troy and Tina, having a violent argument.'

'So Leila can come out of hiding. Wherever she is.' He picked up the paperclip and unfurled it.

'We don't know where she is.' Agnes watched him working the thin wire.

'But you'll hear from her now, won't you?' He looked up at her.

'My concern,' Agnes said, 'is that they're still scared of someone.'

He glanced at her, but said nothing.

Agnes leaned back in her chair. 'Someone at Malcolm's church said that they were very harsh about unmarried motherhood there. She said they gave Tina-Marie a hard time.'

He met her eyes. 'Yes,' he said. 'They wanted us to get married. That's when I began to question it. Lot of pressure, man.'

'Why did you leave her?'

'That's just it, see. The church split us up. The more heavy they got, the more I wanted out. The more I wanted out, the more Tina-Marie put the pressure on me to marry her. In the end, I said, it's them or me. And she chose them.'

'But that must have made things worse for her?'

He flicked at the paperclip wire, and it shot across the desk. 'Yeah, I think it did. They were bad times, man. I wanted to see my baby, and she said not if I wasn't going to be a proper father, so I stopped. That was bad of me, I admit it. But I couldn't get past all that God shit—' He broke off, glanced at her. 'Sorry,' he said.

'It's quite all right,' Agnes said. 'Do go on.'

'You're not like them, are you?' He studied her, leaning back in his chair.

'I hope not,' she replied.

He smiled at her.

'How did you get to join Malcolm's church?'

His hand went to his wrist, turning the cuff-link round and round. 'It seemed like an answer, at the time.' He flicked a glance at Agnes, then went on, 'I was lost, I suppose. I was working out that way, driving for a living, delivery man – staying in a rented flat.'

'Are you from that area?'

He shook his head. 'London, man. My mum's still there. She's from Jamaica, originally.'

'And your dad?'

'I don't have no dad. Mitchell O'Connor, my dad. He went back to Ireland before I was born.'

'So, Malcolm's church—'

'Yeah. Well, I got to hear about them, went to visit. And there it was, the message of a loving Father...' He breathed out through pursed lips. 'Something I didn't know nothing about. So, I signed up. Big mistake, it turned out.'

'And then you met Tina—'

'Man, she was the best thing there. She was so beautiful, in her soul too. Yeah...' He sighed. 'I loved her. I should never have abandoned her there. It was against all I believed, to leave my little girl, but them times, they were so hard, man...'

'And then she left,' Agnes said. 'And she ended up with Troy.'

'I'd gone, by then. My cousin was opening an office in New York, so I joined him.'

'What do you do?'

'Design,' he said. 'IT stuff, you know. Here—' he took a

business card from his inside pocket. 'This is us. My mobile's on there too.'

'Thank you.'

'I just want to help, see?' he said.

'Did you know Helena Padgett?'

He frowned. 'She's the one who's got Leila now, right?'

'Yes. She was in the cult with Malcolm, then she joined us.'

'Yeah. I do remember her. She hadn't been there long, when I left. They were friends, her and Tina-Marie.'

'We need to track them down, now that Troy's been arrested. I think she knew that Leila was in danger from Troy, and that's why she took her away. But now that you're here, they can come back.'

'And then, I can be with my little girl. Unless…'

'Unless what?' Agnes looked at him.

Jared shifted in his chair. 'Do you think she's scared of Malcolm?'

'Do you?'

'I wouldn't trust that man further than I could throw him. After I left, he wanted to adopt Leila. One of the girls there told me, we managed to stop him. But now that Tina's gone…'

'Would Malcolm really pursue Leila now?'

He was about to reply when the door opened.

'Oh, these hospitals, every time it's a different consultant, we have to start all over again, explaining Mother's medication – oh, hello, I'm sorry, am I interrupting?' Shirley put down her carrier bags and began to take off her coat.

Jared stood up and held out his hand. 'Jared O'Connor,' he said. 'We'd kind of finished, hadn't we?' He looked down at

Agnes. 'Tell you what, you should talk to Josie. Tina-Marie's sister. She's the one to ask, I reckon.'

Agnes stood up too. 'Where is she?'

'Up north somewhere. They weren't close. Josie's much older. I could try and find her for you.'

In the hallway he shook her hand. 'Thanks for this, Sister,' he said. 'It's like Danielle said to Ahmed. I'm all Leila's got now. I know what it's like to be abandoned by your dad. This time, I ain't going to do the same.'

Sunlight spilled briefly into the hallway as he opened the front door. He shook her hand again, then left. Back in the library, Agnes slipped his business card into her purse.

'...And we've got a new offer for the Hawker Bequest.' Shirley looked up from her desk. 'Look.' She waved an envelope at Agnes. 'They wrote to us. Malcolm Noble. He's some kind of vicar from the sound of it. Offering five thousand and that's just a starting figure, he says. "Open to discussion." Well, that's certainly going to change things with the museum lot. They're going to have to buck their ideas up sharpish.'

'Malcolm Noble? Where from?'

Shirley peered at the letter in front of her. 'Colnworth, in Essex.'

Agnes reached over and picked up the letter. '...I would be delighted if you would consider me as a serious contender. May I assure you that the terms of my purchase will include a commitment to making the Hawker archive accessible to students and researchers. I am happy to come and visit your order and discuss terms at your convenience. Yours, Pastor Malcolm Noble.'

'He obviously doesn't know the order very well,' Shirley

said. 'The letter's addressed to "The Mother Superior".'

'So it is,' Agnes said. 'And he doesn't mention that he's met me. And that without me he wouldn't even know about the collection being moved.'

Shirley raised her eyebrows at her. 'Really?'

'Yes. I met him. I went to talk about little Leila, it's a long story. And I mentioned the library move.'

Shirley took back the letter from her. 'Well, that is odd. Still,' she added, putting it back in the envelope, 'if it makes the museum people reach a decision at last, your Pastor Whatsit will have done us a favour.'

'Unless Mr Harris makes an offer too. He seems rather interested in it as well.'

Shirley opened a drawer on the desk and placed the envelope in it. 'I can't imagine he can afford it. Far better to have this vicar with his five thousand.'

Agnes glanced at the cabinet. 'It's an odd amount. It's not really very much, considering the value.'

'You could haggle,' Shirley said. 'You could double it, treble it, get enough to set up a whole new day centre, or buy all you sisters a lovely place in the country. Now, shall I tell Sister Lucia or will you?'

'I think she'd rather hear from you than me at the moment,' Agnes said. In her mind she could see a sprawling rural mansion, with high walls and a padlocked gate.

'...you could do traditional monastery things,' Shirley was saying, 'like keeping bees and making wine.'

'I suppose spending hours picking grapes in the rain might help my spiritual path,' Agnes said, 'but I think I'd rather stay in Bermondsey.'

Shirley smiled at her. 'I'll tell Sister Lucia, then. If you see Mr Harris, perhaps you'd better tell him too, it's only fair. He's due in at two. In fact, it would help me enormously if you could be here. I told Mother I'd try to be with her for the ultrasound. She does fret so, she thinks the machines are giving off dangerous rays. I've tried to explain it's just soundwaves, but she says, "Why can't I hear it then, I'm not deaf you know."' Shirley smiled weakly. 'And they never find anything. It does seem a shame, upsetting these elderly people for no good reason, I suppose they mean well...' Her words faded away. She opened a book on Vatican Architecture and began to read.

'Is that the time?' Julius looked up from his desk.

'Is what the time?' She smiled down at him.

'Lunch, I suppose.' He took off his spectacles and polished them. 'It's usually a mealtime when you appear, and it's too late for breakfast.'

'I've brought you a sandwich,' Agnes said.

'Oh dear, not crab—'

'Mozzarella and tomato for you,' Agnes said. 'Crab and avocado for me.'

'Ah. Good.' He put his spectacles into their case and leaned back in his chair. 'How are you?'

'I've been reflecting on pride,' she said.

'Always helpful.' He clicked shut his glasses case.

'I had to return a very nice Mercedes car to the car-hire place today. Athena really couldn't afford it for more than a day.'

'And was that good for the soul?' He put his head on one side, waiting.

'It ought to be.' She began to unwrap a sandwich.

'Relinquishment of worldly pleasures. Non-attachment to false idols.'

'Yes.' Julius nodded.

'But mostly I was thinking, maybe I'll get the Coupé next time.'

Julius smiled at her.

'And anyway, I think I've made a terrible mistake.' Agnes went to the shelves in the corner of his office in search of plates.

'But taking final vows—' Julius began.

His amusement had become concern, and Agnes turned to him. 'Oh, Julius, not that. You mustn't worry about me.' She brought two plates to his desk, then bent and briefly hugged him. 'Not that kind of mistake,' she said. 'It's just that I mentioned the Hawker collection to that Pastor chap in Essex, and now he's offered money for it.'

'Oh.' Julius stared at her. 'And is that a mistake?'

'Something's not quite right,' Agnes said, unwrapping the second of the two sandwiches. She sat down and passed him a plate. 'And Philip's cross with me for discussing Heaven with his wife.'

'I would have thought you're a very good person to talk about Heaven. At least you believe in it.'

'That's just the problem.' Agnes sighed. 'As far as Philip's concerned, I've just encouraged her to believe in more nonsense. He says it's deeply irresponsible and if he could he'd sue us.'

'Oh.' Julius put down his sandwich. 'Oh dear. What would he sue us for? It's hardly deception, if we believe it ourselves.'

'She seems to think she'd be better off in the next world rather than this one, and I suppose, if someone like me supports her in an idea of heaven, she's more likely to take action to – to get there.'

'Ah.' Julius resumed his eating. After a while, he said, 'I can't help thinking that the problem there is not whether or not Heaven exists, but her need not to be Here. In this life.'

'That's what I said to Philip.'

'What did he say?'

Agnes remembered her exchange with Philip that morning. 'I don't think I put it as well as I might have done.'

'Oh dear.' Julius frowned at a piece of tomato. 'I do like the man,' he said. 'I wish we could help.'

Agnes finished her sandwich. 'I can't stay long,' she said. 'I've got to see that book dealer this afternoon. I'll have to tell him about Malcolm's offer.' She stood up and began to put cellophane wrapping into Julius's bin. 'I can't help thinking there's something hidden,' she said. 'Something about the Hawker collection that has a huge value, greater than the books. Maybe not a monetary value, maybe something else...' She glanced at Julius. 'Why are you looking at me like that?'

'Was I?'

'It's the same old thing isn't it?'

'What same old thing?' He frowned at her, affably.

'You think I'm in crisis because of having taken my vows. You think I should concentrate on being a good nun. Instead of being distracted.'

'I wouldn't dream of judging you.' He passed her some sandwich wrapping, and she put it in the bin. 'Searching for something hidden, it's a perfectly respectable thing to do. The problem is when, like Philip's wife, you think you've found it.'

The library was deserted; the lines of books sat neatly under the heavy silence. Agnes leaned back in Shirley's chair and listened to the stillness. Her eyes scanned the shelves.

All these words, she thought. All these thoughts. It's as if there's a constant, silent murmuring. If only I could hear it, then I'd know.

I'd know what? she wondered. I'd know why all these people are circling the collection. I'd know what Alice Hawker was afraid of. I'd know why she died, and why her little boy died, and why Tina-Marie died, and where little Leila is, and why Helena won't bring her back, and what Jonathan Harris thinks is hidden here —

She heard the front door bell ring, and a moment later was showing Mr Harris into the library. As they came in, she had a sense of hush, as if just for a few seconds, when there was no one there to hear, the whispering books had become audible.

'I gather the collection might go to a different home.' Jonathan Harris flicked his jacket out behind him and settled into a chair. 'A Pastor of some kind.'

'How did you hear?' Agnes sat down opposite him.

'Shirley mentioned it. I phoned earlier to check my time.'

'You've gathered right,' Agnes said.

'Who is he?' He leaned forward, pushing his spectacles up his nose.

'He's called Pastor Malcolm Noble.'

'A man of the cloth?'

Agnes hesitated. 'He has a church, yes. Out in Essex.'

'Well, I can't see he'll be much of a threat, then.' Jonathan settled back in his chair. 'No money, obviously. "Pastor"…' He shook his head.

Agnes thought about the restored house, the extensive, well-kept grounds of Malcolm's farm. 'He mentioned five thousand as a starting price.'

Jonathan blinked several times. 'Five thousand pounds?'

'You see, that's exactly what I thought, Mr Harris. Why would anyone see such a value in all these?' Agnes waved an arm towards the shelves of books. 'And yet, for what they are, it's not very much.'

Jonathan flushed pink. He glanced at his feet, as if surprised by their twitching, then looked back at her. 'I can't – I can't imagine… I mean, I know for myself…' He looked at her, helpless.

'Yes, Mr Harris?' Agnes waited.

'I would love to have the collection.' He spoke quietly. 'I haven't been altogether straight with you people,' he went on. 'I'm – I'm a descendant of the Hawker family. Nicolas acquired this house after his first wife died, Alice. Alice Braden, she was, then she became Hawker…' He gazed vaguely at the ceiling, then looked around, as if trying to remember where he was. 'Alice… Anyway, he m-married again, and had a family, and lots of descendants…' He stopped, breathless.

'I see,' Agnes said. 'But why didn't you say all this before?'

He looked at his shoes again. 'I thought, with the library involved, there was no way I could acquire it. Now, with this vicar on to it, it makes me think that I, too, could make a claim to it.' He breathed in, then out.

'But both the museum and Malcolm would make the collection available for research.'

'I could do the same. It's just that within the collection, there will be some items of great relevance to my family history.'

'And what might they be?'

Jonathan scratched at his ear. 'If I knew, you see, I could make you an offer just for those. Then this Pastor could have the other books, although why he thinks they're worth all those thousands...'

'I would assume,' Agnes said, 'that he's only offering such a price because he, too, knows about something of value in this collection – something that's not here on these shelves.'

He thumped his fists on his knees. 'Sister Agnes – if I may make an appeal to you. I'm an only child, both my parents are no longer with us, I'm unmarried and am likely to remain so until my death. This is not to say I'm unhappy, oh no. But you see, my sense of who I am, my sense of belonging in this world if I may put it so, comes from having deep roots, from knowing my place and how far back into time it goes. Very few Englishmen can sit in a room like this and say, "Four centuries ago my great great whatever grandfather lived in this house..." There are very few of us left, you see, and it falls to me to take responsibility. I am an Englishman, Sister. I can say, this is who I am. This is where I belong. It is a great good fortune, if I may say so, to know such a thing, and one not granted to many people.' He stopped, pink and breathless. He produced a large white handkerchief and mopped at his face.

Agnes was aware of an image of herself; a child, standing in a field in Provence, her parents' house behind her. We didn't belong, she thought. We were interlopers even then, my English father, my mother pretending to be something she wasn't. And here's Jonathan, with his roots spreading into the very foundations of this building...

She drew out from the pocket of her cardigan the string of beads, and held it out to him.

He took it, holding it delicately. 'What is—?'

'It's Alice's rosary,' she said.

He almost gasped, staring at it open-mouthed. 'How do you know? Where did you find it? Was it with the crystal?'

'No,' Agnes said. 'I haven't seen this crystal.'

'I have – had – a great-aunt. She did lots of research into our family, into Nicolas Hawker. She was also very interested in magic, you see, and when she died she left me various things – books, magic charms. And she was rather, shall we say, taken up, with this idea of the Hawker crystal.'

'So,' Agnes interrupted, 'your bid for the Hawker collection is in the hope that somewhere in the midst of it you'll find the crystal?'

His feet twitched in their brogues. 'It would be awful if all knowledge of the crystal was lost. And if the crystal is – somewhere – amongst the Hawker things, then, yes, I would like to have it.'

'Does it have a value?'

'To me, personally, of course. To the outside world...' He frowned, then nodded. 'Yes. It must have a monetary value, a thing like that.'

'Worth a few thousand pounds?'

He met her eyes. 'You can't think – why would a vicar want anything to do with seventeenth-century magic?'

'He's not a vicar,' Agnes said. 'He's more of a—' she broke off, wondered what to say. 'It's rather a free church.'

Jonathan was still holding the rosary, and now he weighed it gently in his fingers. 'Alice's rosary,' he repeated. 'They were quite rare, weren't they?'

'From what I can gather,' Agnes said, 'Catholics took to the rosary when their religious practice had to be done in secret.'

Jonathan turned the beads over in his hand.

'Mr Harris,' Agnes said. 'My order is likely to take the highest offer.'

'But they can't,' he said. 'What if the crystal turns up? What if it gets into the hands of someone who doesn't know its power?'

'You think it works?' Agnes stared at him.

He glanced nervously at her. 'My great-aunt said that her grandmother had been told she couldn't have children. And she used the crystal, and when she looked into it she saw a little girl. And sure enough, after that, she fell pregnant with her daughter. My great-grandmother,' he added.

'When was this?'

'Around 1870,' he said.

'So the crystal was in your family then?'

'It seems so.'

'So—' Agnes thought for a minute, then said, 'So it's unlikely it's here. The Hawker Bequest stayed with the building, when the order took it over. But if your great-great-grandmother used it to foretell her daughter—' Agnes hesitated, then went on, 'it would be wherever your family was living then.'

'Sussex,' he said. 'Near Chichester.' He frowned. 'But this vicar might not know that.'

'No,' Agnes agreed.

Jonathan stood up. 'I've taken enough of your time, and I'm short of assistance at the shop.' He held up the rosary, briefly, then passed it back to her. 'Take care of it, won't you.'

Agnes looked at the beads, shiny with age. 'I feel – I feel I've stolen it,' she said.

'Oh, no,' he smiled at her. 'Not from me. Papist, you see. Like Alice. She was the first wife. But I'm – we're Protestant,' he said. His shoulders straightened, and he seemed suddenly taller.

'Yes.' Agnes smiled back. 'Of course.' She opened the front door for him.

On the steps, he shook her hand. 'Well…I'm sorry. I – I should have been more honest in the first place. Well…' He nodded, then left. Agnes watched him go, watched his bustling walk as he reached the street and merged with the London crowds. She thought of his ancestors, this unbroken lineage of aunts and grandmothers that still seemed cheerfully to haunt him.

An Englishman, she thought. And I'm not even properly French.

She wondered about Matthew, and Jonathan, and their striking resemblance.

She went back into the library, fingering Alice's rosary, thinking about the missing crystal. It seemed so phoney, so fairground, somehow, this ball into which you could look and see your unborn children. She stopped, the words still circling her mind. As the beads passed through her fingers, she imagined Alice looking into the crystal and seeing her baby boy. Or maybe it was Nicolas, wanting to know – wanting to know what?

And then once more, the image of Tina-Marie flashed through her head, the violence and the blood and the wide-eyed stillness of her body, and Agnes found a chair and sat heavily into it.

I have to find Leila, she thought.

She looked at her hands. The polished beads trembled in her fingers.

CHAPTER ELEVEN

'But sweetie, really, crystal balls? Seeing the future? And I thought I was the one who went in for all the mumbo jumbo.' Athena held a prawn cracker between long red nails. 'Apart from God, obviously. But then, that's not mumbo jumbo, really, or at least, not when you do it.'

'Thank you.' Agnes smiled at Athena over the top of her wine glass.

Athena glanced around in search of a waiter. The restaurant was subtly lit, lined with bamboo blinds. 'They do a fab soup here,' she said. 'With coconut milk and those green lemony leaves. I might have that.'

'You see, Jonathan Harris thought that this Pastor Malcolm might be after the crystal.'

'Why?' Athena topped up their glasses. 'I hope this wine's OK, I'm not sure Italian red goes with this sort of food.'

'Jonathan thought it would explain why Malcolm's offered so much money, I mean, that he thinks there's something of great value hidden in the collection.'

'But a crystal ball? If it was a book or something, that would make more sense.'

Agnes sipped her wine. 'Mmm,' she agreed. 'I think I might have the spring chicken and jasmine rice.'

'And there's that old diary thing you've been going on about. That would be worth a fortune, surely.'

'They don't count as part of the collection.' Agnes thought about Alice's notebook and diary stacked into the cupboard of her tiny bedroom.

'But this Malcolm might know about them. And this Jonathan almost certainly would, wouldn't he? I mean, it's his family.'

'But Alice's books – they're just lists of housekeeping. And outpourings about how awful her life is. Terror of her husband...terrible grief...' She looked up. 'Jonathan clearly thinks there's a gap, but I can't imagine he means those. There is the odd spell, I suppose. But I really don't see how Malcolm would know about it.'

'Nic would say the museum people should have it all. Regardless of the money.' Athena poured some sparkling water into a glass. 'He's been emailing me, about how wonderful it is that people can access their own family past. Apparently he's traced his grandmother's side to a Jewish lot, terribly exotic apparently, descended from the Rabbis of Prague. I think that's what he said. The idea of Nic being a rabbi is really rather funny. At least, it would be if all this wasn't doing us such harm.' She sipped her water. 'It's as if he's choosing to live in the past. And meanwhile, my life in the present is carrying on without him.'

'The past.' Agnes turned her wine glass around in her hands. 'It's there all the time. Every time I walk into Collyer House, it's as if the steps are treacly and sticky, as if everything that ever happened there is still there somehow, still grabbing at my feet, trying to make itself known.'

Athena waved at a passing waiter. 'Any more ghosts?' she asked.

The waiter came, and they gave their order, and as he went away, Agnes said, 'No. No more ghosts. Not visibly, anyway.'

'The past. It's a bloody nuisance. Jake was saying last night that in a parallel universe he and I did get married. And we're still there, we have a house somewhere, he wanted Hoxton near Justin's studio, but I said it would have to be West, I don't understand East London. We settled on West Hampstead, but I could tell he wasn't entirely happy. Anyway, in this parallel life, he does his art with Justin, and I still help Simon run the art gallery, and we have a house in the country too, Gloucestershire, where the foundry is, and we spend weekends there. And I said, but you can't do that, you can't live in a parallel universe, it's cheating.'

'And what did he say?'

'Oh dear...' Athena stared at the tablecloth.

'Go on—'

'He said, there's nothing to stop the parallel universe becoming the one I live in.' Athena smoothed the white linen of the cloth with her fingertips. After a moment she said, 'Do you know?' She lifted her head. 'In the parallel universe I have a little girl. A daughter. A late pregnancy it was, Jake said. You see, if Nic was here – if he was present in any way at all...' Athena blinked back tears.

'Oh, Athena—' Agnes reached across and took her hand.

'Nic isn't here to fight for me. He's either in the centre, or in Spain, or he's in cyberspace, or he's in the past, not even his past, his grandparents' past...' Athena picked up her wine glass. 'It's like you said. It's sticky, the past. Nic's got all these different threads and he's tangled up in them all and he doesn't even notice that I'm slipping away into another life, a life with a man I once really liked, who could even now offer me the chance of...' She fell silent.

'Motherhood? Really?'

Athena picked up another prawn cracker and looked at it. 'Oh, sweetie, I've no idea.'

'But – have you and Jake – I mean...?'

Athena shook her head. 'The awful truth in all this, is that when I think of Nic, I still get a kind of lurching desire. I fancy the pants off him. Whereas Jake – I mean, yeah, he is gorgeous, but...' She bit into the prawn cracker. 'All I really want is for Nic to behave as if we're having a relationship, that's all.' She turned to catch the eye of their waiter, pointing at the nearly finished bottle of wine on their table and indicating that they'd like another.

'I'm not sure I should,' Agnes began.

'It's for your own good,' Athena said. 'Sleeping in that haunted house, all on your own, at least if you're drunk the ghosts won't disturb you.'

'The order want me to leave the house.'

'For once I agree with them,' Athena said.

'But if I leave, then what happens to little Leila? What happens to Helena? What happens to Alice Hawker, and her story, and the child who died?'

Athena met her eyes. She shook her head. 'The past, you see, sweetie. It's like the edge of a pit, and we're all tip-toeing round it, all the time. And you and me and Nic, we seem to have fallen in.'

* * *

Much later, Agnes drew up outside Collyer House in a taxi – 'Sweetie, really, you can't possibly take the bus at this time of night, here's the money, honestly, I won't hear another word…'

She unlocked the front door and stood in the hallway. She realised this had become a habit, listening to the emptiness of the house before she ventured into any of the rooms. An image came to her, of Alice doing the same, creeping around the empty spaces of the house in the hope of avoiding harm.

There was silence.

She went into the kitchen, switched on the lights, poured herself a glass of water. The clock in the library chimed eleven, although it felt much later. Then, almost immediately, Agnes heard her phone ringing.

She answered it, not recognising the number.

'Is that Sister Agnes? This is Mrs Padgett. I'm sorry to phone so late, but it's important, and you're the only person I can talk to.'

'It's fine, really.'

'I didn't know when you people go to bed. I thought if you're up at dawn with your worship…' The clipped tones hesitated, then went on, 'Anyway, the point is, Helena phoned me. Earlier this evening. She wouldn't say where she was, and afterwards I did that thing on the phone when you get the number, but it said it was withheld or something.'

'What did she say?'

'She said, she was fine, and I wasn't to try to find her because that would make things worse, those were her words. "It'll make things worse." And she asked about you, which I thought was rather perceptive of her, given the kind of person you are.'

'Me?'

'She said, had anyone tried to find her, anyone from the order, like Agnes, she said.'

'And what did you say?'

There was a tiny pause. 'I lied. I said, no, not to my knowledge. I don't know why I lied.'

Agnes heard a slight thaw in the tone of voice. 'Do you have any idea where she was?' she asked.

'None at all. The only clue to anything, was that in the background, I could have sworn that I heard a child. A small child, asking for milk, a milky drink, something like that.'

Agnes realised she was still standing up, leaning on the kitchen table. She sat down on one of the stools. 'It's very kind of you to phone me,' she said.

'Well, to be honest, you're my only hope at the moment. There's one other thought I had,' Mrs Padgett went on, 'and that was our place near Market Harborough. I don't know if you know it round there, it belonged to my mother's family, it's only small, but we kept it on, my husband and I... For some reason, I had a mental picture of her standing in the kitchen there.'

'It's very kind of you to ring,' Agnes said. 'There's no reason why you should trust me, but the truth is, you and I both want Helena to be safe.'

'Yes.' Her voice had softened. There was a pause, then she said, 'What will you do?'

Agnes looked at the scrap of paper on which she'd written the words 'Market Harborough'. 'I don't know,' she said. 'I won't do anything without consulting you.'

'Thank you. I'm – I'm sorry I was rather hasty with you

before. My experiences with you people so far haven't been
happy ones—' she stopped. 'I can give you the address of our
place up there, if you want, although I'm not sure that rushing
up there will do any good.'

'No. I agree. But I could take it down anyway…'

'Do you have a pencil handy? It's Langley House, it's at
Little Bassett, just near the reservoir there. It's off the A508
north of Northampton. But if you're going there—'

'I'll ask you first,' Agnes said.

'Thank you. Thank you so much. She's – she's all I have.'

'I understand, Mrs Padgett.'

'I'm not sure you do.'

Agnes breathed, then said, 'As much as I'm able to.'

'Well, that may have to do. Good night.'

The phone clicked off. Agnes put her phone back in her bag.
She thought about Mrs Padgett's English reserve. She wondered
what had caused it to soften. She thought about Helena, on the
run, with a small child; she thought about Mrs Padgett, sitting
on her chintz sofa every evening, anxious and alone.

Agnes crept through the house and unlocked the library. She
pulled out one of Shirley's reference books, a road map of
Britain. She sat in the light of an Anglepoise lamp and looked
up Market Harborough. She saw the A508. The reservoir. The
site of the battle of Naseby, 1645. The river Welland…

Alice Hawker had mentioned the river Welland, Agnes
remembered. She looked more closely at the map, tracing the
river through the edge of Leicestershire. Cranfield, there it
was. The battle that Alice wrote about must have been this
one, Agnes thought. One day I'll know about the history of

this country. So Alice, before she married Nicolas and came to London, grew up in the same area as the Padgett house.

She stood up and switched off the lamp. She crossed the room in the dim yellow glow from the high windows. She locked the library, hesitated in the hall. There was no sound, not even the traffic on the main road only yards from the house. As she crept up the stairs she thought about Alice Hawker, carrying her candle up to bed, watching the shadows flicker on the walls.

'I lift up mine eyes to the hills; from where is my help to come?' Agnes joined her voice to those of her fellow sisters. 'My help comes from the Lord; the maker of heaven and earth...'

Agnes tried not to yawn. A thin dawn brought a pale life to the leaded windows of the community chapel.

'...The Lord preserves you from all evil. It is he who shall keep you safe...'

Agnes wondered where Helena was. In her mind she saw a sleeping child, a woman watching over her.

After the service she found Sister Madeleine in the kitchen.

'How's everything?' Madeleine said.

'OK. The thing is—' Agnes began.

'Another favour. I can tell by your tone of voice.' Madeleine scrunched her short brown hair into spikes.

'I wondered whether the community car was free.'

'I'm not the person to ask. Sister Anna keeps the rota.'

'Sister Anna probably won't give it to me.'

Madeleine looked at her. 'What is it this time? Off-road rally driving?'

Agnes smiled. 'If only it was. I think—' she lowered her voice. 'I think I may have found Helena, but I don't want anyone here knowing.'

Madeleine blinked. 'Oh. OK. Leave it with me.' She slipped out of the kitchen. Agnes found a chair in the corner and settled with her mug of tea. She could hear strains of conversation from the living room; a dispute about the new setting of the Magnificat – 'But if we start in A Minor, it's too high for most of our voices—' Another voice was complaining about a leaking pipe: 'If he doesn't turn up by Wednesday, I won't answer for the ceiling...'

Madeleine appeared in the doorway. 'I've got you the car,' she said. 'I'm afraid I lied, went on about supermarket shopping. So, the condition is, that when you bring it back, it'll be stocked up with loo roll and stuff. I'll give you a list – margarine, I'm afraid, one of those big tubs. Soap powder. Oh, and tinned tomatoes, that's another thing we need.'

The morning traffic was heavy. At Shoreditch, inching between red lights, grinding through the gears, Agnes found herself considering the possibility of driving up the M1, stuck in the slow-lane at sixty miles an hour. She wondered whether she could persuade the thin young man in the Mercedes showroom to do a deal, perhaps pleading that it was in the service of the Lord. It was a shame, she thought, the Godlessness of youth.

It began to rain. The tower blocks of East London were hunched under heavy clouds. Agnes thought about fields, and farmhouses, and open sky.

She sat at the lights, watching the lines of raindrops on

the windscreen, feeling her spirits rise.

She parked outside the clinic. As she locked her car, she was aware of unusual activity within the glass doors. There were lots of people in the foyer, looking agitated; there was an ambulance waiting on the corner.

She ran into the centre. Beatrice came to meet her. 'There you are. We've been looking for you. Your phone was switched off.'

'What's happened?'

'It's Mrs Sayer. She tried to take her own life.'

'What? Serena?'

'She came in here, about half an hour ago. She said she was looking for you, she seemed very odd, it was lucky I was here, I saw the signs, eyes very strange...and then she collapsed.'

'What had she taken?'

'I tried to keep her awake, tried to find out. We're looking for empty pill bottles in Dr Sayer's room, that's where she was, but she might have taken the stuff before she came here. He thinks she must have stockpiled some of her medication—' She broke off, as Philip's door opened.

He stumbled into the foyer. His skin was papery, his eyes sunk in shadow. He looked at Beatrice, then at Agnes. His voice, when he spoke, was hoarse.

'Life everlasting.' He pointed an accusing finger at Agnes. 'She told me... Dying in order to live. That's what she thought she was doing. My wife,' he added.

'I heard,' Agnes said. She took a step towards him. 'I'm very sorry—'

'So you should be. I hold you responsible.' His hand dropped limply to his side. 'Do you remember, once, a lifetime ago, you asked me what it's like in a world without God? And I told you.'

'Yes,' Agnes said. 'You told me it was a peaceful place, a place of scientific enquiry, I seem to remember.'

'My wife—' his eyes were dark with rage. 'She has left my world and joined you in yours. My wife has chosen death instead of life.'

'She's not dead,' Agnes said.

'Not this time.' He swayed slightly, staring at the floor.

'Philip – you can't hold me responsible—' Agnes stretched out a hand towards him.

'You peddle this nonsense,' he said, recoiling from her. 'You sell people this happy-ever-after. Why shouldn't you be held responsible if they believe you?' He turned to Beatrice. 'I've asked the hospital to ring me back. Take the ward number and I'll go straight there.' He wandered back into his office and slammed the door.

Beatrice looked at Agnes. 'Shall I get you a cuppa, love?'

Agnes sat down heavily into one of the foyer chairs. 'Yes, please,' she said.

The life of the clinic was readjusting itself, settling back into shape. Francis returned, mumbling, to his chair in the corner. Beatrice reappeared with two polystyrene cups.

'I don't wish to speak out of turn,' she handed one to Agnes, 'but that was quite uncalled for. Careful, it's hot.'

'Serena believed she was going to heaven.' Agnes balanced the cup on her knee.

'From what I know of the Good Lord,' Beatrice said, 'He don't need us to rush things. That lady's problems aren't to do with Heaven, they're to do with Earth. Ain't that so? It might just be she finds it easier to talk about Heaven, and if I'd gone through what she's gone through, I might be the same.' Beatrice patted Agnes's arm. 'Don't take it personally.' She jerked her head towards Philip's door. 'It's not my place to say so, but some of the folks in here would be better off if there was more like you looking after them. Too much tinkering with their brains, not enough caring about their souls.' She glanced at the clock above the reception desk. 'Anyway, can't stay here chatting. People live, people die, I've still got my work to do.'

She flashed Agnes a smile. 'By the way,' she went on, 'you watch your step out there. I've seen them little tykes again. Them ones that used to hang out with Troy, there's two of them, one of them's got red hair and a mean little nose, nasty-looking kid. He used to cause trouble when poor old Tina-Marie was with us. And the other one, he threw an egg at the door once, I caught him by the scruff of his thin little neck and made him clean it off. Luke, he's called. Anyway, him and his friend, they were both hanging around here when I arrived this morning. I was going to ask them their business but they legged it before I could.'

'Should we tell the police?'

Beatrice pursed her lips. 'If I see them kids again, then I will. Not that the police can do much unless they really cause trouble.'

Agnes walked out of the clinic, out into the street. A drinks can shot across the kerb in front of her and she turned to see two lads laughing, swaggering, on the corner of the street.

'Hello,' she said, approaching them.

'Hello,' they echoed, laughing some more.

'I could call the police now,' she said.

The red-haired one squared up to her. 'We ain't done nothing,' he said.

'We've met before,' she said. 'You're Troy's friend.'

'He ain't done nothing either,' Ryan said.

'On the night that Tina died—'

'We know who sliced Tina,' the other boy said.

'Shut it, Luke,' Ryan said.

'Them feds have got it wrong with Troy,' Luke said. 'He was just going to teach her a lesson, weren't he? And then that bloke in the Saab came up and started having a fat go at her, and she was like screaming at him to leave her alone, and then she ran away. And he drove off after her.'

'Bloke in a Saab?'

Ryan was staring at the pavement, his hands in his pockets. 'Yeah,' he joined in. 'Posh bloke.'

'American, he was,' Luke said. 'All tanned. Looked fake.'

'Has Troy told anyone all this?'

'He's told his brief, yeah.' Ryan shot her a look. 'But them feds ain't going to listen to a badboy over a rich white man, are they? Anyway, what's it to you?'

Agnes looked at them as they stood there, slouched and furtive. Ryan lit up a cigarette, took a drag, handed it to Luke. 'Better blurt, man,' he said. 'Later on.'

They ambled to the end of the street and disappeared round the corner.

She stood in the rain. Bloke in a Saab, she thought.

At the far end of the main road she could just see the spire of Julius's church.

He'll be there, she thought. I could just walk into his office and tell him, Serena's taken an overdose and Philip blames me for convincing her that there's an afterlife. I'd tell him that apparently my argument was so powerful that Serena concluded the next life was preferable to this one. And Julius would reassure me, just as Beatrice has done.

And yet...

The rain trickled through her hair onto her face.

And yet, without God, as Philip said, there would be no holy wars. No suicide bombers. No happy-ever-after to peddle to the vulnerable.

Without God there would be no Protestants, no Catholics. Agnes turned to face the building, and her eye fell on the ruins of the Jacobean wall. In her mind she heard Alice's words: 'They will kill me, for their God is not my God, my faith is false in their eyes...'

She marched up to her front door, let herself in, called hello to Shirley, went straight to the kitchen, dripping raindrops across the floor, and took out her phone.

She bashed at the keys with her thumb, shaking her wet hair from her eyes.

'Hello – Mrs Padgett, it's Agnes.'

'Ah. I thought I'd hear from you.' Agnes was taken aback by the warmth of her tone.

'And, as you thought—' Agnes began.

'You want to visit the house,' she interrupted.

'I share your instincts about Helena,' Agnes said. 'It's the most obvious place she'd run to.'

'There are spare keys, we leave them with the neighbours. If there's no answer at the house, pop round there to get them.

I'll warn them to expect you. Theirs is the white house on the main road, Mr and Mrs Bewley, very nice people, incomers but they've settled very well...'

'Mrs Padgett,' Agnes began. 'Have you ever heard of Alice Hawker? Her maiden name was Braden. She lived at Cranfield, in the village there.'

'I know Cranfield.' There was a pause, then she said, 'No, I can't say I have. How long ago?'

'In the seventeenth century.' Agnes realised it sounded odd.

'We don't go back that far.' Mrs Padgett didn't seem to think it was odd. 'My father bought the house after the war, it had a bit of land attached and I think he fancied himself as a farmer, but his career at the bank had too much of a hold. He sold off the land for a camping site.' She was silent for a moment, then said, 'Yes, I do know Cranfield. We had a flower arranging competition in their church once. We did rather well, as usual. Betty Atwell did her ivy and chrysan-themum display, it always wins something.'

The rain was easing as Agnes set off for Northamptonshire. The North Circular was washed with watery sunlight, and the sky brightened as she left London behind her. She felt the car engine struggle as she joined the M1. She thought about Serena, lying in a hospital bed. She thought about Jonathan Harris, and the book collection, and Malcolm's offer. She wondered what he was after.

She thought about the leather-bound book shut away in her desk. In her mind, she heard Alice's words. 'I will die. God keep my child.'

All I have to go on, Agnes thought, is a child's voice, a tiny snatch of sound across a phone line.

God keep my child. The words echoed with the whine of the engine, the rumble of the tyres on the tarmac.

CHAPTER TWELVE

The directions were precise. Langley House was a handsome, red-brick building. Agnes crossed the clipped lawn and approached the shiny gloss-painted front door. The doorbell chimed and she waited.

There was no answer.

From the drive she could see the white house belonging to the Bewleys. It would be so easy, she thought, to ask for the keys, let herself in, begin to search the house.

For what? she wondered. What did I hope to find?

There was the sound of footsteps within, and then the door opened a crack. A woman stood there. She wore a long skirt, and had dreadlocked hair wrapped up into a turban.

'What?' she said.

Agnes cleared her throat. 'I was looking for Helena,' she said. 'Helena Padgett. I believe this is her parents' house.'

The woman hesitated, then said, 'She's not here. I haven't seen her.'

'And little Leila,' Agnes added.

The door opened slightly wider. Inside Agnes glimpsed an untidy hallway, coats hanging on a set of hooks. One coat was small and covered in pink flowers.

'I don't know who you mean,' the woman said.

'And you are—' Agnes tried.

'None of your business.' She went to close the door, but something was blocking it. She kicked it out of the way with her foot. It was a red plastic beaker, a child's drinking mug.

'They left in a hurry, then?' Agnes said, but the door had slammed shut.

Agnes stood on the driveway. She wondered what to do now. In the distance, a church bell chimed three.

Agnes got back into her car and set off, slowly, idling through the village, past a pub, a run-down shop, another pub, and then out onto the main road. A sign said Thornby, then Naseby, and then Agnes found she'd turned across towards the battle site itself.

She stopped the car and got out. A breeze rippled the long grass, tickled the branches of the trees. She left the car and began to walk across the field, aimlessly, wondering whether it belonged to anyone, wondering whether she was at risk of attack by farmers armed with shotguns, as she would have been in France.

Soft sunlight drenched the landscape. She listened to the birdsong and thought about the battlefield beneath her feet; how the earth had long since closed over the fallen; how the blood-soaked scars had healed.

Perhaps I'm wrong to chase the past, she thought. Perhaps, with the passage of time, events lose their power, and after centuries, their meaning, until in the end there's just this pretty green hill with the birds singing in the trees.

She set off again, her hands in her pockets. Perhaps I should look forward, rather than back, she thought. Whatever happened to Alice Hawker happened long ago, and it's only my urge to run away that makes me—

Her fingers in her pocket closed over Alice's rosary. She pulled it out and looked at it.

The beads swung there, glinting in the sunlight. When Alice held this in her hand, Agnes thought, there were the bodies of men in shallow graves, still keenly mourned, on this field where I'm standing now.

I will die. God keep my child.

She remembered Tina-Marie – her rage, her laughter, her long, coloured skirts. She thought about the woman at the house. She remembered Jared's words about Tina's sister, Josie. 'Up north, I think. They weren't close…'

Josie. That was the name he'd said.

Agnes strode back across the field, got into her car and drove back to Langley House. She rang the doorbell, and this time, when at last it opened, she said, 'Hello, Josie.'

The woman with the turban stood and stared at her. Agnes pushed at the door, and said, 'I think I'd better come in, don't you?'

Agnes found herself in the hall. She closed the front door behind her. Josie's gaze was still fixed on her.

'You're Tina-Marie's sister, aren't you?' Agnes said.

Josie nodded.

'I'm Sister Agnes. I work in the day centre she used to go to, before she died. I know that Helena took Leila away, and that Helena knew Tina-Marie from Pastor Malcolm's church in Essex.'

'How did you know she had a sister?' Josie's shoulders were slumped, her hands hung at her sides.

'Jared mentioned you.'

Her face brightened. 'You've seen Jared? I thought he was away?'

'He's back. He wants to see Leila. He says he's all she's got now.'

'Oh.' The word came out as a sigh. 'If we'd known he was here... Do you have a number for him?'

Agnes thought about his business card tucked into her purse. 'I can get one,' she said. 'But I need to know what's going on.'

Josie led her past the coats hanging on their hooks, into the kitchen. Agnes noticed that the small pink-flowered coat had gone. The kitchen was warm and untidy. Empty pizza boxes were stacked on the white surfaces. A black bin bag seemed to be overflowing with milk cartons. 'I'm sorry about all this—' Josie waved an arm over it. 'It's all been a bit temporary. I'm going to do serious cleaning before I leave.'

Agnes sat down at the table.

'Do you want some tea or something?' Josie looked doubtfully at the kettle.

'No thanks.'

Josie seemed relieved, and sat down opposite her. She studied her for a moment, then said, 'I'm sorry I appeared unfriendly earlier. We don't know who to trust.'

'I can imagine.'

'We think Troy was after Leila too, you see. We think he's scared of what she was witness to.'

'But he's been arrested and charged.'

'He has friends. Helena thinks she saw someone, about two days ago, a guy called Ryan – nasty guy, red-head, mean face – one of Troy's associates. We're not sure how long we can stay here.'

'Jared really wants to see Leila.'

'That would be great.'

'Can't you come back to London?'

Josie stared at the table. 'You don't know what they're like, Troy's people. And also—'

'Malcolm?'

Josie glanced at her, but said nothing. After a moment she looked at Agnes and said, 'A nun, eh? You don't look much like one.'

'Were you close, you and your sister?'

Josie's finger made circles as she traced the grain of the old oak table. She sighed. 'It makes it worse in a way,' she said. 'I feel I should have looked after her more. Helena says I shouldn't blame myself, but—' she glanced up. 'I knew what Troy was like, I should have protected her better. We were seven years apart, see. My life was so different from hers.'

'In what way?'

Josie wove a lock of hair into the turban on her head. 'She didn't get on with Mum the way I did. Our dad left when we were still at school, and we had to move. I was nearly eighteen, I was all set to go to Art college. But it took Tina much worse. She and Mum had fights, you know… She ran away, got into trouble. She blamed Mum for Dad going, I think.'

'Are you in touch with your dad?'

Josie shook her head. 'I think he went back to France. Started a new family. My mum was hurt when he left. They'd met in Africa, where she was from, Togo. He was working for a French company at the time, Pharmaceuticals. Anyway, he brought her back here, she left her home, her family… We became her life.'

'Where is she—'

'Oh, no, she died, see. Five years ago. It was crap for both of us. But I'd met Karen by then, my partner. She was at law school. It was easier for me. After Mum died, we got citizenship after that, and that's when Tina joined Malcolm's church thing. That's where she met Jared. And when she fell pregnant, they were going to get married – that Pastor was very keen on it. And then Jared went right off it. He couldn't cope with the community any more, so he left. And that's why they split up, because Tina wanted to stay there. There was talk of Malcolm marrying her, I think he wanted to give the baby a proper home. Tina wasn't having that. He's a real bully, everyone says. And I don't share his beliefs—' she broke off and looked at Agnes. 'Sorry. They're your beliefs too,' she said.

'Well, not exactly—' Agnes began.

'Anyway,' Josie went on, 'then it all went wrong for Tina, and she left too. But Jared was in the States by then, and she took up with Troy – early last year it was. And that was a bloody disaster...' Her voice faltered.

'Where's Leila now?'

'Helena's taken her out for a walk, I think. They'll be back soon.'

'Why did Helena pretend she didn't know Tina-Marie, when she joined us?'

'I'm not sure. They were very close. She's Leila's godmother. Maybe it felt safer that way. I know they were both scared of Malcolm, after they'd left. Helena still is, even now.'

'What's there to be frightened of?'

Josie stared at the table. 'I don't know. I don't get it. I only met him once or twice. I just thought he was a phoney. Helena says there's something very dark in his beliefs. Spells and things, magic. She says it's not really Christian at all.'

Agnes reflected that Philip would say there's no difference.

'It's all been so much to get used to,' Josie said. 'Losing my sister. And everyone feels bad, everyone feels they could have helped her. Me, and Helena, and probably you, and her psychiatric team – and even our Dad would, if he ever heard about it. And Jared – he must feel responsible, to have come back. He should have the baby really, he's always cared about her.' She picked up her mobile and glanced at the time. 'I don't mean to be rude, but you ought to leave.'

'I'd love to see Helena—' Agnes began.

'No. Please. She's so scared. If she thinks anyone knows she's here, she'll be off. I want her to believe she's safe here, in her mum's house. Mind you, if that friend of Troy's shows up again, we'll have to leave. We may have to go to my place.'

'Where's your place?'

'Leeds.' Josie stood up. 'Really, I know it's rude of me, but—'

'I understand.' Agnes put on her coat and followed Josie to the door. 'Thanks for all your help.'

'Like I said – we all feel responsible.' Tears welled up in her eyes and she blinked them away.

'Have you heard of Alice Braden? Her married name was Hawker,' Agnes said.

Josie shrugged, shook her head.

'She grew up round here. About three hundred years ago. She had a tragic life.'

Josie smiled. 'There's enough tragedy for me in the present,' she said. 'I can't begin to worry about people in the past. Keep in touch.'

As Agnes drove away from the house, she scanned her mirror for signs of a little girl, a woman walking beside her. The road was deserted; the hedgerows cast long shadows in the afternoon light.

Agnes took the road back to Naseby again, and then on as far as the next village. 'Cranfield welcomes careful drivers,' a sign said. She slowed down, looking around her. There was a war memorial with a patch of thin grass around it. There was a line of uniform houses, boxy tiled roofs and tight little windows, looking worn but not old.

Next to the church there was a red brick house. A mossy roof, leaded glass windows. Agnes took a deep breath and went to ring the bell.

'Can I help you?' A woman stood in the doorway. She had roughly chopped dark hair streaked with grey, a round face, and was wearing a dog collar.

'I'm sorry to bother you—' Agnes wondered what the Protestant, female equivalent of Father was. 'I'm Sister Agnes. I'm – I'm researching the history of this area...the Braden family.'

'Good heavens. This was their house.' She had a brusque, well-spoken tone. 'This is one bit of Cranfield Hall. Most of it's gone, of course. The church acquired it in the seventies, and sold off the land. I'm Sue—' she held out her hand. 'Sue Radlett. I'd invite you in but I've got the PCC here in a minute and they'll take a dim view. Mrs Pike's already here, she's the secretary, she doesn't like people wasting her time.' She glanced over her shoulder. 'Sister, eh? A nun?'

Agnes nodded at her.

'Do come back another time, won't you?' Sue smiled a round, pink smile and Agnes agreed that yes, of course, she'd love to.

Alice's birthplace. Agnes walked slowly down the drive, then turned back to look at it. The windows glinted pink in the last low rays of the sun. Agnes thought she saw an upstairs curtain move.

She wondered whether Alice would haunt two places – or was it revenge, she wondered, that kept her in her husband's house?

It was dark when she reached the outskirts of London. The looming lights of a supermarket on the North Circular Road reminded her of her deal with Madeleine. She found herself wandering the brightly lit aisles, blinking at breakfast cereal, soap powder, special offers on wine and pizza and pomegranate juice...

She drove south through Holloway, arriving at the Hackney house as the bell rang for vespers.

'You could join them,' said Rachel, the novice nun on kitchen duty who was helping her unpack. 'You've only missed the opening collect.'

The words of the Psalms seeped through the building. How soothing it would be, Agnes thought, on the eve of the Sabbath, to stand with her sisters in the choir, to join her voice to theirs. Then she remembered that she wasn't supposed to have the car, and that she still needed it; she remembered that Lucia was cross with her as it was, without the added aggravation of arriving late and unannounced.

'I'd better get back,' Agnes said. 'Thanks all the same.'

The solitary light in the darkness of the clinic signalled that Philip was at his desk. She knocked on his door.

'Enter.'

She walked in.

'Oh, not you.' His face was drawn, his skin chalk-white. His fingers on his biro seemed skeletal.

'I want to help.' She sat down opposite him.

'It's a bit late now.' He continued to write.

'Philip—'

'What?' He put down his pen. 'As far as I'm concerned, this is how it is. My wife, in her sorrow, wanted to bury herself in a pit of despair. And you gave her the spade and helped her dig.'

'And is that where she still is? In the pit I helped her dig?'

'Oh, you don't have to call it a pit. You call it faith. Or Heaven. Or Jesus, who supposedly takes a personal interest in us even though in real life he was just some poor Jewish fellow crucified by the Romans two thousand years ago.'

'How is Serena?' Agnes kept her voice calm.

'Conscious. I've been with her all day. She blames me.' He studied his fingernails. 'From now on, I will have to police her, you see. All medication locked away. All food consumed while I stand over her.'

'Is she in hospital?'

'They're keeping her in. But, for all it means to her, she

could be anywhere. I've sorted out a prescription for anti-depressants, but she won't take them. She doesn't want to come home, she said. She seems to have made a deliberate choice to inhabit a fantasy world. She has a postcard, it's of a painting, I don't know where she found it. It's a Madonna and child, medieval, you know the kind of thing. Well, you're bound to, you live in the same fantasy world. Anyway, she sits and stares at it, and smiles. Just smiling at this picture of the little baby Jesus.' He ran his fingers through his hair. 'Even if she agrees to come home, I know how it will be. We won't speak. I'll feed her. She may eat. I'll put her to bed. I'll sleep in the other room...'

'You should let someone visit her—' Agnes began.

'One of you people? Why on earth would I let you make it worse?'

She met his gaze, his eyes dark with fury. 'Philip,' she said. 'I care. I care about her. And I care about you. You're as much locked away as she is. Surely, if she can find some kind of meaning in her grief – if she thinks that that tiny life wasn't wasted – then you should try to listen to her?'

He shook his head. 'I can't believe how an intelligent woman like you – you don't understand, do you? She thinks that if she prays hard enough to baby Jesus or whoever it is, she'll get another baby. Our consultant knows, and I know, that it's impossible. If you really cared about her, you'd agree with me, that these fantasies are unhelpful and dangerous. Now, if you'll excuse me—' He picked up his pen in his pale fingers.

'If you must know—' She felt tears prick her eyes, and her voice shook. 'I'd rather believe what you believe.'

He glanced up at her.

She went on, 'All I can see at the moment is damage. If I felt it was possible for me to live in your rational, godless world, then I would.' She blinked as the tears blurred her eyes. 'You're right. In my world people call themselves Protestant or Catholic, or Christian or Muslim, and they gather themselves under the banner of their God and they plunder people's lands in their Crusades, they slaughter each other on their battlefields, they strap explosives to their chests in tube stations, they lock up an innocent mother until she dies of grief and even then, they'll say, it's God's will. It's what He wants us to do.'

Philip had put down his pen. He reached his hand slowly towards her across the desk. They sat in silence, in the hum from his computer screen. After a while, he said, 'I didn't mean...when I attacked your God... I didn't mean to attack you.'

She nodded.

'So – if you think these things...?' He stopped.

She took out a tissue and dabbed at her eyes. 'In this world that I live in, Tina-Marie was killed and her little girl is in danger. I have to find out what happened.'

'But why is that about God?'

'On these stones at our feet,' Agnes said, 'Alice Hawker prayed to her God to rescue her, to reunite her with her child. And her husband had God on his side instead. Just as Pastor Malcolm does, or so he says. In all these prayers and psalms and spells and incantations, some great evil has been done. Alice's baby, little Jonjo, died; I have to make sure that Leila survives.'

'And then?'

'Then I will emerge into your world, your world of light and rationality.'

He almost smiled. 'And Serena?'

She stood up. 'Philip – let Julius talk to her. Please.'

'Julius?'

'Trust me.'

'Is there any reason why I should?' He stood up and helped her on with her coat.

'None at all,' Agnes said. 'I must seem as mad as most of your patients.'

'Oh, madder.' He seemed to be about to say more, but fell silent, gazing beyond her into the night.

She hesitated in the doorway, then turned and went out.

She walked round to the convent entrance, wondering about supper. She thought about the community house in Hackney, how they'd all be sitting down to something warm and nutritious like shepherd's pie. She thought about the damp bare larder of Collyer House.

Then she remembered the bag of supermarket shopping still in the boot of the car, the packet of organic smoked salmon, the avocados and lemons and the rocket salad and the rather expensive mayonnaise.

As she sat, some time later, squeezing the last drops of lemon juice over the last avocado slice, she heard the doorbell ring. She went to the front door,

'Who is it?' she called through the letter box.

'Jared.'

She opened the door. He looked crumpled and gaunt. 'I

have to find her.' He came into the hallway and stood there. 'My little girl. I have to find her. And you have to help me.'

He stood silhouetted in the light from the kitchen.

'I've found her,' Agnes said. 'I've found your little girl.'

CHAPTER THIRTEEN

'So, she's OK, is she, little Leila?' Jared held a mug of tea between his hands. He looked cold, with a finely woven tweed scarf wrapped tight around his neck.

'I didn't actually see her, but yes.' Agnes sat down at the kitchen table opposite him.

'Why didn't you tell me you'd found her?'

'I've only just got back.'

'Where is she?' He rubbed at his black curls.

Agnes stirred a spoon round in her mug. 'She's with Josie.' She glanced at Jared.

'Josie? Where?'

'There's a house in Leicestershire, round there. It belongs to Helena's family. I've just spoken to Helena's mother, it's thanks to her that I went up there.'

'Helena?'

'The nun, from my order. The one who was in Malcolm's church.'

'Oh, yeah.'

'They're hiding out there, Josie and Helena, with Leila. They're frightened of Troy's people. And they're frightened of Malcolm.'

He nodded. Agnes looked at him, and then said, 'Do you think Troy killed Tina-Marie?'

'Who else? He's violent, and he's ruthless. And they were seen fighting that night. And what I think is, Leila's in danger from his homies, because she might count as a witness. He might want her out of the way.'

'And you can protect her?'

'I'll take her back to the States.'

'Yes.' Agnes warmed her hands on her mug. 'And Malcolm?' She looked up and met his eyes.

He leaned back in his chair. 'He's a very powerful person, Malcolm is. It's difficult to explain. People feel that they can't escape from him. That's what Tina-Marie thought. I think that's why she took up with Troy, she saw someone strong, someone who'd take on her enemies. She didn't realise that to Troy she'd become the enemy.'

'Malcolm wants to buy our library collection.'

'What, all them old books?'

'Yes. We thought it was odd. He's offered a substantial sum.'

'Tax evasion, maybe?'

'I don't know.'

'You know he's American, Malcolm is?'

Agnes nodded.

Jared wrapped the end of his scarf round his neck. 'When I got there, I did some research on him. He's left very few traces, and I thought maybe he'd changed his name, but then I went through some internet things, and there were some press reports from a few years back, maybe fifteen years – he was arrested on sex offence charges. Two young women, separate incidents, they were working as call girls...they accused him of assault. It never came to trial. I reckon it was soon after that he left the States. And before all that he was in the army somewhere, in the Midwest. Anyway—' Jared pushed his mug away from him. 'When are we going to see my little girl?'

'You'd better phone Josie.' Agnes reached for her phone. 'You can arrange something with her. They're very nervous.' She clicked on her phone, then wrote down Josie's number and handed it to him.

He held it in his hand. 'Thanks,' he said. He stood up. 'I haven't been the best dad in the world. Circumstances made it difficult. But all that's going to change. My mum, she's lived on her own in Willesden, ever since my dad walked out. Anyway, my brother's got a US visa for her, she's going to come and stay with us in New York. She'd love it if Leila was there too. A proper family again.'

They went out into the darkened hallway. At the door, Agnes said, 'What was Malcolm like with women in his own church?'

Jared shrugged. 'You've met him.'

'I don't mean women like me.'

He frowned, briefly, then said, 'He's dangerous. Even now. What I think is, if he fixes on a woman, then she has to play his game. And then, as long as she plays his game, within that community, she gets power, and status, until he moves on to the next one. Sometimes he has more than one at a time.'

'And Tina-Marie?'

He nodded. 'You know how beautiful she was. I think she was always top of his list. After I left I think he...that's why I wanted her to leave too.'

'But you left her there on her own?'

'I had no choice. I couldn't spend another day, singing praises to our Lord...' He glanced at her. 'Sorry, I don't mean to offend. For all I know I'll find God again, it's in my blood. I'm a hybrid, see.' He laughed. 'Protestant and Catholic. My mum a pentecostalist, and my Dad, not that I remember him, Irish Catholic. If I seem a bit anti, that's why.'

'It's OK. I know what you mean. Anyway,' Agnes said. 'It's over. Troy's locked up, you can be with Leila, Leila will be safe...'

He offered her his hand. 'Thanks,' he said. 'Thanks for finding her.'

She closed the front door and stood in the silence of the house. Above her, on the landing, there was a rhythmic padding, like footsteps. As she went up the stairs, it stopped.

In her room she took out her phone and dialled Josie, wanting her to know that everything was going to be all right. She got Josie's voice requesting that she leave a message. She rang off.

She settled at her desk, and took Alice's diary out of the drawer. She turned the pages.

'Our smith did send for me to say that the old horse had lost a shoe, but Nicolas became enraged and chased him from the yard, and then chastised me, saying what was I thinking of, wasting his money on shoeing a horse without use. She's not without use, old Betsy, and even if she was, she's the friend of my girlhood and I love her dearly. But there is no use in trying to explain this to my husband...'

As she turned the page, a bundle of papers fell out. They

were roughly tied, and the writing was thin. Some lines were illegible.

'I write this from Cranfield, where they have locked me up. My parents assure me that it is for my good, and that my reason will thereby be restored...'

Agnes turned some of the pages. A wavering line of ink blots caught her eyes, and she read the name John Joseph. '...I watched the cart process along the path that leads to our house. I stood at my attic window, and saw the little swaddled body, and the maidservant that sat beside him. I could see the tears that stained her cheeks. I ran, then, out of the door, down the stairs and out into the rain, because I knew, I knew that they had brought home to me my child, my boy, my dearest lamb...' The rest was illegible. Agnes turned to another page. '...The Lord has abandoned me, for I did pray to him that I might die and that my boy might live. And now the world is turned upside-down, and I live, if living it be, and my dear child is to be buried in the churchyard here. If the Lord hear my prayers, then let him grant my wish that I will soon be reunited with my boy.' The rest of the page was blank.

Agnes sat at her desk, in the narrow pool of light from her desklamp. She stacked the diaries away in their drawer, and took out her prayer book. She turned to the evening prayers.

'...Whenever I am afraid, I will put my trust in you, O Lord. Oh God, you have noted my lamentation; whenever I call upon you, my enemies will be put to flight; this I know, for God is on my side...'

In her mind she saw the horse and cart, the weeping

maidservant; she saw the drive she herself had stood on, only that day. She imagined Alice Hawker standing at the window knowing that the worst had happened, knowing that God was no longer on her side.

She thought of Jared, phoning Josie to arrange to go to Langley House. She thought of him standing by the neat front door, ringing the bell, reclaiming his child.

'...For God is on my side.' The words made her feel cold. She closed the prayer book and got ready for bed.

'Perhaps you should go on retreat. Is that enough milk in that coffee?' Julius handed her a mug. Outside a single bird chirped in the early morning sun.

'Retreat?' Agnes sipped from the mug.

Julius sat down in his chair. 'Please don't take what I'm about to say the wrong way. But in these last few days, you've been edgy, and nervous. You've been avoiding your community in a way that they must interpret as deliberate.' He took off his glasses and began to polish them. 'You could stay with the Carmelites; you like it there.'

'But I'm not having a crisis.' Agnes peered into the biscuit tin that was on his desk. 'Do you only have digestives?'

'All this focus on the past,' Julius said. 'Everything you've said, about this poor Catholic woman and her dead child.'

'But it's true.'

'It was true three hundred years ago.' He picked up the biscuit tin. 'These are rather boring, aren't they. I could open another packet.'

'No,' Agnes said. 'I'm meeting Athena for a Sunday brunch after this. I ought to be at my community, but—' she stared at her hands on her mug. 'As you've just pointed out, they're not very pleased with me at the moment.'

Julius picked up a biscuit and put the tin down on the desk. 'I don't want to put ideas to you that aren't your own, but, when we take final vows, we give up our past. We become in some sense people who occupy the present. And maybe, because you're not quite comfortable with that, you're seeing past events as some kind of clue to the present.'

'You mean I'm wrong?'

'I mean that something that happened three hundred years ago can't really have any bearing on poor Tina-Marie and her little girl, surely.'

'It's just that Alice Hawker is haunting me, that's all.'

'Oh, that house. Those noises. I know. You should move out.' He brushed biscuit crumbs from his jumper. 'If you like, I'll come and sprinkle some holy water. That's known to lay ghosts to rest.'

'I thought you didn't believe in ghosts,' Agnes said.

'I'm perfectly happy with them, as long as they're metaphorical.'

'So, Father, for what exactly would my ghosts be metaphors? Or do I know the answer to that question?'

He smiled at her. 'You can't run away from the order for ever.'

'It's not for ever,' she said. 'I gave Jared Josie's mobile number. He'll phone her. He'll arrange to see little Leila. He wants to take her to the States.'

Julius looked up at her. 'So – everything's all right, then?'

She returned his gaze. 'Yes. I suppose it is.'

* * *

Athena brought two round white cups to the table. She sat down and peered out of the wide window. 'Look at this Sunday crowd. I'm used to having the Market to ourselves in the week, and now, just because we've made it fashionable, everyone's trooped down here to have a look.'

Agnes laughed.

'I got some apricot jam, I hope that's OK.'

'It will remind me of my childhood,' Agnes said.

'Oh dear. I should have got marmalade instead.' Athena stirred some sugar into her coffee. 'So – how's the hunt for that poor little girl?'

'I've found her. Everything's going to be all right. I can become a proper nun, as Julius was just explaining to me.'

'Oh, it's all right for him to say. Julius is already a saint, it's easy for him.'

Agnes smiled at her. 'And how are you?'

'Oh, fine, you know. I thought I'd found the perfect pair of shoes yesterday, and so I bought them.' She sipped her coffee, leaving a moustache of foam across her lip. 'Black suede, pointed toes, lovely.'

'And?'

Athena sighed. 'And then I got home, and I found they're rather like another pair of shoes I already own, in fact, extremely like them.'

'Two perfect pairs, then?'

'Well, yes.' Athena dabbed at her lip with a paper napkin. 'It makes it hard to choose. And then I spoke to Nic and he said, if you want a baby, then that's a choice you must make.'

'Oh.'

'Just like the shoes, only with more serious repercussions for the rest of my life. Perhaps.'

'But—' Agnes put down her cup. 'But – he's mad, Nic is. He loves you. How can he let you go? Has he found someone else?'

Athena shook her head. 'I'm sure he hasn't. His mistress is History. He's telling himself all these stories about his Sephardic grandmother and her ancestral line to medieval Prague, and none of the stories include me.'

'Do you still love him?'

Athena's eyes welled with tears. 'More than anyone. I just don't know how to reach him any more.'

'Can you go out there and win him back?'

Athena spread some jam on her brioche. 'I said to him, on the phone, shall I come out next weekend? And he said, he was going to the Jewish museum in Toledo or somewhere, he wouldn't be there. And I can't go during the week, Jake and I are full-on hanging metal seagulls from Simon's ceiling.'

'How are things with Jake?'

Athena gazed out of the window. 'Oh, look, it's coming on to rain,' she said. She turned back to Agnes. 'Jake? We get on really well. We haven't...we haven't yet – you know. Gone to bed. Jake says he respects my need to sort things out with Nic.'

'But surely, if you wanted to, I mean, with Jake...?'

'That's just the point, isn't it, kitten? There's Jake, being funny and gorgeous and sweet – and I look at him and think, if I really fancied you I'd jump on you right now. And Nic – if I hear his voice on the phone, even after all these years – I have to sit down and catch my breath.'

'Mmm.' Agnes watched the rain splash against the window.
'I know what you mean. And don't say I'm a nun.'

'Wouldn't dream of it. Even though you are.'

Agnes walked back home through the rain. Everything will be
all right, Julius had said. But Athena will be with Jake when
she ought to be with Nic; and Serena is retreating into a world
without her husband. And Jared will take Leila to America.

In her mind she heard Alice's words: the world is turned
upside down.

She thought about the funeral cart coming to a halt outside
Alice's window.

'Oh dear, Agnes, it's such short notice.' Shirley flapped across
the library to greet her. 'You'd think he'd have told us before
the weekend, and now it's Monday and he'll be here in a
minute. He's just phoned, he's on his way, he said.'

'Who?' Agnes hung up her coat and switched on her desk
lamp.

'Pastor Malcolm. He's coming to see us. Now. I wanted to
print out a list of the titles he might be interested in, but
there's no time. I do think he could have given us more notice.'
She perched, bird-like, at her desk, and flicked bits of paper
into a pile.

'But he's based in Essex.'

Shirley blinked at her, her head on one side. 'You look
tired.'

'I am a bit.'

'He said he would be in London anyway, just passing. He

made it sound quite informal. "Just call me Malcolm," he said when I addressed him as Reverend—' The doorbell rang and Shirley jumped up and left the room. Agnes heard their voices in the hall, and then she reappeared, followed by Malcolm Noble. He approached Agnes, an arm outstretched. 'Sister. What a pleasant surprise,' he said as they shook hands.

'Hello.' Agnes gestured to a seat, and all three sat down.

'I'm here to testify to my commitment,' he began. 'I have thought about this more and more, I have prayed for guidance on the subject, and the Lord tells me that I should become the guardian of this collection. Not only that, but I, in turn, should endow your community of christian women with whatever financial recompense they think fit.'

He beamed from one to the other. There was a small silence, broken by Shirley. 'May we know exactly what has sparked your interest, Rev – Malcolm?'

In answer he began to gaze around the room, at the ceiling, at the book-lined shelves. 'Collyer House,' he said. 'So much history.'

'How do you know?' Shirley's hand went to her glasses as she peered at him.

'Shirley—' Malcolm leaned forward, as if his words were for her alone. 'I'm someone who works with the light. I have seen the workings of the Lord and how it heals, how it makes the broken whole, the sick well...just as our Lord Jesus did. And as God grants us gifts, it behoves us to make use of them.'

Shirley glanced at Agnes, as if in hope of translation.

'What gifts, exactly?' Agnes watched him as the full beam of his attention transferred to her.

'I have known of Collyer House for some time. It was built by Nicolas Hawker, wasn't it. And he was someone who knew something of the mystic arts.'

'You mean magic?' Agnes tried not to sound tetchy.

'More than magic.' He leaned back in his chair and interlocked his fingers. 'Nicolas Hawker had the Jerusalem Crystal.'

'But he never went to Jerusalem.' Shirley's tone, too, was rather short.

'No, but the story goes that the crystal that he acquired had come from a glass maker in the Holy Land, probably about eleventh century, via the crusades. And it had been kept in this country by an alchemist, who passed it to one of his disciples. And eventually, a descendant of this man joined a church that Hawker attended, and it seems that Hawker offered a lot of money for it. And as far as we know, it's been here ever since.'

'Malcolm,' Agnes said. 'We don't know where it is.'

He looked from one to the other. There was a sudden chill in his expression. 'But – but you must know. The Bequest has been here all along.'

'We think some other Hawker descendants ended up with it,' Agnes said.

'But there were books of spells and magic.'

'We have the books,' Shirley said. 'There.' She pointed at the cabinet. 'Although, if you're going to use the spells, you'll have to be good at Latin.' She smiled at him, but he didn't smile back.

He swivelled in his chair to look at the cabinet, then turned back to them. 'My offer would have to include the crystal.'

'That's all very well,' Shirley said, 'but if he passed it on to his descendants, they already have the rightful ownership of it.'

Malcolm frowned at her. 'It must be here,' he said. 'No one has heard mention of it for a long time. It's very distinctive, it has the greek letters Alpha and Omega carved into the base. I only know about it from doing very painstaking research, ever since Helena—' he stopped himself, then went on, 'And, there's another reason it should come to me. Apparently, the crystal was cursed. And the curse is inherited through the Hawker line, because Nicolas came by it wrongly, in some way. It could be doing untold harm, if his descendants still hold it.'

'Surely—' Agnes tried to speak in a tone of reasonableness. 'Surely a man of God can leave behind all thought of curses, or spells or magic? Doesn't our faith liberate us to believe in something greater?'

He turned to her, and managed to summon up his warm smile. 'Ah, sister – better, surely, to acknowledge the darker side of the Lord's creation, than to pretend it isn't there.'

Shirley stood up. 'Well, all this talk of crusades and alchemy sounds very unlikely.' Agnes wanted to applaud, but managed to nod instead. 'But we'll keep our eyes open in case your crystal turns up.'

He got to his feet. He stood crookedly, as if being thwarted had thrown him off balance. 'Right.' He walked slowly to the door. 'Well, I'll keep in touch. My offer stands, of course. But without the crystal, the value of the collection is much diminished.'

Out in the hall, he began to pull on his coat, when the doorbell rang. Jonathan Harris was standing there.

'Mr Harris,' Agnes said. 'Do come in—'

She stood back from the front door. He shuffled in, damp and pink under a tweed cap which he now took off and clutched between both hands.

'I've been thinking—' he began, breathless.

Shirley gestured to Malcolm. 'Well, well,' she said. 'Mr Harris, this is the Reverend Noble. How appropriate that you should both meet.'

The two men stood in the dim daylight of the hallway. Jonathan peered up at Malcolm from under his gingery lashes. Malcolm smiled and put out his hand. 'Mr Harris,' he said. 'You must be the book dealer. A pleasure to meet you. Shirley mentioned you.'

'And you,' Jonathan began. 'You're the Reverend who's offered a huge sum—'

'Some things have a value beyond money,' Malcolm said. 'Wouldn't you agree?'

Jonathan unhunched his shoulders. 'If it's the crystal you're after,' he said, 'it's quite likely that it's no longer part of the collection.'

'And how would you know that?' Malcolm looked down at him.

'Let's just say, I have privileged knowledge.' Jonathan returned his gaze.

Malcolm's eyes narrowed, then he allowed himself to smile. 'Well, all I know is, I want to help these ladies find a good home for the collection. And that is still my aim.' He offered his hand to Shirley, then to Agnes. 'I'll be in touch,' he said.

The front door closed behind him.

'Well,' Shirley said. 'I would like a cup of coffee. Would you, Mr Harris?'

They went into the library, and Shirley filled a kettle and tutted over the mugs.

Jonathan sank into a chair. 'I don't know what to make of it all.' He shook his head. 'So – Pastor Noble—' He shrugged and looked up at Agnes.

'He's determined to make some kind of deal which includes the crystal,' Agnes said. 'Although, he didn't mention the missing books.'

'But if they're not here—' he began.

'That's just what I said.' Shirley raised her voice above the noise of the kettle. 'That crystal is obviously the only thing he really wants. And him a man of the cloth, to dabble in the dark arts, even if it is a load of nonsense. Glass blowers in medieval Jerusalem, I mean, really.' She clinked instant coffee loudly into mugs.

'You know—' Jonathan leaned forward in his seat. 'When I heard about him, I thought I'd do some research on him, this Pastor. I thought there'd be a website, which there isn't, which I thought was odd; if it's a proper church, they all have websites these days...' He stopped to breathe. 'The idea of allowing a man like that to acquire ownership of...' His gaze went to the shelves of books and he shook his head.

Shirley brought three mugs of instant coffee over to her desk, and for a while there was quiet while milk was poured and sugar stirred.

'I know what I've got to do.' Jonathan broke the silence. 'I've got to find the crystal. I'm pretty sure it's not in this house, almost certain. If I can track it down, then I can prove it was passed on to us through the family line – and then that so-called Pastor can't have it. And then he won't want the books either, and we can go back to the plan as was, and the museum can have the Hawker archive. And if the crystal ever turns up, well, I don't have much money, as you know. I only have the claim of my own ancestral lineage. Financially, I can't begin to say I have greater rights over the collection – but morally, it seems to me that I do.'

He sipped his coffee.

Agnes's phone rang.

'Hello?'

'It's Jared. I've tried and tried that number you gave me for Josie. It's not answering. I'm really worried now. I'm worried that Malcolm's gone up there—'

'He hasn't.' Agnes wandered over to the window. 'I've just been with him. Here in London.'

'Oh.' Jared's relief was audible. 'I don't know what to do,' he said. 'I'm thinking of just driving there myself to find them.'

Through the high window, Agnes could see a crow settle on the clinic roof, black against the red tiling. 'Do you think it would be OK?' Jared said.

'I can tell you where the house is.' Agnes watched the crow as it sidled along the gutter. 'You go up the M1 to Northampton, and a bit beyond...' While she gave Jared the directions, a second crow landed next to the first. There was a noisy flutter of black wings, a squawk of beaks, and then one flew away.

'Thanks,' Jared said. 'I'll keep in touch.'

Agnes rang off. She crossed the library to join the others.

'Are you all right?' Shirley looked up, concerned. 'You're very pale.'

'Me? No, I'm fine. Thanks.' Agnes sat down with them.

'Mr Harris was just saying that one of his father's cousins might still be living in the Sussex area.'

'She'd be very old by now, but it's worth a try. If the Chichester branch of the family ended up with the crystal, you see...' His eyebrows flickered up and down. 'She might be able to shed some light, if she's still with us.' He stood up. 'Well, thank you ladies, for your understanding. I sense that we all three share a feeling about our Pastor Malcolm that all is not what it appears.' He looked from one to the other, his cheeks flushed. He picked up his coat and then bowed to them each in turn, and headed for the door, followed by Shirley.

A sudden loud cawing made Agnes look towards the window. Two more crows had landed on the roof. They stood in a line, hopping and shifting blackly in the rain.

CHAPTER FOURTEEN

Philip looked dreadful. He was standing at the front of the main meeting room in the clinic, a sheaf of notes in his hand, delivering a speech which consisted mostly of numbers. Agnes tried to listen, but all she could hear was various sums of money. She looked around the room at the assembled group of architects, health professionals and user-group representatives. Francis was sitting in the corner, with Julius next to him. Francis's white hair was even more dishevelled than usual, and he looked from person to person, smiling. As Philip went through some kind of projected figures for return on the sale of the site, Francis was wearing an expression of great authority, and as Philip finished, Francis nodded as if in total agreement.

'...So in conclusion, ladies and gentlemen,' Philip was saying, 'it is imperative that the main operation of the clinic and drop-in centre transfers to the main building of the hospital by the end of the month. The site buyers have set their terms and we must abide by them.'

He sat down. He looked worn, drained by the act of speaking. There was a hubbub of worry and dissent. People began to stand up, form groups, pose questions to each other. Francis thanked everyone for coming and then slipped out of the door.

Agnes went to find Julius. 'Does that mean the library too?'

Julius was about to reply when Philip joined them. 'Agnes wants to know whether she has to move the library by the end of the month too,' Julius said to Philip.

'I'm afraid so.' Philip glanced at Agnes, then back at Julius. 'Thank you for your help,' he said to him.

'It was nothing.'

Philip turned to Agnes. 'Julius came to speak to my wife. In hospital. I don't know what he said, but she's agreed to come home. She even ate some lunch, after you'd gone. The nurses told me. I'm going to pick her up in a minute.' He looked at Julius. 'I don't know what your magic is,' he said, but Julius interrupted him.

'No magic,' he said.

'Not even God?' The grey weariness of Philip's face lightened briefly.

'I wouldn't know about that,' Julius said. 'We just talked about grief, and loss. And we talked about death, and about how sometimes life has to carry on in the face of death.'

'And none of that is God?' This time Philip did smile.

'Oh, yes,' Julius said. 'All of that is God, of course. It's just, you don't have to call it God. If you don't want to.'

'Are you really telling me,' Philip said, 'that the difference between your viewpoint and mine is just a matter of description? Because I won't accept that.' He looked at his watch. 'And one of these days we can argue this properly, but I do have to go and take my wife home.' He seemed to be about to say more, but instead he nodded at Julius, then left the room.

Julius and Agnes walked round to the door of Collyer

House. 'People do complicate things, don't they?' he said to her. The drizzle had cleared, and the late afternoon sky was streaked pink. 'It's always seemed very simple to me. Perhaps I'm missing something.' He kissed her cheek, then went on his way.

In the library, Shirley was sitting on the floor surrounded by stacks of books and large cardboard boxes. 'I'd heard,' she said, when Agnes told her that they had about three weeks to clear the whole collection. 'I bumped into that nasty developer chappie on my lunch break. If he wasn't literally rubbing his hands together as he told me, he might as well have been.' She picked up a book. '*The Stations of the Cross – A Lenten Journey*,' she said. 'Any ideas?'

'Which box is which?'

Shirley pointed at various heaps of books. 'That pile is to go to your convent house. That pile is to be disposed of, subject to Sister Lucia's approval. And that pile is for Jonathan Harris to take away as he thinks fit – assuming we're still doing business with Mr Harris.'

'*Stations of the Cross* had better go into the convent box.' Agnes placed it on the pile. She surveyed the shelves. 'This is going to take longer than three weeks.'

Shirley sighed. 'Particularly if we don't have Mr Harris. What did your convent say about Mr Noble?'

'Sister Lucia was going to talk to the Provincial about it.'

'Well, I think I should tell Just-Call-Me-Malcolm that he's got three weeks to come up with some money.'

'I think you should.'

Shirley went to the phone and Agnes took her place on the

floor. She stacked books into piles and listened to the one-sided conversations; Malcolm seemed untroubled by the news, and she heard Shirley agree that indeed, God's will no doubt would be done. Jonathan, it appeared, was more concerned, and Agnes listened to Shirley's reassuring tones, as she read the titles on the spines of books and put them into boxes.

'Oh dear.' Shirley returned to her desk. 'Mr Harris was in a bit of a flap. "But how am I going to be able to make my claim to the collection in such a short time...?" I tried to say we were on his side, without giving too much away.'

'*Bathing in the Jordan – a Baptismal Promise.* What do you think?' Agnes held up a battered hardback.

'Surely not,' Shirley said, and Agnes passed it to her for the 'Dispose Of' box.

They settled into silence, lifting books from shelves, placing them in boxes. The windows above them grew dark; a half-moon crept into their frame. The convent clock chimed six, and Shirley yawned. 'I ought to go home,' she said.

'Yes, of course.' Agnes had been standing, writing lists of titles, but now sank into a chair.

'I suppose we've made some progress.' Shirley frowned at the box destined for Jonathan Harris. 'That's already full,' she said. 'I don't know how we're going to manage without him.' She stood up and took her coat down from its hook, then stopped. She went back to her desk and took a key from the drawer and went over to the locked corner cabinet which housed Nicolas Hawker's collection. She began to pull all the books out from their shelves, in ones and twos, stacking them on the desk as if they were fragile.

'What are you doing?' Agnes watched her in surprise.

'I know it's ridiculous,' she said, 'but what if this darned crystal was here all along?' She took some more books out, and Agnes got up and helped her, until the cabinet was empty, and the desk was covered in beautiful volumes, leather-bound, gold-edged. They looked at the empty cabinet.

'It was worth a try.' Shirley shook her head. 'Have you had anything else from here?'

'Only Alice's diary and notebook, and her rosary box.'

'Let's hope Mr Harris's elderly cousin can help, then.' They replaced all the books, and Shirley locked the cabinet. She tucked the key back into her desk, and put on her coat. 'I'm too late for the fishmongers, now. Mother does like a bit of cod. She'll have to manage with an omelette for once.'

In the kitchen, Agnes's phone trilled through the darkness.

'Hello?' Agnes switched on the lights.

'It's me, Jared. I'm there, in the village. I went to the house, it's deserted. I hung about, in case they came back. But it's all in darkness. I'm outside now.'

'What will you do?' Agnes sat at the kitchen table.

'I don't know. There's a pub with rooms in the next village, I thought I'd stay there and check this place out again tomorrow. I've tried the number you gave me for Josie, it's been switched off all day. Agnes, I'm that worried, I am, I don't know what to do.'

'I can't really help, from here. I've only got Josie's number too.'

'Well, look, I'm on this number. Call me if you hear anything. I'll stick around here for tonight.'

* * *

Agnes cooked herself an omelette. She thought about Shirley's mother eating omelette too, and wondered whether she'd be quiet and obliging about it, or whether the absence of a bit of cod would lead to an evening spent in silent hostility, or even raised voices and slammed doors. She wondered what Shirley would do when the library move was over.

She went to her room and took out Alice's diary, and turned to where she'd left off before.

'O Lord, rebuke me not in thine anger, neither chastise me in thy hot displeasure; Have mercy upon me O Lord for I am weak; O Lord, heal me, for my bones are vexed. Depart from me, all ye workers of iniquity; for the Lord hath heard the voice of my weeping.'

Agnes put the book down on her table. She wondered when these words had been written. Was this when Nicolas was treating her badly, in the early years of the marriage? Or later, when she was locked away? Or even later, when she was back in Cranfield, living in the terrible shadow of Jonjo's death?

She wondered how the diary had come to be in London, stuffed away in a corner with the rosary, undated, uncared-for. It was amazing they'd survived at all, she thought.

She picked it up again. '...For the Lord did send his wrath upon us, he sent flames from Heaven, that the whole of London did burn, with flames leaping up to the sky. And I spoke of these things to my husband, and I said that it is written that the first death will be by fire and the second death will be by water, and just as Noah was not believed when he went into the Ark, so it will be when these things come to pass in times to come. And my husband did mock, and say, well, then, it is as well that we built our house so strong. And so I was silent thenceforth.'

Agnes turned the page, and her eye was caught by the word 'crystal'.

'Today I tried to make my case, to plead with my husband. For either the crystal or myself will be proved to be a liar. I threw myself before him and said, will you take the word of this piece of glass, or of your own wife, she who is promised to you? And he answered me not, but did harden his face towards me and did leave the room. And so did I curse the crystal then, that it should be held to be honest whilst I was held to be a liar. For thus is my fate sealed and I feel it with dread in my heart. And so this night will I find a place to hide it where no one shall see its hellish face again.'

Agnes imagined her, alone, kneeling perhaps, lifting floorboards? Or climbing into the rafters...and if so, where? At Collyer House?

And might it still be there, the crystal, after all?

Agnes closed the book and went to bed.

At some point in the night, she was woken, by a noise, she thought. A loud clatter. She wondered if she'd dreamt it. She lay still and listened. At first she heard nothing. Then a soft rhythmic thudding along the landing.

She switched on her light. The sound was coming towards her.

She pulled on a jumper, picked up her phone, and opened the door. The footsteps stopped, then started again, this time at the staircase. Agnes followed them, resolving never to read Alice's diaries at bedtime but only in daylight hours.

The padding sound seemed to descend the stairs. It was only then that Agnes, standing at the top, noticed that the library door was open. Through the gap she could see a streak of light, like torchlight, motionless across the floor.

She fled back to her room and dialled the local police number. Eventually she got through, and reported that someone had broken into her house, while she was asleep, yes, she was still there, no, there was no sound at all from downstairs, do I think they've left the premises? I've no idea but I'm not going to go in there to find out...

She sat and waited. Even the soft footfall had stopped. She ventured back out on to the landing, clutching her phone. There was no sound, no police siren outside. She took a step downstairs, then another. She found herself in the hallway. She pushed the library door wide open and turned on all the lights.

It was just as she and Shirley had left it. Stacks of books, boxes, half-empty shelves. The Hawker cabinet was wide open, the door swinging as if it might fall off. Some of the books had tumbled to the floor. And there, lying next to them, his torch fallen from his hand, was Jonathan Harris.

CHAPTER FIFTEEN

'Unconscious,' Agnes repeated into her phone. 'Not dead, no. But in a bad way. Serious blow to the head. Please hurry.'

And then, almost immediately it seemed, they'd arrived, flashing blue lights and ambulance sirens, and Jonathan had been strapped to a stretcher and taken away, and the CID men had been wandering about and the nice woman police officer had taken her statement.

'There have been previous attempts on this address, haven't there?' The policewoman had pen and notebook poised.

'Yes,' Agnes agreed.

'Have you had sightings since, anyone hanging around?'

'Well, yes.' Agnes remembered her conversation with Luke and Ryan. 'There were two lads, friends of Troy Henson.'

'Ah. Troy Henson, eh?' The policewoman made some notes. 'They'd have had to know what they were doing.' She pointed to the gap in the high window where the glass had been removed. 'And then they surprised your friend.'

'But how did he get in?'

The policewoman frowned. 'Are you sure no one else has keys?'

'Only the nuns in my order.'

The policewoman smiled.

'If Jonathan had carved out the window pane, then his attacker could have followed him through it.'

The policewoman became serious again. 'I didn't get a detailed impression of him, but you'd have to climb over the adjoining roof to get level with the windows in this room.' She looked around the library. All the lights were on and there were murmured conversations, as fingerprints were taken, locks were examined.

'A library,' the policewoman said. 'Anything of value? Anything that might make someone go to all this trouble?'

Agnes remembered Jonathan Harris's anxiety earlier that day, when Shirley had explained that the library had to be moved. 'I think the injured man—' she began, then stopped.

'Or his attacker?' The policewoman prompted.

Agnes thought about the leather volumes of the Hawker archive. She thought about the spells and clues hidden in their pages, at least if Malcolm was to be believed.

'I can't imagine,' she said, 'that Luke would have any idea of the value of anything here at all.'

'Well—' the policewoman stood up. 'It's lucky for us that your friend survived. And for him too, of course,' she added. 'Here's my card. Call me if you think of anything else.'

And then, somehow, they'd gone, and the library lights were all turned off, and a damp sluggish dawn crept over the rooftops. Agnes sat in her kitchen, in the misty light of the new day, with a mug of tea. She felt she ought to make a list: arrange window boarding up, phone a glazier, alert Shirley, that sort of thing. Of course, she'd have to report the whole thing to Sister Lucia, who would insist, absolutely insist, that she move out of the building at once.

Outside, a burst of birdsong heralded the morning.

It was Malcolm who'd said that the crystal was cursed; it was Malcolm who'd said that the curse was inherited through Nicolas Hawker's line. It was Jonathan who was found, injured, in a heap of books from the Hawker archive.

Jonathan had broken in; and then someone had attacked him. All the evidence was that skill had been used, with glass cutters and copy keys. And yet, was it likely that someone like Jonathan would have the skill to—

Her train of thought was interrupted by the rhythmic sound of footsteps, again. She thought about sightings of dogs, of women in puritan dress, of guttering candles throwing shadows through the banisters. Perhaps Jonathan's attacker was constantly here, she thought, and not earthly at all. Then there was a louder, ticking noise, the gurgle of pipes, a chiming of the clock, and she remembered that the central heating came on at six.

She stood up, deciding that she might as well run a bath, sort out some clean clothes, and arrange an early meeting with Sister Lucia.

'Of course, I insist, absolutely insist that you move back here at once.' Sister Lucia sat back in her chair and folded her arms.

'Yes, Sister.' Agnes's hands were clasped together in her lap.

'Whatever is going on in Collyer House, it is clearly unsafe.'

'Yes, Sister.'

'When they told us we'd have to give it up, all those months ago, I was terribly resistant. Now, I have to say, it will be a relief not to have sisters staying there, with all these burglars haunting the place. You can have Sister

Brigitte's room, she's over in France at the moment.'

'And the library?'

Sister Lucia sighed. 'There's dear Shirley, of course. Perhaps you can pop over during the next few days and help her.'

'Yes, of course, Sister.'

Lucia frowned at Agnes, as if waiting for something more. 'Well,' she said, after a moment. 'Good. That's settled then.' She stood up, and opened the door of the study for Agnes to leave. She was still standing there, still frowning, long after Agnes had gathered up her coat and left the building.

'Sister Lucia says I've got to leave Collyer House. At once.' Agnes sliced her croissant in half and spread butter on it.

'Mmm?' Athena looked up from her cup of coffee. 'Well, sweetie, after all these goings on—'

'I must phone the hospital soon and see if Jonathan's come round.'

'Who?' Athena was gazing out of the wide glass window.

'Jonathan – the man who got knocked out.'

'Oh. Yes.'

Outside the morning crowds passed by, dark-suited men, sharply heeled women, hurrying through the slanting sunlight.

'I've already spoken to Shirley. I said she didn't need to go in, but she said she'd rather see the damage for herself.'

'Mmm.'

'Are you all right?' Agnes said.

'Me? Um, yes. I think so. The thing is, sweetie, last night Jake said that he was serious. About us. He means it, about playing houses and having children.' Athena spooned milk froth around the edge of her cup.

'But – but that's crazy.'

'Is it?' Athena met her eyes. She was pale, thin-lipped; from tiredness or from lack of make-up, Agnes wasn't sure.

'Do you remember when I told you, how Nic said, if I want a baby, that's what I've got to do?'

'Yes, but – Nic didn't mean it, did he?'

'Didn't he?'

'Even I can see,' Agnes said, 'that that's how he works. He's got all that honest, lay-your-cards-on-the-table, tell-it-how-it-is psychotherapy stuff, that means you say the exact opposite of what you think.'

'So what does he really want to say?'

'I imagine, he wants to say what any normal person would want to say. Which is, please don't leave me, I love you, I need you, don't let this Jake character deceive you into leaving.'

'Oh.' Athena stared down at her untouched brioche. Tears welled in her eyes. 'Well I wish he'd said that, then, last night, on the phone, instead of saying that whatever I do he'll always be my friend.'

'He said what?' Agnes put down her cup. 'What kind of man is he? Why isn't he fighting for you?'

'He thinks that he had an aunt on his mother's side, who was in Germany in the thirties and who didn't survive the camps. He said he might have to go to Auschwitz or somewhere.'

'What's that got to do with anything?'

Athena shrugged.

Agnes took a bite of croissant. After a moment she said, 'Don't listen to me. What do I know about it?'

'What do any of us know about it?' Athena dabbed at the

corner of her eyes. 'Except Jake. He's delighted. He's all set for me to move in with him; and Andrea from the gallery needs a place to stay, so she could rent my flat for a bit. And then later on, Jake says, we can sell both our places and find a new one, it's up to me...'

Agnes watched a brisk man in a well-cut suit talking loudly into his mobile phone. He stopped still, then thumped his briefcase down at his feet for emphasis. She turned back to Athena. 'Do you remember,' she said, 'when it was all about passion?'

Athena sighed. 'Oh yes. Passion.'

'And now it all seems to be about property prices.'

'Are we getting old?' Athena tried to smile.

'I used to think that when I took my final vows, something huge would happen, a moment of great illumination, some kind of reward for having done the right thing at last.'

'And?'

Outside the man finished his call. He frowned at his case, then picked it up and stalked away.

'It just seems to be more of the same,' Agnes said. 'Only more difficult.'

'You'd think God would lay on some fireworks,' Athena said. 'Given that he can do anything. It's not much to ask, after all you've done for him.' She broke off a piece of brioche and nibbled at it. 'That's what's making me feel old. Fireworks. Or rather, the lack of them. If Nic could be arsed to come and fight for me – or if Jake was capable of setting my world on fire – or both – at least I'd feel alive. Whereas, all I'm doing is looking in shop windows. And that would be OK if it was Prada, but these days I'm either looking at three bedroom mansion flats or different sorts of prams. It's no sort of life, is it?'

'Prams,' Agnes said.

'What?'

'It's just a bit odd. I mean, when you don't even know whether you and Jake are physically able to—' A birdsong tweeting interrupted her.

Athena rolled her eyes. 'I wish you'd sort out your ringtone,' she said.

'Hello,' Agnes said into her phone.

'Hi, it's Jared.'

'Where are you?'

'Still in Leicestershire. Listen, does Malcolm have a Saab?'

'Yes. Though he wants to upgrade to an SL—'

'I think I saw him drive past.'

'Are you sure?'

'It looked just like him. And the numberplate had JC in there somewhere. I remember that from before.'

'Oh. It must be.'

'I tried the house again this morning. There's still no answer. I think I'd better come back to London, I don't know what else I can do up here.'

'OK.'

'I'm worried sick. I just don't know where they can have gone.'

'I'll try Helena's mum again, if you like,' Agnes said. 'She might have some news.'

'That would be great.'

'And maybe I'll call Malcolm's church; find out where he is too.'

'Yeah. I don't trust him at all.' He was silent. 'The thing about Malcolm is, he always gets what he wants. That's what's so frightening about him. Speak later on, eh?' He rang off.

Athena had eaten most of her brioche. 'Oh well,' she said. 'If God won't lay on the fireworks, at least you can chase kidnapped children around the countryside.'

Agnes smiled. 'If only my order would see it that way. As it is, I've got to move back into the community house, after this library break-in.'

'I don't blame them, sweetie. It obviously isn't safe in that weird old house.'

'Safety.' Agnes picked up her coat. 'Since when did you and I ever value being safe over anything else?'

Athena began to wrap her scarf around her neck. 'It's terrible, sweetie. The end of danger. You locked away in your cell for ever and ever. And me discussing property prices and whether we should have a place with a garden. I've always lived in flats, I'm completely out of my depth. Apart from when I was a child in Greece – but I don't think it's fair to ask a London estate agent to find me an olive grove, even in West Hampstead.'

Shirley was standing in the middle of the library, her arm outstretched, issuing instructions to a man with a ladder.

'Can you tell your lad out there to hammer quietly?' she was saying. 'This is a library, you know.'

Above them, the carved out window was neatly boarded up. Shirley turned to Agnes. 'It could have been worse,' she said.

'The order want me to move out.' Agnes ran her finger along Shirley's newly dusted desk.

'Well, I must say, I wouldn't want to sleep here any more.'

'I'll still help with all this.' Agnes gestured to the boxes.

Shirley surveyed the room, her hands on her hips. 'It's a daunting enough task as it is, without all these break-ins. What do you think he wanted? And why couldn't he have just asked us?'

'Jonathan?'

'Who else?' Shirley picked up a book and glanced at its spine, then put it in a box.

'When you spoke to Malcolm yesterday,' Agnes said, 'did you get him on his mobile?'

Shirley frowned. 'Yes,' she said. 'Yes, it was his mobile.' She settled down next to one of the boxes and began to sort through a pile of books.

'So he could have been anywhere.'

'I suppose so.' Shirley glanced up at her. 'You're not suggesting he was here last night?'

'I don't know. Someone must have assaulted Mr Harris.'

'He might have fallen over.' Shirley frowned at a book and put it on one side. 'He might have climbed up to get at the Hawker books and lost his balance.'

'But why go to such lengths, if you're him? As you said, he could have just asked us.'

Shirley put two books in the Dispose Of box. 'It makes me think the previous burglary attempt was him as well and not those horrid boys. Well, perhaps when he wakes up he'll tell us.'

Agnes went to the desk and picked up the phone. She

dialled Mrs Padgett's number, and heard the English voice give the number she'd just dialled.

'Hello, it's Sister Agnes.'

'Oh.' There was a catch in her voice, then she said, 'Is Helena still at the house?'

'We think not.' Agnes tried to sound reassuring. 'Jared, he's the father of Tina's child, he's been in the village since last night. He couldn't see any signs of anyone.'

'Oh.'

'Do you know where else they might have gone?'

'No. We have very little family. There's no one Helena could impose on in that way. Perhaps they've gone to where this other woman lives.'

'Perhaps.' Agnes listened to her anxious breathing. 'Mrs Padgett, I'll let you know as soon as I hear anything.'

'Thank you.' She made her polite goodbyes and then she'd gone.

Agnes dialled the office number for Malcolm's church, and asked the young, female voice if Malcolm was there.

'No, I'm afraid he isn't.' The voice was hesitant, and possibly Australian, Agnes thought.

'Are you expecting him back soon?'

'He has some business to attend to. But I'm sure he'll be back soon, in the next day or two. Can anyone else help you? Marina's here, you could talk to her.'

Agnes remembered poor Marina and her hoovering, and wondered how much she would know; very little, she decided. She thanked her and rang off. Almost immediately her mobile tweeted at her. As she answered it, Agnes reminded herself to find out how to change the ringtone.

'Hello, it's Philip.'

'Oh. How are you?'

'I haven't phoned for a chat.' He sounded rough, abrupt. 'The hospital phoned here, trying to get through to you. Jonathan Harris has regained consciousness and is asking for you, apparently. Does that mean anything to you?'

'Yes. Yes, it does.'

'Good.' He hesitated.

'How's Serena?'

'She's back home. As you know.'

'And—' Agnes began.

'Well, then,' Philip interrupted. 'Goodbye.' He rang off.

Agnes walked along the hospital corridor. The fluorescent light gave the walls a greenish tinge. Jonathan was sitting up in bed, concentrating on a newspaper. He looked thinner, somehow, his hair more grey than ginger. He raised his eyes from the paper as Agnes approached, tried to smile, winced.

'Ow,' he said.

'That bad?' Agnes pulled up a ragged plastic-covered chair.

'Everything hurts.' He arranged a pillow behind him and settled back on to it. 'The police said I'd had a lucky escape. It was one blow to the head, but a pretty forceful one, apparently. Could have done a lot more harm. Anyway, nice of you to come.'

'I was worried about you.'

'They said it was you who found me.'

'Jonathan—'

He held up one hand. 'I know, I know, you're going to ask what on earth was I doing there. And you'd have every right to.'

'So—?'

He looked down at a pyjama button, as if surprised to find it there. 'Desperation,' he said. 'When Shirley said three weeks, I panicked. I need to find—' he stopped himself, then went on, 'I must have the Hawker collection, you see. The idea that that preacher might get his hands on it, and I don't trust him at all with the crystal, if that ever turns up, I'm afraid I wasn't thinking straight, I thought if I just crept in and had a look—'

'You could have asked us,' Agnes said. 'Shirley shares your view of Malcolm.' As do I, she almost added.

'I know. I'm sorry. It was stupid of me. More stupid than I realised.' He tapped the side of his head where it was swollen, then winced.

'But to go to all the trouble of cutting out a window—'

'Oh, no—' Jonathan blinked at her. 'That wasn't me. That was whoever hit me on the head.'

'So how did you get in?'

Jonathan looked down at his pyjamas and blushed. 'I – um – broke in. Through the door.'

'Right.' Agnes looked at him. 'So who do you think hit you on the head?'

'I wish I knew. The police showed me some photos, and one of them was of that lad who'd been hanging around, and it's true, I did see someone who looked just like him, earlier on in the evening, when I did my recce.'

'Luke?'

'Yes. That's the one.'

'And what would he want with our collection?'

'Well, I suppose it has a value.' Jonathan shrugged, then winced.

'And where did he learn to remove whole panes of glass?'

'At burglar school?' He managed a smile. 'I don't know. For all I know it was that preacher.'

'Malcolm may have an alibi. Then again, he may not. But even if it was him—' Agnes heard a trolley approach, was aware of a savoury, not very pleasant smell '—even if it was him, he must think there's something really valuable, to go to all that trouble.'

Jonathan shifted on his pillows. 'If one believed in magic, and had read about the crystal, then maybe it would be enough.'

'And what were you looking for, Mr Harris?'

His hands were warm and pink against the starched whiteness of the sheet. 'I told you,' he said. 'I need to have the Bequest. I have a moral right, without the financial assets...'

'Yes. So you said.' The meal-time smell was getting nearer. 'Do they really make you eat dinner at five in the afternoon?' Agnes asked.

Jonathan seemed to breathe again at the change of subject. 'They say I can go home tomorrow. I can't wait. I'm used to having dinner at about nine, a nice glass of claret and a steak or a chicken breast – I don't take kindly to this mince and mash arrangement at tea-time. At lunchtime it was cauliflower. I think—' he broke off, and tilted his head. 'What's that? Can you hear birdsong?'

'Oh.' Agnes snatched her phone from her bag. 'I'm sorry. You're supposed to switch them off, aren't you?'

'No one does.' Jonathan lay back on his pillows as Agnes answered the phone to a clipped English voice.

'It's Emily Padgett here.'

'Oh. Hello.'

'Helena phoned me. I did that thing where you dial it afterwards and it gives the number. Have you got a pen?'

Agnes pulled a receipt out of her bag and scribbled down the number. 'How was she?' she asked.

'Well, they're all three together. They seem to have gone further north. She wouldn't tell me where. She's frightened of Malcolm Noble, I think, but she gave very little away. She told me not to worry. As if I'm not going to worry. If she knew what it was like to be a mother...'

'Thank you for letting me know,' Agnes said.

'Well, it seems you're our best hope. Unless I start driving around the country in search of her myself, which I have to say, I'm rather tempted to do.'

'I'll keep in touch,' Agnes said.

She clicked off her phone and dropped it into her bag. Jonathan was watching her. 'It seems that Malcolm's influence extends rather far,' she said.

'Well...' Jonathan shifted his head on his pillow. 'It does tend to make people dangerous if they think that God is on their side – present company excepted, of course,' he added.

Agnes smiled at him. 'Will you be all right?'

'Oh, I think so, yes. I'll be glad to get home.'

She stood up. 'Mr Harris – do you remember anything about the attack?'

He shook his head. 'That's what the police kept asking. Nothing at all. They tell me it might come, I might get flashbacks.'

'There's a rumour,' Agnes began. 'About a curse.'

Jonathan wrinkled his nose. 'A curse?'

'Something to do with Nicolas Hawker having taken what wasn't rightfully his.'

A shadow crossed his face. Then, with some effort, he smiled. 'Oh, there's always curses.' His tone was light. 'Any family with a heritage as old as mine, there's bound to have been some gypsy or a witch or two, someone who uttered a few dark words two or three centuries ago, the odd ghost, even...' He shook his head. 'I wouldn't worry about me.'

'Well—' Agnes did up her coat. 'Come and visit us in the library, won't you. Shirley will be glad to see you.'

She walked back along the corridor in the fluorescent hum. It was getting dark outside, and she could hear rain against the high windows. She felt as if she'd visited an orphanage, or a home for abandoned dogs, as if Jonathan was waiting for someone to claim him. But then she imagined him sitting on his own with his glass of claret, and thought, perhaps he's OK as he is.

She thought about his flustered answer just now, telling her he'd broken in last night. The police had found no other sign of a break-in, apart from the pane of glass. But then, she tried to tell herself, people don't just materialise in buildings. Not real people anyway.

In the streets, people hurried through the dark, through driving rain. Shirley had gone home, leaving her a note. 'I've done what I can. See you in the morning. PS: There's a message from your order.'

Underneath her note was another one. It said, 'Sister Lucia

phoned. They're expecting you in the house for supper.'

Agnes locked the library and went straight up to her room. She took out her phone and the scrap of paper and dialled the number that Mrs Padgett had given her. A nervous female voice answered.

'Helena?'

'Who's this?'

'It's Agnes.'

'Oh. Did my mother—'

'I'm afraid so.'

'Josie said you'd called on us at Langley.'

'Yes.'

'We had to move on.'

'What are you frightened of?' Agnes sat on the edge of her bed.

There was silence.

'What can Malcolm do?'

'We've seen him.'

'To speak to?'

'No. We saw his car at Little Bassett. That's why we left.'

'Why does he frighten you so much?'

Agnes could hear her breathing. 'You won't understand,' Helena said.

'Jared wants to see Leila,' Agnes said. 'He called at Langley House yesterday.'

'Did he? We'd had to go by then.'

'Can I tell him where you are?'

There was a silence. Then Helena said, 'I'll ask Josie. I'll ring Jared, OK. Have you got his number?'

Agnes dictated Jared's number. 'Helena—' she said.

'Yes?'

'You can't live like this for ever.'

'You saw what happened to Tina-Marie.'

'But that was Troy, he's in prison.'

Helena's voice was edged with nerves. 'Please don't ask me to explain. I'll call Jared. Tell him.' She rang off.

Agnes sat on her bed in the dim light from the streetlamp outside. She dialled Jared. 'I've spoken to Helena. She's still with Josie and Leila. She said she'd phone you. I think they're at Josie's place.'

'Oh, thank God,' he said. Agnes could hear the relief in his voice.

'Malcolm was in Little Bassett, it seems. You were right. They saw him too. From a distance.'

'Bastard.'

'Why are they so frightened of him?'

'He's a very powerful guy. And he believes in himself to the point of madness. Those of us who got away...' His voice tailed off. 'I'll go up there,' he said. 'I'll see my little girl. Thanks,' he added. 'I really appreciate it.'

Agnes looked around her. She looked at the wooden cross hanging on the wall, at the icon of St. Francis, at her books by the bed, at Alice's diary stacked with them. She took her holdall out of the wardrobe and began to pack things into it. Slippers, nightwear, clean clothes. The French edition Bible that had been her mother's. She picked up Alice's things, weighing the leather-bound books in her hand.

It seemed wrong, to take them out of this house, away from the flagstones that still held the imprint of her step. It seems wrong to be leaving at all, Agnes thought.

She wrapped the notebooks in a blanket and stacked them under the bed.

She had an image of Athena, packing up her clothes to go and live with Jake. She looked at her one small holdall and imagined Athena's serried ranks of suitcases. It would take a taxi, perhaps two, Agnes thought, to move Athena's things. All I have to do is catch a bus across the river.

All I have to do is walk away.

The house was quiet. She listened for a pad-pad of footsteps. There was only silence. She opened her door, hoping to see a guttering candle moving along the corridor, a white puritan collar, even a growling mass of fur. There was nothing.

She picked up her bag and went along the landing. The house felt calm, benign. Only now, she thought, can it admit me as one of its own. And now is too late.

She double-locked the front door. She stood on the steps in the rain, her holdall at her side. Her fingers in her pocket closed around Alice's rosary.

You are still with me, she said to Alice.

And I am still with you.

CHAPTER SIXTEEN

In the morning there were bells ringing. There was chapel, then more bells. There was breakfast, conversation, chores to be shared out, arrangements to be made. At ten past ten Agnes caught the bus to Collyer House, feeling as if she'd lived a whole day.

She looked out of the window at the slate grey morning. Her phone rang.

'Sweetie – where are you?'

'I'm on a bus. I stayed at the convent last night, I'm going back to work in the library.'

'I'm at Jake's. I stayed here last night.'

'Oh. And?'

'I'm looking out over Clapham Common, it's quite pretty really.'

'But – did you—?'

'South London, sweetie, it's never going to work. I'm staying in my own flat from now on. Andrea will have to find somewhere else.'

'I had to have breakfast with about ten other people.'

'How awful.'

'What are we going to do?' Agnes watched a cyclist disappear into the tiny space between two buses. She held her breath.

'And Nic phoned,' Athena said.

'Nic?' The cyclist emerged unscathed and raced ahead through the traffic lights.

'He said would I mind if he didn't come over for the gallery opening after all, he really needs to visit the Holocaust place that week...'

'What did you say?'

'I said, fine. What else can I say?' Athena's voice wavered at the other end of the phone. 'I could ask him if he's having an affair, there's always Chantal the housekeeper I suppose—'

'If she's Marie's daughter she'd be about eighty-two.'

'Oh. Good.'

'I'd better go,' Agnes said. 'This is my stop.'

'In answer to your question,' Athena said, 'I've no idea what we're going to do.'

The library was looking less like a library and more like a series of empty shelves.

'You've worked very hard,' Agnes said to Shirley.

Shirley was sitting at her desk. 'And no burglaries, for a change,' she said. 'Coffee?'

Agnes thought about the cheap cornflakes and instant coffee she'd had for breakfast. 'No thanks,' she said.

Shirley went over to the kettle and switched it on. 'The problem is,' she said, 'we're all rather stuck now. Until we know who's taking what, all those boxes in that corner will just have to stay there. I can send those three there off to your convent, Sister Lucia has confirmed she wants them. But the others...' She spooned coffee into a mug. 'If only Mr Harris could come up with an offer, he could take all the books and the Hawker archive. How is he, by the way?'

'He seemed quite cheerful. Big bump on the head, but it could have been worse, he said. They're letting him go home today.'

'Well, the police seem to think it's those horrible young men. I told them about Malcolm Noble too, they said they'd investigate.' Shirley brought her mug over to her desk and sat down. 'The only other thing to do, is for you to take the Hawker stuff over to the convent. Your order can keep it until someone makes a decision about the money.'

Agnes glanced at the cabinet. A ray of dusty sunlight glanced across the glass doors, picking out the gold on the leather spines. 'I suppose it all depends on Malcolm's offer,' she said. She stood up and went to the desk phone. 'Do you mind if I make a call?'

Mrs Padgett sounded breathless as she answered. 'Oh, it's you, I've just got back from visiting my husband. Any news?'

'I spoke to Helena,' Agnes said.

'And?'

'I think it's going to be all right. Jared's going to go up there, I think they're at Josie's place. Then he can take his daughter, and everyone can come back.'

'I hope it's that simple.'

'Mrs Padgett – why are they so frightened of Malcolm?'

'I wish I knew. From the moment she left that church, she was terrified of him. I thought she'd be safe once we'd rescued her. I wasn't happy about her joining your lot, as you know, but even then, I thought, at least she can stop being frightened of that man. But now, here she is, on the run from him, practically. I think Josie knows more about Malcolm than she's letting on. And while the child and Helena are with her, they're all in danger.'

Agnes could hear her mobile ringing in her bag. 'Mrs Padgett, I've got to go. I'll keep in touch.'

She grabbed her mobile and answered it, and heard Jared's voice.

'I'm on my way, just thought I'd let you know. You were right, they're in Leeds, at Josie's. Leila's fine, can't wait to see her. Thanks for everything.'

'That's OK. Good luck.'

Agnes sat at her desk. She looked at her phone. 'The thing is,' she said, 'if Malcolm was lurking in Leicestershire, he wasn't in London to hit poor old Mr Harris over the head, was he?'

'I'm sorry?' Shirley looked up from a large piece of paper she had on her desk. 'I'm writing a list,' she said, 'so everyone knows where all the books are.'

'Unless he came back, late that night, sawed away at the window up there, climbed through, found Jonathan at the cabinet and attacked him.'

Shirley took a ruler and drew a column down the page. 'That Malcolm would have to want it very much, wouldn't he? To go to all those lengths. He'd have had to follow poor Mr Harris, to know that he was here, wouldn't he? And I still don't know exactly what Mr Harris was looking for. Anyway, there was nothing missing, so he can't have found it.' She drew another line.

'Jonathan lied to me,' Agnes said. 'He lied about how he got in. He said he broke in, but the police said the door was opened from the inside, probably by the person who'd already got in through the window and who then attacked Jonathan.

Which means Jonathan was already there, with no obvious method of having broken in. And when I asked him what he was looking for, he lied again, went on about his moral right to the collection. And then I mentioned the Hawker curse, and he pretended to find it funny, but something troubled him.'

Shirley looked up from numbering her columns. 'How do you know he was lying?'

'I just do.'

'What else would he have been looking for?'

'I don't know.'

'Surely not the silly old crystal.' Shirley went back to her list. 'And you can't suggest he just materialised in here, he must have got in somehow. There.' She put down her pen. 'All the boxes are numbered, and all the book titles will be listed here with their box number next to them, so if Sister Lucia has second thoughts, she can retrieve the books she wants.'

Agnes saw her pink-faced triumph. 'Shirley, I don't know what we'd do without you.'

At lunchtime she went next door to the clinic. Julius was sitting in the reception area, deep in conversation with Francis.

'...now Father,' Francis was saying, 'there's no use you telling me that Him up there is going to listen to any word of mine, not after the way I've treated Him. Not that I blame Him, mind, I'd be just the same if it was me on the fluffy white cloud up there, and a pillock like me down here trying to make amends.'

'Ah, but Francis,' Julius said, 'it's the making of amends that matters.'

'But Father, tell me honestly, how the devil would he know that I'm trying to make amends. I mean, rationally speaking?'

'I'm not sure it's so much to do with the reason as with the heart,' Julius said.

'Reason's what I'm after, Father.' Francis rubbed his stubbly chin with his fingers.

'I knew I'd find you here,' Agnes said.

Julius looked up. 'Telepathy again?'

'No. Because it's Wednesday.'

'Ah. Yes. The rational explanation.'

'There you go, Father.' Francis pointed at Agnes. 'And she's a woman of the cloth.' He stood up, and shook Julius's hand. 'Thank you for putting me straight, Father. I have an appointment now which mustn't be missed.' He smoothed down his ragged jacket and ambled out of the clinic doors.

'Well, then.' Julius looked up at Agnes. 'How are you?'

'I've moved in to the main house.' She sank on to the seat next to him.

'And how is that?'

'Social. Busy.'

'Oh dear.' Julius fiddled with the edge of a file on the table in front of him. 'But no black dogs?' He smiled. 'And now you're going to tell me you can bear ghostly dogs better than you can a chores rota.'

'Couldn't have put it better myself.' She glanced towards Philip's door. 'Do we know how Serena is?'

'According to Philip, she's slightly better—' Philip's door opened, and he appeared. He saw them, appeared to flinch, then approached.

'Hello,' he said.

'I was just telling Agnes here,' Julius began, 'that Serena's a bit better.'

Philip pursed his lips. 'Well, up to a point. She seems not to want to kill herself any more. For now. But there's a whole new game going on.'

'Oh yes?' Julius looked up at him, waiting.

'She's praying for a baby. She's praying to your God. Perhaps that pleases you both? She says, if her faith is strong enough, she'll conceive. It's medically impossible. So, this is the situation. Either your God answers her prayers, or she'll be thrown back into suicidal despair. You can see my problem. Or perhaps you can't.'

'Philip—' Agnes began.

'Well? Can you give me any guarantee that this so-called God will do something about it? I mean, he's supposed to be loving, isn't he? And all-knowing? And if you can't give me any guarantee, then how on earth do you people continue to believe?' He looked down at Julius. His eyes had deep shadows of exhaustion.

Julius rested his hand on Philip's arm. 'Tell your wife, that we'll be praying with her.'

'Is that the best you can do?' Philip said. 'A stupid false hope?'

'I'm afraid it is.' Julius patted his arm. 'We're not doctors, like you. We can't do medical miracles.'

'Doctors like me don't use words like miracles. We call it science.' He turned, slowly, and walked back into his office. The door slammed behind him.

'Well,' Julius said.

'What?' She looked at him.

'If it was all true, wouldn't it be grand.'

She smiled.

They parted at the door of the clinic, Julius back to his church, Agnes back to the library. Shirley's calm had been replaced with fluster.

'Oh, dear, it all happened while you were out. Malcolm's letter arrived at your order this morning, confirming his offer, bank details and everything. Sister Lucia has asked Mr Harris to respond, and he's in despair, poor man, says he can't find that kind of money, it will have to go to Malcolm. And Lucia says she's had no response at all from the Oxford people, she doesn't know what to do.'

'Has anyone spoken to Malcolm?'

'No, it's all in the letter.' Shirley surveyed the empty shelves. 'I suppose Mr Harris can have the books that no one else wants. Malcolm says he wants the Hawker Bequest, and also a few of the religious books to expand the library at his community.'

'I'm not sure he'll approve of this lot,' Agnes said, as her phone tweeted at her from her bag.

'Agnes, it's Helena. It's awful—'

'What's happened?'

'Malcolm has taken her.'

'What?'

'Leila. Malcolm has got her.'

CHAPTER SEVENTEEN

It was as if time was suspended; the snaking wet darkness of the motorway a continuous night. White headlights streamed past; the windscreen wipers of the order's car kept up their rickety rhythm.

Agnes had told Madeleine that she needed the Metro, and Madeleine, sensing the urgency in her voice, had handed her the keys. And now it was after eleven, and the blue signs, looming out of the dark, counted down her approach to Leeds.

She followed Josie's directions, finding herself circling the city, following signs to the waterfront. New buildings stretched sparkling away into the night sky, their clean lines broken only by the skeletal ghost of a disused factory or a derelict warehouse.

She got out of the car. The city seemed quiet here after the noisy rumble of the Metro's engine. She could hear water lapping in the distance. She approached Josie's block and rang the intercom. The lobby door clicked open. She took the stairs to the second floor, glad to stretch her legs.

The door opened a tiny crack. 'Yes?' It was a woman's voice, not one Agnes recognised.

'I'm Sister Agnes.'

'Oh.' The door opened wider. 'I'm Karen.' A hand was offered, which Agnes took. 'I'm Josie's partner.' She had wide, dark eyes, straight short black hair, a white collar, thin black jersey and trousers. 'Come in. It's hardly a party, as you can imagine.'

She showed Agnes into a bright living room. Wide windows were softly draped with cream blinds. Three forms were sunk in cream sofas, three faces looked up as Agnes came into the room. Jared, Helena and Josie.

Jared jumped up and crossed the parquet floor. 'It's my fault,' he said, taking her hand. 'He must have followed me. I was so keen to see her...' His voice crumpled, and he flopped back onto a chair.

'The police—' Agnes began.

'They were here.' Josie stood up and began to clear away empty mugs. 'They've gone for now. They're checking airports, railway stations, you know. It'll be on the news.' She picked up a tray and carried it through to the kitchen. Agnes heard her talking to Karen.

Jared put his head in his hands.

'What happened?' Agnes settled into an armchair.

'We were here, waiting for Jared,' Helena said. 'Us three. We heard the doorbell go, we were completely off guard, it was so stupid of us.'

'I saw his car.' Jared chewed on a fingernail. 'I was parking mine in the car park across the way there, I was all set to come up, I'd just phoned, hadn't I—' Helena nodded. 'And I saw this car,' he went on, 'and my mind was sending me warning messages, and I got to the lobby door of the flats here, and I thought, Christ, that's it, of course. I was phoning Josie's number, wasn't I, trying to say, don't open the door, and as I got through I heard it all, screaming, crying. I was about two seconds behind him…' He stopped, breathless.

'But the lift—' Agnes began.

'No,' Helena interrupted. 'It was all so fast, he grabbed her and ran, down the fire escape, Jared came up in the lift just as he'd gone, we shouted, he followed him down the stairs—'

'I saw his car pull out,' Jared went on. 'Nearly ran in front of it, he swerved. I jumped in mine, but I'd lost him as soon as he hit the loop road away from the waterfront.'

'We'd phoned the police by then,' Josie said. 'And that's when we phoned you too.'

The story over, a hush fell. Jared raised his head, seemed about to speak, leaned back on the cushions.

'Why—' Agnes began. 'Why does Malcolm want Leila?'

Glances flashed between all three. Helena broke the silence. 'He thinks—' she looked at Jared, who gave a barely perceptible nod. 'He thinks he's her dad. He's sure of it.'

'And he isn't?' Agnes's eyes rested briefly on Jared.

'No,' Jared said. 'It's part of the madness.'

'But he – he could be?' Agnes asked.

Josie sighed. 'While Tina-Marie was with him, in that church – they had – they had a bit of a thing.'

'More than a thing.' Jared spoke with barely veiled rage. 'Malcolm gets what Malcolm wants. She was the most beautiful woman there. She didn't stand a chance.'

'And…' Josie went on, 'that's why he thinks that Leila is his.'

'So – he won't harm her?' Agnes was aware of a chill in the room.

Again the looks exchanged. Jared said, 'We think not.'

'He's not that mad,' Helena said.

'Where might he have taken her?' Agnes asked.

'Essex maybe,' Helena said.

'Unless he's going to try to go abroad,' Jared said.

Karen appeared from the kitchen, with a fresh tray. 'Here's toast,' she said. 'And tea. Unless anyone wants a beer or something?'

People shook their heads, reached for mugs, plates. Karen settled on the arm of Josie's chair. 'Karen says,' Josie began, 'that he might try and get DNA testing done.'

'There are loads of those places,' Jared said. 'It doesn't help us find him.'

'If you got the police to send out his description,' Karen said, 'to all the clinics...'

'The problem with that,' said Jared, 'is that he'll find out she's not his. And I'm not sure he'll just come quietly back and hand her over. He's not that kind of guy.'

There were tense nods of agreement from the women.

Agnes put her mug down on the glass table. 'Tina-Marie was killed,' she said. 'And Jonathan Harris, who is Malcolm's rival for our rare books collection, was attacked. And Luke and Ryan gave me a very good description of a tanned American.' She looked at each face in turn. 'Just how dangerous is Malcolm?'

No one answered. Then Karen said, 'People who think they've got God on their side will stop at nothing.'

Josie nodded.

Jared ran his hands through his hair. 'And with Malcolm's past record on women...'

'It's about certainty, see,' Karen said. 'In my experience. People who have fixed belief systems, they see everything in black and white. If he thinks it's his child, then he wants her with him. It's probably quite simple as far as he's concerned.'

Outside, distant windows twinkled in the city darkness. 'What on earth are we going to do?' Agnes said.

'I just want to go looking for him,' Jared said.

'The police are doing all they can. We should sleep.' Karen stroked Josie's arm. 'All of us. If we can.'

The sun rose over the canal, flooding the white blinds with coral light. Agnes kicked off her duvet, remembered she was on Josie's sofa, sat up, wrapped her cardigan around her. Helena was still asleep on the other sofa. Agnes wandered into the kitchen. She found the kettle, put it on.

Karen emerged from her room, followed by Josie, who opened cupboards, found teabags, then Jared appeared from the spare bedroom. Helena sat up, rubbed her eyes, smoothed her hair, went into the bathroom.

Karen picked up the phone. Agnes heard her ask for one of the police team, heard, after a long pause, a brief conversation. Karen hung up. 'No news. No sightings at airports, at least.'

Helena came out of the bathroom. She took the mug of tea that someone handed her and wandered over to the window, gazing out. Then she lowered herself onto the sofa, and turned to Agnes. She looked bleached out and tired, her pale hair falling around her face. 'I'll have to come back to London,' she said. 'I've come to the end of running away.'

Agnes sat next to her. 'You weren't running away,' she said.

'I made a promise to Tina, that I'd look after her child. I've failed to keep it. I might as well just lock myself up in the convent for the rest of my life.'

'We'll stay here,' Josie said. 'We'll wait for news.'

'What will you do?' Helena turned to Jared.

Jared lifted one of the blinds. He looked at the urban skyline, misty pink and blue across the water. 'I just want my baby back,' he said.

They joined the motorway, heading south in the early morning traffic, Agnes bent over the wheel, the windscreen steaming up, the car heating rattling through the airvents.

Helena shivered next to her.

Somewhere around Leicester, Agnes pulled into a motorway service station. 'Petrol,' she said. 'And coffee.'

Helena sat huddled by a sticky table in the glaring light. Agnes put a mug of coffee down in front of her and sat down. 'You did what you could,' Agnes said, and waited.

Helena shook her head.

'No, listen to me,' Agnes went on. 'You knew Leila was in danger, and you removed her from the danger as best you could.'

'And the danger still found her.' Helena looked at the mug of coffee but didn't pick it up.

'We'll get Leila back,' Agnes said.

Helena met her eyes, then stared at the table again. 'You don't know Malcolm,' she said.

'What's he like, then?'

She picked up her spoon and stirred it round in her mug. 'When I'd been at his church about a year, maybe eighteen months...' She took out the spoon. It lay on the table, making a small puddle of coffee. 'He wanted to have sex with me, you see.' She glanced up at Agnes. 'That isn't what he called it. He'd have people around him, he'd give them special roles in the community, some of the men would run the business side of things, and the women...' She traced a circle in the puddle of coffee with her fingertip. 'Usually one at a time, you'd get to stay in the house with him instead of the accommodation block. Until he got tired of you.'

'And so – did you...?'

'No. I refused. He tried to anyway.' Her voice shook.

'You mean he would have—'

'Yes. He would have raped me. Except that he was interrupted, someone came to the door...'

Agnes felt a shiver of memory, as if from a previous life. 'So,' she said, 'did you leave after that?'

'Oh, no. Not for ages. I thought it was my fault, you see, I thought I must have provoked it.' She gave a thin smile. 'It's hard to understand, I know, but we were so caught up in the life there. It felt joyful, it felt as if we were doing the right thing. Malcolm didn't speak to me at all after that. And then he went back to Tina anyway.'

'And she didn't mind?'

Helena bit her lip. 'A lot of the women felt privileged. And he's probably quite attractive. I mean, if you like—'

'Men?'

Helena managed a smile. 'Yes.'

'And when he got tired of Tina-Marie—'

'Oh, he didn't. She was so beautiful, you see...I think if that man was ever capable of love, she would be the one.

But after he attacked me, she came to her senses. And Leila was growing up, and she realised that Malcolm was behaving like her father and she didn't want that. So we both left.'

'When Tina-Marie was at the clinic, you pretended not to know her.'

Helena brushed a lock of hair away from her face. 'We felt it was best that way. We were scared.'

'Of Malcolm?'

She nodded. 'He was so sure he was Leila's father, we thought he'd try to track her down. I thought it would be safer. If he tracked me down I'd just deny any knowledge.'

'Helena – the police have charged Troy with Tina-Marie's murder.'

She was silent for a moment. 'If you're asking me whether Malcolm could have killed her...' She met Agnes's gaze. 'I don't know. When she came to me, when she was frightened, it was Troy she was scared of. He was the one threatening to kill her, he's that sort of man. And as far as I know, Malcolm didn't know where to find her. Not then, anyway.'

Agnes stood up. 'Come on. Let's get back to London.'

Helena left her untouched coffee and followed Agnes out to the car park. They drove in silence. At one point Agnes passed her her mobile and Helena phoned Josie. She spoke to her briefly, then rang off. 'No news,' she said. 'Josie's there, and Jared's there too. Karen went into work today, she's a barrister, she's got a big case on. The police have gone to Malcolm's church, he's not there.' She stared out at the passing fields. 'They've got to find her,' she said.

* * *

Agnes parked the car outside the community house. They let themselves in quietly and crept to Helena's room. Helena sat on the narrow bed. 'I'll have to tell them I'm back,' she said.

Agnes hesitated in the doorway. 'Your mother,' she began. 'She does worry so.'

Helena smiled. 'I'll phone her too.'

Shirley looked up as Agnes walked through the library door.

'Oh, there you are. Everyone's cross with you.'

'I'm not surprised.' Agnes sat down heavily at her desk.

'Not me.' Shirley went over to the kettle. 'I'm not cross. I know it's all about that poor little girl. But you ought to tell your Mother Superior where you are, she's been asking for you.'

Agnes sighed in agreement.

'And the police have tried to arrest that Luke, apparently. They went to his flat, but he wasn't there.' Shirley poured tea into a mug.

'When?'

Shirley put the mug down in front of her. 'This morning. Early on. Mr Harris told me. They want him to try and identify his attacker, but he says he can't remember a thing.' She straightened up and surveyed the room. 'I tried to tell her, Sister Lucia, my work is done here. Everything's listed. I've written down the Hawker stuff too, but I've kept it in the cabinet. Everything else is in boxes. I'd like her to release me, if truth be told. Mother does need me.' She bent down to pick up her handbag; the movement made her seem suddenly old.

Agnes reached out and touched her elbow. 'But—'

Shirley looked down at Agnes's fingers, then met her eyes. 'But what?'

Please don't give up your life to your mother, Agnes wanted to say. 'Shirley,' she tried. 'There's other work. You're a skilled person...'

'My heart wouldn't be in it,' Shirley said. She looked at her watch. 'I promised Mother I'd be back at lunchtime. As all this is done.' She looked around at the boxes again. 'Your order really ought to make up its mind – we can't leave all this here. And the Hawker things need a better environment, acid-free paper lining, that sort of thing. I'll be in in the morning.'

She picked up her coat and hung it over her arm, smoothing the folds. Agnes heard the front door shut behind her.

I ought to phone Sister Lucia, she thought.

She stood up and wandered over to the Hawker cabinet. She unlocked the doors and gazed at the faded leather spines. She pulled out a book at random.

'"...In nomine dei Patris, dei Filii, Dei Spiritus Sancti, Amen,"' she read. In the name of the Father, and of the Son...

She flicked through some of the other books. They seemed all to be religious texts, all in Latin. She turned the pages more slowly, hoping to find...what, she wondered.

She thought of Jonathan Harris's desperation, his urgent attempt to claim the archive for himself. She thought of Leila, and her heart clenched as she wondered where she was, how she was.

She put the books back on the shelves and sat at her desk in the fading daylight. It is here, she thought. Hidden here, in this library, somewhere in these shelves, there is something that people want. A crystal, a book, a piece of paper, a magic spell. Something to prove – what? Their inheritance, perhaps; a claim to wealth. A genetic heritage; their lineage, their paternity.

Their paternity.

She raced out of the library and up the stairs to her room. She unpacked Alice's diaries from their hiding place and began to turn their pages, scanning the faded ink lettering. She paused over recipes, lists of expenses, turning the pages, putting down one book, picking up the other. She remembered seeing the words, somewhere in these books, a reference to the crystal.

And then, there it was.

'Today I tried to make my case, to plead with my husband. For either the crystal or myself will be proved to be a liar. I threw myself before him and said, will you take the word of this piece of glass, or of your own wife, she who is promised to you. And he answered me not, but did harden his face towards me and did leave the room. And so did I curse the crystal then, that it should be held to be honest whilst I was held to be a liar. For thus is my fate sealed and I feel it with dread in my heart. And so this night will I find a place to hide it where no one shall see its hellish face again.'

Somewhere the crystal is hidden. And Jonathan Harris must know that, and Malcolm knows it too.

Agnes sat on the bed that had been hers. But what do I do, she thought. Take up the floor? Hope that the crystal survived the re-building of this house over three centuries?

And then she thought, Alice was in Leicestershire when this was written. Nicolas must have looked for the answer in the crystal, and finding the answer, incarcerated his wife in the house in Leicestershire and come back to London. So, had she really buried the crystal it would be there, in Cranfield, not here at all.

She took Alice's rosary out of her pocket. She held it in her hand. She thought about Alice's thin fingers, scrabbling under the floor to hide a crystal ball. She thought about her child, after his death, being brought to her in Leicestershire. She thought of her grief, her heart shrinking in pain until it ceased to beat for ever.

She remembered the night that she'd opened the door of this very house to find the body of Tina-Marie. And now, Leila was with Malcolm.

And what does Malcolm know about the crystal? Does he know that Alice buried it somewhere in the middle of England? Does he know what Nicolas knew? Does he ask what truth might be revealed were he to gaze into it as Nicolas did three hundred years ago?

She picked up the rosary and went out onto the landing. The house was in darkness.

Show me, she willed.

She listened to the silence.

She went back to her room and found her candle, still standing in its dish, a box of matches on the side. She lit the candle and carried it out into the corridor. She watched the flickering shadows, waiting.

Then she heard it, the pad-padding sound of footsteps approaching her from nowhere. As they passed, she thought she felt a breath of air, the swish of skirts close by along the carpet. She followed the sound, the candle held out in front of her. Down the stairs, the sound still just ahead. In the hall the steps paused, then started up again, down the passage towards the kitchen. At the door of the cellar the steps stopped.

Agnes opened the cellar door. In front of her, the wooden stairs descended into darkness. Next to her, in the dusty brickwork, was another door. She turned the handle, which moved, stiffly. She pushed the door open and stepped through it, pushing a curtain to one side.

She blinked in the light, in the open space. She was standing in a narrow corridor. She could hear voices ahead, a phone ringing. As she passed along the passageway, she realised she was in the clinic.

She rounded the corner and found herself in the reception area. Philip was standing by his office door, and he looked at her as she approached, her candle still held in front of her, the rosary swinging from her other hand.

'Agnes—' He turned to face her. 'What the hell do you think you're doing?'

CHAPTER EIGHTEEN

She sat in Philip's office, as the noise of the clinic quietened around them.

'I can't do it,' he said. He was sitting opposite her, his chin resting heavily on his hands.

'Leila's life depends on it.' Her candle, now extinguished, sat on the desk in front of her.

He lifted his head. 'Try and see it from my point of view, Agnes. You appear in my clinic looking as if you'd seen a ghost, carrying various trappings of superstition, going on about secret doors. You then say that you want me to allow you access to my patients' files and that otherwise people might die. You can see, surely, that I'm unlikely to respond well.'

'There was a perfectly rational explanation,' Agnes said.

'Well, that makes a change.' He sat, slumped, unsmiling.

'I need proof,' she said. 'I need evidence.'

He glanced at her. 'How odd. For all these years you've clearly been prepared to believe all sorts of rubbish, with not a shred of proof.'

'Please don't tease me.'

'Oh, if only it was teasing.' He sighed. 'My wife is just the same. She's invented a God, some supernatural being who has her best interests at heart, apparently. Everything's going to be all right, because of Him.' He shook his head. 'It breaks my heart.'

'Philip – Tina-Marie's daughter is currently with a man who's dangerous to her. I need to get her back.'

'And how will my records help?'

She looked at him, then stood up. 'You're right. I can't explain.'

'It's been on the news,' Philip said. 'The police are hunting for him. And you come in here and say that a ghost told you?'

She gazed down at him. 'I don't believe in ghosts,' she said. 'Not even Holy Ones?'

Agnes's eyes narrowed. 'How will you feel if Leila comes to harm?' She picked up her candlestick and went to the door.

'Agnes—'

She heard his computer whirr into life.

'I don't understand a word you're saying.' He was staring at his screen, clicking the computer mouse. 'But that seems to be normal for me these days. And if anyone finds out what I'm doing, I'll probably lose my job. Here—' he beckoned her over, pointed at the screen. 'What do you want to know?'

She drove across London Bridge. The windscreen wipers rattled against the drizzle. The river flowed sluggishly under the black night sky. There was a rumble of thunder.

What if I'm too late, she thought.

She inched north through the late rush-hour traffic, through Holloway, Archway, to the A1, the M1. She sat in three solid lanes of traffic, changing lane from time to time in the vain hope of speeding up.

In her mind she could see Tina-Marie's file as it had appeared on the screen. There was nothing, of course; a few dates, notes of consultations, recommended prescriptions. She'd scrolled through the sparse details, and all the time, Philip had been there, asking her the same question: just because Alice's life was destroyed, why does the same thing apply to Tina-Marie?

She had been unable to answer him. He had switched off his computer.

The rain became heavier, and the traffic thickened and slowed around her. In her mind she could see the red brick house, the leaded windows.

She pulled out her phone, and dialled Josie's number.

'Hi.' Josie sounded exhausted.

'Any news?' Agnes checked her mirror for watchful police patrolling mobile phone use.

'No. Jared's out, he couldn't stand another evening pacing the flat. He's got mates in Mirfield, apparently. It's just me and Karen here. What about you?'

'I'm on the M1. I'm going back to Cranfield.'

'Why?'

'I – I don't know.'

'Oh.' Agnes could hear Karen's voice in the background. 'Well,' Josie said, 'keep us posted.'

'I will.' She clicked the phone off and threw it on to the passenger seat.

Philip thinks I'm mad, she thought. And he's an expert. She saw the rhythmic slow passing of headlights, like the flicker of a candle flame, like the soft beat of footsteps along a corridor.

Perhaps this is how madness feels.

* * *

It seemed to be the middle of the night when she arrived in the village of Cranfield but the church clock said twenty to ten. She parked her car and got out. The rain had eased, but the night sky was swollen with a threatening storm, the village muffled under the opaque clouds.

She looked at the vicarage. She thought, I could just knock on the door. And what would I say?

She went back to her car and sat in the driving seat for a while, watching the rain stream down the windscreen. Perhaps I am mad, she thought. Perhaps it's the deep pit of the past, as Athena said, and I've just fallen in.

She remembered the Psalm copied out by Alice in her diary: 'Save me, O God, for the waters are come in unto my soul; I sink in deep mire, where there is no standing; I am come into deep waters, where the floods overflow me. O God, thou knowest my foolishness, and my sins are not hid from thee...' She recalled Alice's words: that the flood would wash clean the sins of the house itself.

The rain battered hard against the roof of the car. Agnes got out, locked the car, marched up to the vicarage door and rang the bell.

The door opened, and Sue Radlett was looking down at her. 'Oh.' Recognition sparked across her face. 'It's you. Hello. Gosh.' She peered out at the downpour. 'Bit Old Testament, isn't it. You'd better come in. Either that or build an ark.'

The vicarage was warm and light; the ancient walls obscured the rain's noise. Over her black vestments and collar was draped a thick embroidered cardigan. 'Do you know,' Sue said, as she led Agnes into the lounge and gestured to one of several armchairs, 'after you appeared the other day, I had someone

SHADOW OF DEATH   261

else mention the family here, the Bradens. Mavis, it was, her sister used to be the cleaner here until she died. She lives in the village, she's terribly old, World War One baby from what I can gather. Anyway, happened to bump into her out by the old Post Office the other day, and we got talking, and she told me all about the history of this house. And she said, how brave I was to put up with living here. I wondered what she meant, and she said, didn't I notice, none of the children ever walked past this house. Well, to be honest, they've no reason to, it's not as if it leads anywhere, but she said, when they were children, the school was up the lane here. It's closed now, of course, all the little ones have to get the bus to Market Harborough to school...Where was I? Oh, yes, she said, when she was a kid, they'd go all the way round past the Colonel's, it's a good half-mile detour, rather than walk past the Braden house. As far as they were all concerned, a witch lived here and they weren't prepared to risk it.' She stopped, catching her breath through a brisk smile. 'I'm so sorry, I'm sure you didn't come out in this awful weather just to hear a lot of nonsense. Can I get you something? A hot drink?' She shrugged her bright cardigan further onto her shoulders.

'I wondered...' Agnes searched for the right words. 'I'm looking for...' Philip would assert that I was clinically insane, she thought. 'Sue – would you mind if I looked in your cellar?'

The rain hammered at the windows, poured down the guttering. Agnes sat at the kitchen table and placed Alice's diary carefully in front of Sue.

'It's this house, you see. It must be here that she hid the thing.'

'Why do you want it? If you and I share the same religion, then surely you believe, as I do, that matters of the occult are best left alone?'

Agnes closed Alice's diary. 'There's a child in danger,' she said. 'And the crystal is the lure to get her back.'

Perhaps I am mad, she thought. But then, Alice was deemed to be insane by everyone around her. And yet, it's her truth that has survived.

Sue fetched a large torch, frowning at it as she switched it on. 'Thought it might have run out of batteries,' she said, handing it to Agnes. 'Seems to be OK. The cellar door is here...' She led the way to a door painted in blue gloss paint, and unbolted it. 'Mice and all sorts,' she said. 'Do be careful.'

Agnes shone her way down a few creaking wooden steps and stood on the cracked floor. She could see garden tools, a single rubber glove, bright yellow in the torch's beam. An old tin of shoe polish. She realised she'd been expecting floorboards, something she could lift up, something that would reveal a deeper, hidden space. And here she was, standing on the very earth where Alice's forebears had built their house.

She stood there feeling foolish, as the drains gurgled loudly with the rainfall. Then she went back up the steps, into the warm kitchen.

Sue was sitting at the table, leafing through Alice's diary. She looked up. 'Find anything?'

Agnes shook her head. 'You must think I'm mad.' She sat down at the table.

Sue smiled at her. 'No. I don't think you're mad.' She closed the diary and passed it across to her. 'I can see why one might feel the need to do this poor woman justice.' She stood up. 'There's a portrait of Alice up on the landing. Come and see it.'

Their footsteps were soft on the thick stair carpet. 'It's a nightmare for the insurance,' Sue was saying, 'the commissioners want me to lock it away as they have to pay, but I've refused so far. I think, well, it was her house, she has the right to survey it. It's the two of them in the painting, look.' She stopped at the top of the stairs, puffing slightly, and pointed at the wall. 'I'll put on the light.'

Within the oval frame there were the tiny brushstrokes of a portrait. Two figures gazed out.

Agnes saw the wide white brow, the pale red hair pinned back, a collar of pearls; she looked at the hazel-green eyes that stared out across the centuries. Next to Alice there was another young woman, encased in stiff lace. She too had pale red hair and hazel-green eyes.

'Who's that?' Agnes pointed at the child.

'It's Alice's little sister, Catherine. She inherited this house, apparently. Mavis told me all about it.'

'Sister?'

They started back down the stairs. 'There was a dispute,' Sue said, 'after Alice died, between the Hawkers and the Bradens. Nicolas tried to claim all Alice's property as his own. But Alice's family were Catholic, and her husband was Protestant, and they were determined that he shouldn't get his hands on Alice's inheritance. There was a house in London that was theirs too, apparently. The Bradens managed to keep this place, but the London house was disputed for years.'

'Who won?' They reached the kitchen, and Agnes sat back down at the table.

Sue chased a cat from a chair and sat down too. 'I imagine the Hawkers did. The early years of the eighteenth century weren't very kind to Catholics. Or to women, for that matter.'

'Perhaps that's why she's haunting Collyer House,' Agnes said.

'Alice? A ghost?'

'So they say.' Agnes decided not to mention footsteps and black dogs.

'Justice,' Sue said. 'That must be what she's after. Not that I believe in ghosts,' she added. 'But I do think the past must be taken seriously. And if there's a wrong to be righted...'

'But after all this time—'

Sue looked at her. 'It seems to me, that if you live in our tradition, where every Sunday we take an event that happened two millennia ago and celebrate it as if it were yesterday...what I mean is, we're people for whom the past is a living, present thing. This poor woman...' she pointed at the diary, which lay on the table – 'is crying out for the truth.'

Agnes stared at her. She was just wondering whether to hug her, when she was aware of loud music coming from under the table.

'Your phone?' Sue prompted.

'Ah. Yes.' She snatched it up and answered it.

'Hi, it's Helena.' The voice was whispering. 'I'm on the convent phone, I'm not supposed to be in the office. Are you in Leicestershire still?'

'Yes. I'm in Cranfield. Long story.'

'My mother rang. Her neighbours called her, they're worried, there are lights on at Langley House, they knew we'd left.'

'Oh. Is it—'

'Josie thinks it might be Malcolm. And she said you were nearby, that's why I'm calling.'

'I'll go over there,' Agnes said.

'Call on the neighbours and get a key, then you can surprise him.'

'If it's Malcolm and Leila—' Agnes said.

'We're praying so. Josie said she'd tell Jared, he's on his way for all I know.'

'I'll go right now.' Agnes hesitated. 'How are you?'

'Not good. I had a long session with Lucia.' She paused, then said, 'It's the rest of my life I suppose.'

'Me too. I think it's driven me insane.'

'Oh, not you.' There was a brief pause. 'You're one of the sanest people I know,' Helena said.

Agnes wondered whether her blush was audible. 'I'd better get going,' she said. 'I'll keep in touch.'

She rang off and looked at Sue. 'Either I'm mad, or I'm right.'

Sue patted her arm. 'You don't look very mad to me. And living round here, I've become an expert in mental disturbance. The English countryside, you know. My last parish was in urban Liverpool – so restful compared to here. Still,' she stood up, brushed herself off, 'takes all sorts. Do come and see me again. And look after Alice, won't you.'

Agnes parked at the white house, picked up the keys from the Bewleys, who were chatty with the drama of it all: 'Only, we saw the lights go on, early this evening, and it did worry us, and so we spoke to Emily, and she said she'd ask her daughter...'

She crossed the village green in the pouring rain, aware of the muddy water soaking through her shoes. She reached Langley House. It was in darkness, apart from a dim yellow glow from an upstairs room.

Agnes went round to the back door, reasoning furiously to herself. If I ring the bell, she thought, then he gets warning. If I let myself in, the shock might make him more dangerous.

It's all very well for Sue, she thought, but this is definitely mad. Probably clinically insane. She found herself wishing that Philip was with her. An expert, she thought, that's what I need.

She took the key, placed it in the lock and opened the door. She stood in the darkened kitchen, dripping wet. She closed the door silently behind her.

From upstairs came a noise; a footstep. A voice. A child's voice. 'But I'm not sleepy.'

Agnes felt faint with relief. She could hear someone answer, a male voice, indistinct. Then, 'Hush, Leila.'

Malcolm's honeyed tones, Agnes thought.

'I can't find Tubby Bear,' the child said.

'He's there, he's in your bed there,' Malcolm answered.

'She's not a he.'

Agnes could hear Malcolm's attempt to soothe the child, to find the bear. It was time to take action. She strode into the hallway and called up the stairs, 'Hello.'

She could hear the shock reverberate through the silence.

'It's me,' she called. 'Sister Agnes.'

A light went on above her. Malcolm's face appeared through the banisters. She saw his chalk-white fury, his lips tight with rage; then the mask, the smile, the descent downstairs, one arm outstretched. 'Agnes,' he cooed. 'What a pleasant surprise.'

'Where's Leila?' she said.

'In bed.'

'No I'm not.' Leila stood, tousled and blinking, at the top of the stairs.

'Well, you ought to be.' Malcolm spoke kindly.

'I want Auntie Josie,' she said. 'Where's Auntie Josie?'

Agnes looked up at the child. 'She'll be here soon,' she said.

Malcolm's face was like stone as he climbed the stairs. 'Go to bed,' he said, his voice rasping. 'I need to talk to Sister Agnes.' He walked Leila back to her room, then came down and led Agnes into the kitchen. He switched on the solitary ceiling light.

'What led you here?' he said.

'Alice's crystal.' Agnes watched him.

His eyes flickered with interest as he met her gaze. 'But—'

'Did you know Alice's family home was in the next village?'

'I had no idea.' He stepped back slightly with surprise.

'More to the point,' Agnes said, 'what led you here? And why did you take Leila from her aunt?'

Malcolm breathed in, then out. 'Isn't it obvious?'

It was as if Alice stood next to her, in the cold chill of the room, the dim light which stuttered with the storm outside.

'You believe she's your child,' Agnes said.

'I know she's my child.' He allowed himself to smile.

Agnes thought of Tina-Marie lying dead on the steps of the house. She looked at Malcolm's icy composure.

'Why now?' she said. 'Why step in now?'

'Because her mother's dead.'

'But why wait until now?'

'I had to be sure.' For a moment he considered her, then took her arm. 'Why don't we both sit down? I think there's some decent whisky in the larder here.' His grip was tight as he propelled her across the kitchen and onto a chair.

She sat and watched him as he opened cupboards, finding glasses, retrieving the bottle of single malt.

'Islay,' he said. 'My favourite.' He poured two generous shots of whisky, and handed one to her. He sat next to the table, leaning on it, his glass in his other hand.

Agnes felt cold and stiff, sitting upright where he'd placed her with such force. 'Everyone's frightened of you,' she heard herself say.

He smiled at her. 'Even you?'

'Should I be?'

He raised his glass. 'Cheers.' He took a large mouthful of whisky, then said, 'Of course you shouldn't be frightened of me. And neither should they. If a father wants to do what's right for his little girl, where's the fear in that?'

'Why was Tina scared, then?' Agnes felt the whisky warming her. She wondered if Malcolm carried a weapon.

'Tina? She wasn't scared of me. If she was scared, it was of the Lord. It was the pricking of her own conscience.'

'What had she done wrong?'

'She had denied me my rightful place in the eyes of God. And she'd denied her child a father. "Male and Female, created He Them." That's what God wishes for us.'

'And so you were very angry with her?'

His face was pale in the light from the single bulb. 'No, sister, not angry. I felt the hurt of the Lord. And that was my hurt too.'

'You knew best, then?' Agnes felt a sensation of heat, a rising rage.

'No, Sister. God knows best. But, yes, I knew how to hear what he was saying.'

'And so, when Tina disobeyed God's will—'

'I was disappointed.' He picked up his glass, found it was empty. He opened the bottle and offered it to Agnes, who nodded. He poured two more shots of whisky for them, then said, 'She was a lovely woman, Tina. I was sad when she left us. She came under the influence of bad people. I should have protected her better.' He put his glass down on the table.

'And how would you have done that?'

He clasped his hands together in front of him. 'If I've been guilty of anything, Sister, it is in being too welcoming. Too trusting. My church is an open church, as Jesus wished it to be. But some of my people abused my trust, broke the Lord's commandments. And when Tina left, it was with one such person.'

'Helena,' Agnes said.

He picked up his glass again. 'Yes. Helena.'

'I know Helena very well, and I can't think of a single commandment that she breaks.'

'Well, Sister. Your community might allow for unnatural practices. As I said, "Male and Female created He Them". I hold to Biblical law.'

'I assume you mean homosexuality,' Agnes said.

'Indeed, Sister, I do.'

'Well, in our community we're celibate.'

'But desire, Sister. Action is one thing, but if one's heart still resides in a place of wrongdoing—'

'Doesn't God love us as we are? As he created us?'

A gust of wind rattled the windows, and the single bulb above them swung gently to and fro, shifting the shadows in the room.

'Desire is the Devil's work,' Malcolm said. He spoke quietly.

'There are questions to which I need some answers,' Agnes said. 'Firstly, why did you leave America, when you could have done such good work in the churches there? Secondly, if, let's say, someone were to break in to our library in Collyer House, what would they be looking for? What is of such great value there that it's worth stealing? Thirdly, how can you be so sure that Leila's your child, when we both know that Jared has an equal claim on her?'

His smile was full of false charm. 'The first is simple. God called me to do his mission here. Secondly, I can't imagine why anyone would break in. However, assuming the Jerusalem Crystal is in Collyer House, it would be terrible if it fell into the wrong hands. More terrible than anyone realises, perhaps. There are great powers invested in that crystal, and they could do terrible harm. Thirdly...' He turned his glass in his hand, and his fingers were warm with refracted light. 'I can trust you with this, Sister. I have certain knowledge. The sort of powers that people call Dark, or Black – the Dark Arts, they call them... I have access to such things. I have trained for years, and I have reached a certain level of mastery in these things.'

'Witchcraft, you mean?'

'People will give it all sorts of names.' He shook his head in feigned sorrow. 'There was a time when our church would have seen such scholarship as virtuous. Where the devil resides, you see, we must drive him out. Where he has power, we must tame him. In studying the occult, I have tamed the devil.'

'So – the devil told you that Leila was yours?'

'No, Sister. God told me. God, using powers that had been reclaimed from the Devil.'

'But surely—' A sudden burst of rain cascaded down the window. Outside was thick darkness. It felt very late. 'Surely,' Agnes went on, 'this is blasphemy. To suggest that God borrows his power from the devil...?'

'That would be blasphemy, I agree, Sister. But you misunderstand. The devil works on Man; but if Man has the insight to offer the devil's power to God, then God can use it. And so, when I did the spell for Leila, it was God who told me she was mine. But that's why I need the crystal, because at the heart of the wisdom of that glass ball is a very particular gift, that will tell a man what he needs to know.'

'So, you're saying that the missing crystal is the Knights Templar version of a DNA test?' In the distance, the church clock chimed the half hour, dampened by the storm.

She feared he might get angry, but he smiled instead. 'Yes, Sister. Exactly that.'

'It's not in Collyer House,' she said.

He put down his glass and leaned forward towards her. 'It's not?'

'I think Alice hid it in her family home. From what I can gather, from her papers...'

'Where—?'

'Here, if I'm right. Up the road, in Cranfield Hall. Well, what's left of it.'

'Is the house still there?' His voice was uneven, his words fast.

'Some of it. It's the vicarage. But the bit she lived in, the bit she hid the crystal in...' Agnes shrugged. 'It's anyone's guess.'

Malcolm jumped to his feet. He put out his hand to shake hers. 'Thank you, Sister. When I thought it was in Collyer House, I knew how important it was to find it, I was concerned to find it wasn't there. But now everything has fallen into place—' He snatched up his coat and began to put it on.

Outside, Agnes heard a car approaching, headlights slicing through the rain. The engine stopped.

'And Leila?' Agnes said.

He paused, one arm stuck mid-sleeve. 'Ah. Leila.' He looked at Agnes. 'Would you mind, I mean, I know it's a bit of a favour to ask you...'

There were footsteps lightly down the stairs, and a sleepy head in the doorway, and there stood Leila, clutching Tubby Bear to her chest. She looked from one to the other, not knowing which of the two strangers to go to. She rubbed her eyes, as if to check whether she was still asleep.

And then there was a knock at the back door, a male figure in the glass, and Agnes opened it. Jared stood there. He looked dishevelled, his face tight with anxiety, his jacket awry across his shoulders. He saw Agnes and almost stumbled with relief, looked beyond her to see Leila, standing half-awake in the kitchen.

'Leila—' He put out his arms towards her.

The child looked at the man in the doorway, backdropped with black sheets of rain. She opened her eyes wide and began to scream.

CHAPTER NINETEEN

Agnes signalled left and joined the slip road leading away from the motorway. She circled a deserted roundabout, pulled into an empty warehouse driveway, and parked. She switched off the engine.

Silence. Only the quiet rhythmic breathing of the sleeping child lying across the back seat, tucked in with blankets and seat belts.

The rain had eased, at last. The night was softening to grey; notes of birdsong pricked the air.

Agnes checked her mirror as a car approached from the motorway and then sped past.

I'll catch up with Jared in London, she thought. He must have overtaken me ages ago. No one driving a brand new Toyota would bother to wait for an ancient Metro.

We'll be in London in an hour, and then Leila can be with Helena, and then when she feels safe, she can get to know Jared.

He is her father, after all, Agnes thought. Tina would have known the truth. For all Malcolm's magic tricks.

The night sky was growing thin over the warehouse roofs. Leila stirred, murmured in her sleep, settled again. Agnes saw the eyelashes against her cheek as the soft light touched her baby skin, and felt a tightening fear in the pit of her stomach.

She remembered Jared standing in the doorway, the child, screaming at the sight of him. For an instant, Agnes had caught Jared's expression, a blaze of rage that flashed across his face and then was gone, as he knelt down, put out his arms to her and said, 'Baby, Daddy's here. Everything's all right.'

And Leila had scrunched her hands into fists, her face grey with exhaustion and fear, and had screwed up her eyes and screamed, and her screaming didn't cease until Agnes had picked her up, and held her close, and carried her to the car, had shut the doors, whispering to Leila that everything would be all right, that soon she'd be with Helena and Auntie Josie. She'd driven to the vicarage, with Jared and Malcolm following, and Leila had fallen asleep in the car.

The Reverend Sue Radlett had proved herself unflappable, listening to Agnes's apologies, Jared's explanations, Malcolm's insistent requests to search the cellar, the grounds if needs be – and in the midst of it all she'd produced a bottle of baby milk, somehow, and some spare bedding.

Agnes had explained, quietly to Jared, that it would be terrible for Leila to be taken away by him now, and he had grown calm and agreed that he would meet Helena later on, and get to know his child gradually. Malcolm had sat in Sue's lounge, threatening Jared with a court hearing once he had his definitive proof of paternity. Jared had faced him, shouting, challenging him to do so, and Malcolm had made an elaborate show of swapping phone numbers. Then Agnes had set out for London, with Jared following in his own car. They'd left Malcolm offering Sue apparently huge sums of money for permission to dig up the garden on the site of the original Cranfield Hall. Sue had nodded, smiled, given him the address of Evelyn Pike, secretary of the PCC, assured him that his claim would be given top priority, and said, yes, of course he could look in the cellar, it wouldn't be the first time such a request had been made.

Agnes had driven as fast as she could through the deserted night streets, to the motorway, and now was on an industrial estate somewhere in North Hertfordshire, watching the sun rise, trying to catch a thought that was just out of reach.

Perhaps I'm wrong, she thought. Perhaps she didn't recognise him. Perhaps all she saw was another stranger, another person taking her further away from the people that she knew. But then, Agnes remembered, as soon as we were in the car she'd quietened, staring fretfully out of the back window, gradually nodding into sleep, her fingers curled around the ear of Tubby Bear.

She took out her phone and dialled the convent number and got the answering machine. She was about to speak, to ask that Helena ring her, but stopped. They'll be beginning to stir, she thought, there'll be tea being made, in silence, in the kitchen; there'll be going across to chapel. No one will get this message, and even if they do, it'll only annoy them.

Helena will just have to be surprised, she thought.

Helena will be delighted.

She thought about Athena, contemplating motherhood so late in life. She leaned over to the back seat and tucked the blankets more firmly around the sleeping child.

All she wants is her mother.

Agnes found she had tears in her eyes. She turned back and started the engine. As she joined the motorway, she checked her mirror again for the Toyota. For a moment, she thought she saw it, slipping between two huge supermarket lorries, but when she looked again, it had gone.

Half an hour later she was joining the early rush-hour traffic heading into London. The roads shone wet in the silvery dawn, and gutters ran with rivers. As she approached Finsbury Park, there were signs diverting the traffic: 'Road closed due to flooding'. She edged her way to Hackney and parked outside the convent.

Leila stirred and sat up. She looked around her, frowned, and hugged her bear.

Agnes unfastened the thermos padding and handed her a bottle of warm milk. 'We're going to see Helena,' she said. 'And soon you're going to be back with Auntie Josie.'

They walked into the convent hand in hand. In her other hand, Leila held the bottle of milk. Agnes was clutching Tubby. Helena appeared in the chapel door, took one look at the scene and began to laugh, then cry, then she snatched up Leila in her arms and cuddled her. For the first time for days, Leila smiled.

Agnes turned to Helena. 'I need to talk to you,' she said. 'Privately.'

The convent lounge echoed with cartoon voices from the television; Leila sat on the sofa, sucking her thumb, her fingers curled round Tubby's ear.

In one corner sat Agnes and Helena, keeping their voices low against the squawk of naughty penguins.

'Sister Lucia's cross,' Helena said. 'It's all too inconvenient.

I've had to explain that her father will take Leila away very soon.'

'Not too soon,' Agnes said.

'But he's her father.'

'Yes,' Agnes said. 'He's her father.' Leila gave a delighted chuckle at the television, and both women looked at her and smiled. Agnes turned back to Helena. 'She was terrified of him,' she whispered. 'Her face, last night, when he appeared in the doorway...'

'But it was the middle of the night, she'd already been abducted by Malcolm...'

Agnes sighed. 'That's what I keep telling myself. I'm sure you're right.' She yawned. 'I've been awake all night,' she said. 'Can you phone Josie? Can you tell her Leila's safe?'

'Sure.' Helena frowned. 'What do we do about Malcolm?'

'Oh, Malcolm's bound to turn up. He was offering pistols at dawn to Jared.'

'I think perhaps he's insane. I've thought so for a while.'

'I must go to sleep,' Agnes said. 'Do you think I'd be missed if I went to bed?'

'I'm not sure you can. Last night's rain was so heavy, it came in on the side of the house where your room is. Rachel's up there with towels and things. And Collyer House is even worse, apparently. That funny bookseller's been on the phone fretting about the archive, insisting we move it right now.'

Agnes yawned again.

'You can have my room,' Helena said.

The afternoon rainclouds were gathering again as Agnes parked outside Collyer House. The clinic driveway glistened.

The proportions of the entrance looked odd, as if something had shifted. As she approached, she realised that the doors of the clinic were fixed open, that people were milling around them; the floors inside had an odd smooth sheen, which came into focus as she grew nearer and became a river of water.

'...Never happened before,' Beatrice was saying. 'Never flooded like this all the time I've been here. Don't get it.'

'...The wrath of God is upon us.' Francis was standing, declaiming, by the doors. As Agnes approached he winked at her.

'Oh, it's you.' Philip stalked past, his hands in the pockets of his white coat. 'Six inches of filthy water. Thank God we're moving anyway.'

There was shouting behind them, and Agnes turned to see Jonathan Harris, jacket flapping, hair awry. 'The archive,' he was saying. 'It's all still there.' He seemed much larger and generally healthier than when she'd last seen him in hospital. 'Thank goodness you're here,' he said to her. 'No sense out of your order, can't get hold of Shirley.'

'How are the bruises?' she said.

'Bruises?' His eyebrows puckered. 'Oh, bruises. Nothing that a decent glass of Bordeaux couldn't fix. Come on, I need to see the damage.' They waded their way out of the clinic and went round to the side of the house, picking their way through the puddles to the door. 'It won't open,' Agnes said, turning the key in the lock.

'It's swollen,' he said. 'The water's higher here.' He put his shoulder to it and shoved, and it gave way, creaking loudly.

They stood, their eyes adjusting to the dim hallway.

'Terrible,' Jonathan muttered, his eyes on the floor.

The parquet made little hills and turrets where it had lifted, and water trickled in between them. Where the floor sloped there was a stream. They tiptoed to the library and opened the door. Jonathan went to the archive cabinet. 'Thank God,' he said. He opened one of the doors, touched the leather spines. 'It seems OK.'

The boxes on the floor were sodden. Some had come apart, and books showed through the gaps.

'Save me, O God, for the waters are come in unto my soul; I sink in deep mire, where there is no standing; I am come into deep waters, where the floods overflow me.'

'What did you say?' Jonathan turned to her, nursing two of the books in his arms.

'It's a version of a Psalm. It's from Alice's diary. She wrote about sins being washed clean.'

Jonathan looked around the room. Then his eyes fixed on hers. 'Alice's diary? You've never mentioned it before.'

'Is that what you're looking for?'

His gaze shifted to the floor, then back to hers. 'It may be.'

'Jonathan – why can't you tell us?'

His toe tapped against a swollen parquet tile.

'You've risked so much,' she went on. 'You've risked Malcolm following you—'

'It was him, apparently. That policewoman came to see me, and I remembered someone shouting in an American accent. I told her what I could, it was all rather fragmentary. But why would he try and kill me?'

She sighed. 'All I know is, both you and Malcolm are chasing the history of this house as if your lives depended on it. He's talking rubbish but probably means it, and you're telling us nothing at all.'

'I need to see Alice's diary.' He looked at the two books in his arms, and placed them back in the cabinet. 'Please.'

Agnes went over to the desk, took the diary out of her bag and placed it on the surface. Jonathan approached it as if it were alive, as if it might scuttle away if he moved too fast. He sat down and began to turn the pages. He seemed to be scanning them, rather than reading.

There was a knock at the library door, which was wedged open by the uneven floor. Jonathan didn't look up. Agnes glanced across and saw the ginger-haired young man half-hiding in the doorway. 'Matthew,' she said. 'Do come in.'

He shuffled in, his eyes on Jonathan. He began to speak to him, but Jonathan held up a white-gloved hand. 'Listen,' he said. '"And so did I curse the crystal then, that it should be held to be honest whilst I was held to be a liar. For thus is my fate sealed and I feel it with dread in my heart. And so this night will I find a place to hide it where no one shall see its hellish face again."' He turned to Matthew, then to Agnes. 'Is there more about this hiding place?'

'Not that I've found,' she said.

'Is there anything else, any more papers, about the house, for example?' He broke off, as if he'd said too much.

'No. Only expenses, lists of bills, problems with horses.' Agnes watched him as he flicked another glance at Matthew. She looked at Matthew's pale skin, his hazel-green eyes. 'Why are you two lying?' she said.

'Lying?' Jonathan blinked at her.

'You're related. You must be. There's something about this

house, or the crystal, or something to do with you both being descendants of the Hawker family?'

Jonathan closed the diary and handed it back to her. He took off his gloves, pulling at the fingertips with extravagant gestures, and put them in his pocket.

'And if not the Hawker family,' she glanced towards Matthew again, 'then the Bradens.' She looked at Jonathan. 'You're descended from Alice's side, aren't you? You and Matthew?'

Jonathan seemed to freeze as he met her eyes.

'But,' she went on, 'Jonjo died. Her only son.' Her gaze went past Jonathan to Matthew. 'There's a portrait of Alice,' she said to him. 'And her sister, Catherine. You look so like them.'

Matthew touched Jonathan's arm.

'We have to go,' Jonathan said.

Agnes held the diary in her hands. 'Jonathan – how can I help you if you're lying to me?'

He stood in the doorway, Matthew fidgeting at his side.

'We have to go,' he said again.

Agnes heard the front door scrape the ruined floor as they went outside.

She sat on the edge of a chair. The air felt thick to breathe. There was a cloying, damp smell. Through the windows the heavy grey sky deepened to twilight.

Outside in the hallway she heard footsteps. The library door edged open. Serena stood there. Her face was doll-like, porcelain white.

'Hello,' Agnes said.

'I thought I'd find you here.' She stood, motionless, her

hands clasped tightly in front of her. 'He won't miss me, I've been helping next door with the clear-up, but...' She took an uncertain step further in.

'Sit down.' Agnes indicated the other chair. 'It's not too soaking wet.'

Her heels clicked on the floor as she approached and sat down. 'The thing is—' she bent her head, and her soft hair fell forward across her face. 'You have to talk to him.'

'To Philip?'

Serena nodded at her. 'He'll listen to you. He likes you.'

'He's got a funny way of showing it.'

'No, really.' Serena fixed her blue eyes on her. 'He said that you were much too clever to be a nun. And he likes clever people. So that proves he likes you.'

'Oh. Right.'

'The thing is—' again, the clear level gaze. 'I can't make him see. I have to have a baby. He doesn't understand. When we make love—' she glanced at Agnes. 'I hope you don't mind me being honest.'

'No, it's fine.'

She smoothed a lock of hair behind her ear. 'When we make love, I pray for it to happen. A baby, I mean. And Philip gets angry with me.' Her hand went to the pearls at her neck. 'He's often angry. He's angry about what I eat, he says it's not enough, he says it's a sign of depression. And he's angry because I won't take all these pills he wants me to take, he gets them from his doctor friends, sometimes I think I'm more interesting to him when he can discuss my symptoms with Doctor This and Doctor That from his medical school days. And then, when I pray, he gets angry and starts going on about "Little Baby Jesus"—' she stopped, and looked at Agnes. 'Is that blasphemy?'

Agnes shook her head.

Serena tucked her hands into her lap. 'I've always believed. My family were Catholic, I went to a convent school. It's not fair of Philip to make out that I'm being mad or childish or wrong. Do you know, I got out my rosary the other day, I haven't touched it for years, it's a family heirloom, ivory, beautiful. And I sat there with it, and I just started saying it, just to see what it felt like, those old words...and then he came in, and—' She hesitated, then went on. 'I was frightened of him, actually. I thought he was going to throw it across the room. Anyone would think it was witchcraft, the way he responded. And what's so stupid is, that he's the one being unscientific. Because after the baby that died, the "ectopic pregnancy" as he always calls it, I asked the consultant if there was any chance at all of me conceiving again. And he said, there was a very slight chance but it was so unlikely that I shouldn't count on it at all. And there's Philip going on about me praying for a miracle, but actually, I'm working on the basis that if there is a chance, however small, that I could conceive again, then I might as well believe in it.' She stopped, breathless. 'Anyway, I decided to come and talk to you because he won't listen to me, so you've got to tell him.'

'What do you want me to tell him?' The room had grown dark. Agnes reached for the lamp, but didn't switch it on.

'That if this carries on, I'm going to have to leave him.'

'But, Serena – he loves you.'

Serena shook her head. 'He should have married someone clever. He liked me being pretty, and I know how to cook and all that, I'm good at being a wife – but now I'm a challenge. I'm trouble. If he loved me...' Her voice tailed off, and her eyes filled with tears.

Agnes thought of Philip. Every time she'd seen him over the last few days he'd been wrung out, pallid and desperate. She looked at Serena, trying to find the words to reassure her.

Serena had grown calm again. 'I've always believed in God,' she said. 'It's just that before, it didn't affect him. It didn't challenge him. And now that I'm mourning the loss of our child, it does. He wants to call me depressed, or mad, or something.'

'But Serena—'

Serena met her gaze. 'What?'

'You tried to kill yourself. If Philip is showing terrible anxiety, it's not surprising. He's trying to help you the only way he can.'

Serena considered her. 'I didn't think you'd be the one to defend him. I thought you knew about faith.'

'I know something about love too.'

Serena shifted on her chair. 'When I was seven, my baby sister died.'

In the silence, Agnes realised that the library clock was no longer ticking.

'It's always been there,' Serena said. 'This feeling.'

'What feeling?'

'That I should have died instead.' Her voice was steady in the gathering shadows. 'My parents told me she was in Heaven and that I wasn't to worry, but I always felt guilty. My father died not long afterwards. And now, here I am, an only child, and my mother's very unwell... We're all alone, my mother and I. I want to be able to make it better before she dies.'

The rain began, lightly against the windows.

'What can Philip do?' Agnes said.

Serena took from her pocket a scrap of paper and handed it to her. 'Here,' she said. 'It's his mobile number.'

Agnes took the paper, with its neat line of digits. 'And what shall I say to him?'

'He has to pray with me.'

'Serena—' Agnes faced her. 'He won't. It's too much to ask.'

'Well then I'll leave. Tell him.' She stood up. 'When he and I got married, I thought he loved me as I was. As I am. And everything's proved me wrong. When he talks to me, it's only to offer me pills. What he doesn't understand is that the pills are to cure him, not me. If I take the pills, I'll feel worse, but he'll feel better.' She managed a thin smile. 'It kind of sums up our marriage at the moment.'

Agnes walked out to the hall and opened the front door for her. Serena stood there shyly, then offered her her hand. Agnes held it briefly in her own, then Serena turned and went down the front steps. In the street, she stopped and took a fold-up umbrella out of her bag, which opened like a turquoise flower.

Agnes sat in the dark damp air of the library. She looked at Philip's mobile number on the scrap of paper. She slid it into her bag.

Who am I, she thought, to tell Philip that his wife's love is slipping away from him. Clever nun or no.

In the corner stood the Hawker cabinet. Tomorrow, Jonathan was going to take all that away. Then the room would be empty.

She stepped carefully across the floor to the door, picking her way through the puddles.

'Save me, O God, for the waters are come in unto my soul...'

She left the library and went up the stairs. She sat on the landing, in the dark, and listened.

Silence. No creaking, no footsteps.

She put her hand out and touched the radiator. It was warm.

Even the central heating has gone quiet, she thought.

Alice is no longer here.

She stood and walked along the corridor to her room. She opened the door, listening still. No footsteps, no creaking of floorboards.

She shut the door of her room and went back downstairs. She looked at the damp carpet on the lower steps. She remembered what Julius had said, about holy water and the laying to rest of ghosts.

Perhaps London rainwater will do just as well, she thought.

Alice Hawker, rest in peace.

She took out her phone and dialled the convent in Hackney. A familiar voice answered.

'Helena, thank God. It's Agnes. How's things?'

'Fine. Leila's very happy, she's talked to Josie on the phone; Josie's on her way down here. She's had the police round, they're looking for Malcolm, they said they'd go and see if he'd gone back to Essex. They were trying to treat it as a "domestic" but Karen's keen to press charges for kidnap and assault.'

'Has Jared come?'

Helena hesitated. 'No. Josie and I thought it was odd. He knows she's here, doesn't he?'

'Yes. Can you—' Agnes took a deep breath. 'Can you tell Lucia I'm staying at Collyer House tonight?'

'Why?'

'I'm not sure. But – tell her it's about flood damage, then she might not be cross.'

Helena laughed. 'She's furious about Leila being here, as it is. She's trying to be charitable, but you can tell.'

Agnes sat in her room at Collyer House. She flicked through Alice's diary, wondering what Jonathan had been looking for. She thought about Serena's desperate need for a family; she thought about Jonathan's search for his inheritance. She thought about the house in Provence. Memories flickered through her mind, of her mother's straight-backed insistence on manners, her father's distant and sporadic benevolence, her pony, her endless solitary walks through sunlit fields of lavender.

And now I'm here, she thought, looking around the bare room. A convent cell.

For Alice, this house was a prison. For me, it's about freedom, the shedding of all the ties that bind.

The moon had risen, a glimmer of light through the window. She thought about her final vows, about all that she'd renounced. She was aware of the beginning of an idea, a gathering sense of hope, of happiness, even. She reached for her phone, thinking she might call Julius and say, You were right, everything's going to be OK—

There was a loud knock at her front door.

She checked her watch. It was late for callers.

The knock came again.

She got up, and went downstairs, turning on lights as she did so.

'It's me, Jared,' came a voice.

She opened the door.

He was looking trim, she thought, and well-rested. 'We wondered where you'd got to.' She stepped back to let him in.

He looked around him. 'What happened here? The rain too?' She nodded. 'I've been at my cousin's,' he said, 'in Dalston. Their cellar's completely waterlogged. Pumping it out and everything, they are.' He followed her into the kitchen. The strip lighting flickered into life.

He stood in the corner of the room. 'I didn't know what to do,' he said. 'I was going to come to the convent house, it's not far from Georgie's. And then I thought about my little girl, and I thought, I don't want to scare her. It's like what you said, I'm going to have to go slow. Get to know her again. Let her get to know me. How is she?'

'Helena's looking after her. I left her laughing at children's telly.'

He flung himself down on a chair. 'Good. After Malcolm's adventure, I'm surprised she trusts anyone at all. It was stupid of me to turn up like that, when I did. I wasn't thinking, I was just so desperate to see her.'

'Josie's partner wants Malcolm arrested, according to Helena.'

He glanced up at her. 'Good,' he said.

'What does Malcolm want?' She sat down opposite him.

He looked at her, shrugged. 'He wants power. And money.

And what I think is, he owes. That farm site, he bought that off some bloke, some property developer. And I think he still owes for it. All this talk about the crystal and magic, either he really thinks it has magic powers and it's going to solve all his problems, or he thinks he can sell it for a fortune and make the money back that way.'

'And Leila?'

'Malcolm's used to getting everything he wants. When Tina refused him, he thought, at least he'd get Leila. It's revenge, for him. He doesn't care about anyone.' He shook his head. 'I'll go and see her in the morning. I'll give Helena a ring first. I was just upset, you know. That wasn't how I thought it would be, my little girl being so scared of her own dad.' He stood up. 'Perhaps it was the rain. Perhaps that's what it was. The night her mother died, it rained so hard that night. Well, I'll call on them in the morning.' He rested a hand on Agnes's shoulder, then left.

CHAPTER TWENTY

Agnes ran up the stairs in the empty house, grabbed her bag, found Philip's mobile number which Serena had given her. Outside the traffic rumbled through the London night, the London rain. She sat on her bed and punched Philip's number into her phone.

'Hello?' He sounded tired, or perhaps drunk.

'It's Agnes.'

'How the hell did you get this number—'

'Please, not now. It's too important.'

'What, it's too important to plot with my wife to bring me to Jesus?'

'Oh, God, Philip – this isn't about your wife.'

'No?' The voice was mocking and unsteady.

'It's about Tina-Marie. You've got to check your files for me again.'

'Who the hell do you think you are, phoning me at this time of night and demanding that I break all my codes of practice, if not the law itself?'

'I need evidence.'

'More? We didn't find anything last time. Which private file do I have to raid now?'

'Leila's.'

Philip made a harrumphing noise. 'I don't have anything separate from her mother, you'd have to go and ask her GP, if she has one. And I don't suppose the GP would be too happy.'

'I just need to know one thing. I know that her mother requested DNA testing. I just need to know the dates.'

He was quiet, then said, 'Is that all?'

'That's all.'

'I can probably get that. Although why I should help you, after all your conspiring with my wife earlier today. She told me she'd been to see you—'

'She told me she was thinking of leaving you. And I told her that you loved her.'

Agnes heard Philip breathing. Then he said, 'Did she say that?'

'She wanted me to talk to you about it, and I refused. She said that I was to ask you to pray with her. And I said, it was too much to ask of you.'

A siren cut through the silence. He said, 'Of course, I do. Love her, I mean.' Then he said, 'She has gone so far away from me.' The siren faded into the night. 'Agnes – come to the clinic tomorrow morning. I'll do what I can.'

A chill had settled on the house. Agnes lay restlessly in bed, listening to the rain. When she did sink into sleep, she dreamed of rising tides of water washing everything away.

By dawn the rain had eased again. Agnes sat at the kitchen table with a mug of tea, looking out at the clear pearly light, checking her watch, every ten minutes, every five.

She got up and went into the library. It seemed no more damp than it had been yesterday. The Hawker cabinet was dry.

At seven-thirty she dialled Helena's number, and got a voicemail message. At eight there was a commotion at the door, which turned out to be Shirley arriving with stacks of crates.

'I'm taking everything away,' she said. 'It can't stay here.'

'But Jonathan—'

'Oh, bugger Jonathan,' she said. 'I'm fed up with all of them. Malcolm's pretending he can buy it all, and Jonathan's breaking in in the middle of the night – or at least, creeping through secret passages from the clinic, as you discovered. We should have stuck to what we'd planned, that nice museum library in Oxford. I've agreed with Sister Lucia that it can stay with you in Hackney until Jennifer from the museum arranges to pick it up.'

'Oh.' Agnes watched her carrying crates into the library.

'You look dreadful,' Shirley said.

'Thank you.'

'Don't mention it. Are you going to help me with these books?'

Agnes looked at her watch again. 'Yes, of course. I've got about half an hour until Philip gets in.'

Helena was surprised to see Agnes arriving, breathless, at the convent house.

'You're in time for chapel,' she said. 'It's only nine-thirty.'

'Has he phoned? Has he been here yet?'

Helena frowned at her. 'Jared?'

'Yes, Jared.'

Helena looked at her watch. 'He called about twenty minutes ago. He's on his way.'

'Take Leila and go somewhere. Anywhere.'

'Why?' Helena stared.

'I have to talk to him.'

'But—'

'Please—'

Helena looked at her. 'OK. We'll go to the swings.'

Agnes sat in the lounge of the convent house. Green brocade curtains framed the window. The pale carpet was streaked with sunlight. She looked out to the street and saw him. He pulled up in the Toyota. He got out, locked the car and walked up the steps.

She opened the door before he could ring the bell, and led him through to the lounge.

'I thought it would be Helena.' He smiled, settled into an armchair. 'Where's my baby then?'

'They'll be here in a while,' Agnes said. She sat on the sofa, her hands on her knees.

'So?' He darted a questioning look, his head to one side.

Agnes breathed, then passed a piece of paper across to him. 'I found this,' she said.

He took it, looked at it. He shrugged, made to hand it back to her.

'It's a request for DNA testing. Made on the 27th January. That's about ten days before Tina died.'

He frowned at it, shrugged. 'Nothing to do with me, mate.'

'It's requested by Tina, for Leila.'

He looked at it again, then handed it back to Agnes. 'Never seen it before. Does it give the result?'

'No. I don't know the result,' Agnes said.

He shrugged. 'Means nothing, then.'

'Leila recognised you,' Agnes said. 'The night you appeared, when Malcolm had taken her – she knew who you were.'

He shifted in his seat, tried a smile. 'Well, I'm her dad.'

'You were there, when Tina died,' Agnes went on.

'No, I told you before, I was in the States—'

'How did you know it was raining, then?'

He sat back on the chair, his hands firm at his sides. He opened his mouth, began to speak, stopped.

'You said,' Agnes went on, 'that the night that Tina died, it was raining heavily. Do they do the south London weather forecast in Manhattan?'

He met her eyes, but was silent.

'And before that,' she went on, 'on the 27th January, you and Tina requested DNA testing of Leila.' She put the sheet of paper on the table in front of him.

'I wasn't here, I can prove it—'

'Did she forge your signature?'

'I've never seen that paper before in my life.' The colour rose in his cheeks.

Agnes glanced at him. 'Didn't she show it to you?'

'On that date you said, I was in the States. I told you, I can prove it.'

'But nearly a fortnight later, on the night she died, you were here.'

He stood up. 'Troy's pleading guilty,' he said. 'What's all this about?'

'Troy's not pleading guilty to murder. He's admitted they had a fight the night she died, that's all.' She looked up at him, and saw again the same flash of rage she'd seen at Langley that night with the rain pouring down, the child's screams.

Now he was staring down at her. He opened his mouth as if to speak, closed it, turned to go. Then he was by the door, out in the hallway, shouting something incoherent – '...Not staying here to be accused of lying rubbish by a nun.'

She heard the door slam, heard the Toyota beep, the engine revving, the screeching round the corner and out into the main road.

She leaned her head in her hands.

Helena found her, slumped on the sofa.

'Oh God—' Agnes raised her head. 'You didn't see him, did you?'

'No.' Helena looked around the room. 'You OK? Where's Jared?'

'Leila—' Agnes half rose, staring beyond Helena into the hall.

There was singing from the doorway, something about a robin in a tree, a sweet wavering voice. Then Leila appeared, in her coat and pink wellingtons, humming quietly to herself.

'She's just here. She's fine.' Helena rested her hand on Agnes's arm. 'What is this?'

Agnes rubbed her forehead. 'I've just accused Jared of lying to us, and now he's run away.'

Helena sat hard onto a chair. 'You did what?'

'He was here, in London, the night Tina died. I'm sure of it. And he and Tina requested DNA testing on Leila, a couple of weeks or so before that.'

'What did he say to all this?'

'He denied it all. He ran off.'

Helena considered Agnes. 'Are you sure you're...I mean, wouldn't it be better if we let the police talk to him?'

Agnes leaned her head back and closed her eyes.

'You look terrible,' Helena said.

Agnes nodded.

'It's that house,' Helena went on. 'All that haunting. It's got to you. All this talk of paternity and revenge. There's nothing to say that Jared had anything to do with Tina's death—'

Agnes opened her eyes. 'Paternity,' she said. 'It's all the same. Nicolas Hawker, and Jared...' She jumped to her feet. 'I'm going back to Collyer. Look after Leila. Don't let her out of your sight. If Jared tries to take her away, call the police.'

'Josie will be here later—'

'Good. You can both call the police.'

Agnes let herself in, pushing hard against the warped front door. From the library came a hammering noise. Shirley was crouched on the floor, surrounded by pieces of wood, which Agnes recognised, after a moment, as parts of the Hawker cabinet.

'What are you doing?' Agnes was aware of the heavy damp smell, which seemed to have worsened.

Shirley looked up. 'I'm taking the cabinet over to your convent house.'

'But—'

'It's a valuable piece of furniture, I thought the nuns ought to have it.'

'But – breaking it up—'

'It's in two parts. Plus the two drawers. It's quite easy to put back together, better that than pay to hire a van, I thought. Can you help me carry it out to the car?'

Agnes bent to pick up a drawer. As she did so, part of the wooden base dropped out and landed on the floor.

'Careful—'

Agnes stared down at the drawer in her hands. 'I've been so stupid,' she said. 'And so has Jonathan. Look. It has two floors, this drawer.'

She put the drawer down and picked up the other one. She turned it over and began to unslot the false base. As she did so, a bundle of papers slid out from between the two slats of wood.

Shirley looked at the papers in Agnes's hands. 'You'd have thought, with all the burglary attempts, someone would have found those by now.'

Agnes untied the faded ribbon, and unfurled the papers. 'Do you have Jonathan's phone number?' she said. 'I think these belong to him.'

Jonathan and Matthew sat side by side. Jonathan held the papers up to the light that came in through the library window. 'These are they,' he said to Matthew.

'Deeds to this house,' Agnes said.

Jonathan nodded at her.

'Alice had a sister,' Agnes said. 'Catherine. And that's why Nicolas tried to make Alice a prisoner, because he knew that this house belonged to the Bradens.'

Jonathan and Matthew exchanged a glance. 'After Alice died,' Jonathan said, 'Nicolas tried to claim this house. But Alice's father had put this house in trust for Catherine. And the Hawkers wouldn't accept it.'

'And you are Catherine's descendants?' Agnes looked from one to the other.

'Nicolas Hawker stole it.' Matthew clenched his fists as he spoke. 'This house was built on Braden land.'

'And you're a Braden?' Agnes asked him.

He nodded. 'We both are.' He tapped Jonathan next to him with his fingertips. 'We're all that's left.'

'Why didn't you tell me?'

Jonathan scratched his head, leaving his hair in tufts. 'Without the deeds,' he said, 'we had no claim. No proof.'

'But – if you've inherited from the Bradens – that makes you Catholic. Both of you.'

They exchanged a glance. It was Jonathan who spoke. 'Technically, yes. But not in conscience.'

'Why didn't you say?' Agnes addressed Jonathan.

'We hoped to get there first, and then we were going to tell you.'

'Did you think we'd steal all this from you?' Agnes smiled at him.

Jonathan nodded. 'Judging on past form of monastic orders, it seemed quite likely. As it is, I'm not convinced your order will take kindly to giving up their share in the value of the site.'

'How will you prove it?' Agnes said. 'Doesn't Nicolas Hawker's will override your claim?'

'Not now that we can prove that the property was never his to leave.'

'And the crystal?' Agnes said.

Now Jonathan smiled. 'I'd like to have the crystal, if it ever turns up. But it's not essential.'

'But for your shop?'

Jonathan looked at Matthew. 'I'm an only child,' Jonathan

said. 'My cousin Jean is an only child. Matthew is Jean's child. We've agreed to share the proceeds of this site. I can pay off my debts and relocate my shop somewhere more fortuitous.'

'Assuming you win in the fight with my order and the NHS.'

Jonathan smiled. 'I'm more optimistic about the NHS part than your order.'

After they'd gone, Agnes sat alone in the library. She was aware of the clock's silence, as if time itself had stopped. Waiting, she thought. Waiting to find out what Malcolm was going to do next. And waiting for Jared.

She picked up her phone. She flicked through all the options until she found Ringtones. Then she flicked through all the Ringtone options, and selected one that sounded like a real phone. An old-fashioned phone. It sounded like the heavy Bakelite telephone with the twisty wire in her parents' house. Athena will be pleased, she thought. She remembered that Athena was due to call, and dialled her number. She heard it ring and ring, then switch to voicemail. She checked the number on the phone. Then she tried the art gallery. Eventually, she heard Simon answer.

'It's Agnes. I just wondered where Athena was—'

Simon interrupted her. 'Agnes, thank God. No one had your number. She's in hospital—'

'What?'

'Jake's with her.'

'What's happened?'

'They were driving stuff up from Gloucestershire, from the foundry. There was an accident—'

Agnes wondered if she'd screamed out loud. 'No,' she said.

'She's OK. She's conscious. But—'

'Where is she?' Agnes tried not to shout.

Simon gave her the hospital address, the ward number. 'There's a phone number there too, but it doesn't work. And I can give you Jake's mobile—'

Agnes wrote everything down. She thanked Simon and hung up.

Jake was smaller than she expected, and pacing the hospital corridor. As she approached, he held out a limp hand. 'You must be Agnes,' he said. He had kind green eyes, untidy hair, worn jeans.

'Where is she?'

'She's OK,' he said. 'She's got a broken leg, concussion—'

'Can I see her?'

He pushed open the door to the ward and she followed him along the lines of beds, breathing in the hot clean brightness of the hospital air. She could hear a voice, '...and can you bring my other cashmere sweater, you know the one, the nice one, yes – and underwear – and my sunglasses...What? No, not for the sun, silly – they wake me up at dawn, I've got two black eyes as it is, no one's going to see me looking like this at that time in the morning...OK. Bye.'

Athena saw Agnes, beamed, switched off her phone.

'You're not supposed to use them in here.' Agnes bent and kissed her.

'How else does one live? Fab to see you, sweetie.' She looked bruised, her face had livid patches around her eyes. Her hair spilled in tangles across the pillow. 'You met Jake, then. Jake, Agnes. Agnes, Jake.' They nodded at each other, then Agnes drew up a chair. 'Nice pyjamas,' she said, eyeing the pink gingham brushed cotton that Athena was wearing.

Jake hovered by her bedside. 'Can I – shall I get—'

'Coffee?' Athena prompted him. 'That would be great. You'll have to leave the hospital to find anything worth drinking, though.'

He kissed her forehead. 'See you in several hours, then.'

'He's nice,' Agnes said, surveying his departing form. 'So, what happened?'

'Well, I was driving – my Polo, you know – up the M40. And some lorry pulls out in front of me, and so I swerved to avoid it, and thank God there wasn't anything else in the fast lane, and I went straight into the crash barrier. And I can't really remember anything after that. Jake was in the passenger seat, but it was the driving side that took the damage, obviously. I have since cross-examined Jake, and he absolutely assured me that I wasn't doing anything like changing the music or fixing my make-up at the time. I hope he's not lying. Anyway, apart from all this,' she indicated her face, 'I've just got a broken leg, it turns out. The car's in a terrible state, the cast-iron owl flew right through the windscreen. The police had to rescue it, they said it had landed in a tree but I think they were teasing.'

'It'll give you a chance to upgrade,' Agnes said.

'It's the leg that worries me.' Athena flicked at the sheet, revealing a thick plaster from ankle to thigh.

'It'll heal,' Agnes said.

'Of course it'll heal. But how am I going to fit *that* into those lovely strappy wedges I bought last weekend?'

Agnes smiled. She pulled up a chair and sat down. Athena

shifted her position, wincing. 'He just hangs about,' she said.

'Who?'

'Jake. One minute we were driving through the countryside singing along to something, Celine Dion or someone; then there were ambulances and stuff. And when I wake up I find he's changed.'

'Changed?'

'He's hopeless, it turns out. He didn't let anyone know I was here, Simon was worried sick and he didn't even think to find your number on my phone. He can't make a decision. I was barely conscious yesterday, but I still had to tell him that no, I didn't want the vegetarian meal option last night and to go for the kosher one, obviously. And I sent him back to my flat with a list, and look at what he brought—' She pulled at her pyjama top. 'It's horrible.'

'I know.'

'You said "Nice pyjamas".'

'I was just being polite. I thought, with you being an invalid...'

'I didn't even know I still had them, God knows where he found them.' Athena winced again. 'And he didn't bring my hairbrush. He keeps saying he ought to be at the gallery, and I keep thinking, well, just go there then.'

'Have you been in touch with Nic—' Agnes stopped. Athena's attention was taken by something beyond her, her gaze transfixed. Agnes turned and saw a man approaching – sun-bleached hair; a tall, loping gait. He was weighed down with carrier bags, and as he approached he began to recite a list. 'Cashmere sweater, the nice one. Underwear. I brought you some pyjamas too—' he fished in a bag and produced something flimsy in pale blue silk. 'Sunglasses.' He put down all the bags by the bed. 'Hairbrush, I thought you might need it. Also, chocolate, flowers, and a carton of pomegranate juice.' He turned to Agnes and kissed her on both cheeks. 'Great to see you,' he said. 'How's it going?' He was tanned, dark-eyed and sparkling.

Athena was gazing up at Nic with a look that even the bruising could not hide. Nic bent down and wrapped his arms around her and buried his face in her neck. 'Babe, I'm so sorry,' he murmured. 'I've been a bloody fool.'

'No you haven't...' Athena's voice was muffled against his chest.

'Yes I have.'

'No you haven't...'

'Have—'

Agnes got up from her chair. Jake had appeared at the end of the bed. He held three paper cups, precariously stacked one on top of the other. He stared in front of him for a moment, then turned to Agnes. 'So that's Nic, is it?' he said.

CHAPTER TWENTY-ONE

It was dark when Agnes left the hospital. The streets were wet, but the sky was clear and pricked with stars.

She walked up the drive to Collyer House.

She paced the hallway. She wondered if she was hungry. She wondered what was left in the fridge.

She heard a car draw up, heavy feet on the steps, a thump on the front door.

'Who is it?' she called.

'You'd better let me in.' The voice was loud and unsteady. Malcolm, Agnes realised.

She opened the door.

He was red-faced and breathing hard. 'You have something I want,' he said.

'I'm surprised you haven't been arrested,' Agnes said.

'Alice's diary. Where is it?'

She stared at him. 'Alice's diary?' Behind him the streets glistened in the moonlight.

He pushed past her, into the hall.

She turned to follow him, to switch on the light. 'I could call the police,' she said.

'I wouldn't do that if I were you,' he said.

She looked at him, puzzled. It was then that she saw the

gun that he was holding.

'Now—' he said. 'The diary.'

'It's in the library.'

'We'll go and get it, then, shall we?'

She walked ahead of him, into the darkened room. She found her bag, reached into it, drew out the diary.

She held it out to him, looking at the gun in his hand. 'Where on earth did you get that?' she said.

'I brought it over with me, from Ohio. I thought, you never can tell when it's going to come in useful.'

'When did you get it?'

'When I was a soldier. Colt.45 it is, the best.'

'Does it still work?'

He took the diary from her hand. 'You want me to try?'

She shook her head. 'No,' she said. 'Not particularly.'

He waved the gun towards a chair. 'Sit down,' he said. She did so. He sat opposite her. He put the gun in his lap, and began to turn the pages of the diary.

'When Tina died—' Agnes began.

He looked up at her. 'Yes?'

'She'd requested DNA testing, on Leila.'

A flicker of surprise crossed Malcolm's face. 'Do we have the result?' The diary and the gun now lay across his lap.

'No,' Agnes said. 'Not yet.'

'Well—' he picked up the diary again. 'I know that Leila's mine. And I'm going to claim her. I've asked them to meet me here—'

Agnes heard the stagey tones of a telephone ringing, then remembered it was hers. She bent towards her bag—

'Don't answer it.' Malcolm waved his gun at her.

Agnes straightened up.

He went back to his reading. 'It must say where it is, the crystal,' he said, more to himself than to her.

'Why are you so sure that Leila's your child?'

'She told me. Tina told me that she was.'

'When?' Agnes glanced at the gun lying in his lap.

'And she told Jared she was mine,' Malcolm said.

'Was this after the DNA testing?'

He shrugged. 'I didn't know about the testing.'

'Who do you think killed her?'

'I assume the police know what they're doing.' Malcolm turned a page.

Agnes went on, 'Ryan and Luke said you were there. The night that she died.'

Malcolm looked up from the diary.

'Luke said that the police had got the wrong man, just because Troy and Tina had a fight that night, but after the fight, when she ran away, you followed her. He described you.'

Malcolm gave a tight smile. 'And you believe them, do you?'

'He said it was typical of the feds, as he called them, to pick on Troy.'

'Well, if you want to trust the word of that weaselly red-head—'

There was a knocking at the front door. Malcolm jumped up. 'Go and answer it,' he said. 'I'm right behind you, so don't try anything.'

Helena and Josie stood on the doorstep. 'You called us here.' Helena smiled at Agnes. 'We've brought Leila, as you asked—' she stopped, her mouth open, as she saw Malcolm standing behind Agnes.

'Come in,' he said.

He ushered them into the library, waving the pistol. Leila stood with Josie, clinging to her legs.

'Why?' Helena said.

Malcolm smiled at her. 'You know why.' He picked up the diary and put it in his pocket. He stretched out his other hand to Leila. 'Come on,' he said. 'You're coming with me.'

Helena took a step towards him. 'No—' she said.

Malcolm aimed the gun at her.

'I'll come too,' Josie said. She took Leila's hand, and they crossed the room towards Malcolm, who then directed them towards the door. They went out to the hall, with Helena close behind. Agnes followed. She felt light-headed, as if she might fall. She put her hand against the wall to steady herself.

Malcolm opened the front door.

Jared was standing on the steps. 'You saved me knocking,' he said.

'We were just going,' Malcolm said.

The evening sky was leaden and icy. Jared saw the pistol. He stepped aside. Malcolm and Josie walked down the steps on to the drive. Leila was between them, clutching Josie's hand. She craned her head round to look at Josie, looking for a clue, trying to find out why there was danger, why there was silence, why there was their breath making clouds in the cold night air.

Jared walked up behind Malcolm and placed a hand on his shoulder.

'Give me the child,' he said.

Malcolm turned and faced him. 'No,' he said.

'Give me the child. Let her go,' Jared said.

'She's my child,' Malcolm said.

Agnes was leaning against the door frame. She was aware of Helena behind her. She dug her phone out of her bag and passed it to Helena. Helena slipped back into the house.

'This is our fight,' Jared was saying to Malcolm. 'This is between you and me. If you care about Leila, you won't want her to get hurt.'

'No one's going to get hurt. I'm her father. Leila's going to come and live with me.'

'You're crazy,' Jared said.

Leila was tugging her hand away from Malcolm, but he grabbed her wrist and held it tighter. She began to cry. Josie knelt down next to her, murmuring reassurances.

'You're the one who's crazy,' Malcolm said. He waved the gun towards Jared.

'I saw you,' Jared said. 'I saw you the night that Tina died. You got out of your car, in the street out here—'

'Tina and I were discussing Leila's future,' Malcolm said.

'You were yelling at her.'

'She was lying to me. I was angry.' Malcolm levelled the gun at Jared. 'Now, if you've got any sense, you'll move out of my way.'

'I'll get you arrested—'

'I'll kill you first.'

'Kill me if you must,' Jared said, 'but let the child go.'

He took a step towards Malcolm.

Agnes heard police sirens in the distance. The sound swelled towards them, then faded away.

Malcolm was aiming his pistol at Jared. Josie, holding on to Leila, was watching Malcolm's other hand, where his fingers gripped the child's wrist.

An armoured van drew up, sleekly in the darkness. Then a car. There were doors swinging open, there was shouting, 'Police—'

Malcolm whirled to see what was happening, dropped Leila's wrist. Josie scooped the child up and ran up the steps, into the house.

Malcolm turned back to Jared. He began to shout at him, waving the pistol in his face. 'The devil will curse you. The Lord himself sees into your blackened soul...'

The police marksmen advanced on him.

'...The poison of your marriage bed will be the death of you...' Malcolm was still shouting, as Jared stepped back from him, as the four police officers surrounded him and bundled him away. '...The flames will engulf you, even as the wrath of God did come upon the people of Sodom and Gomorrah...'

The doors of the police van slammed shut. There was the squeal of the engine, the siren blaring into the night.

Agnes found herself sitting on the steps. Behind her, Helena burst into tears.

CHAPTER TWENTY-TWO

WPC Yvette Newland closed her notebook and put it back in her pocket. 'I wonder if that gun of his was loaded,' she said. 'Perhaps it was some clapped out old thing, just for show. The labs have got it now, anyway.'

The kitchen was warm and brightly lit. Agnes got up and switched on the kettle, again.

'I'm glad I didn't have to find out.' Jared leaned back in his chair.

Helena appeared in the doorway. 'Can we go now? Leila's asleep.'

'Where will you go?' Agnes asked her.

'The convent house, for now. They can sleep in my room.' Helena yawned. 'Then Josie can get back to Leeds tomorrow.'

WPC Newland stood up. 'Yes, of course you can go. I ought to go too.' She stretched her arms, her fingers interlinked behind her head. 'That Reverend's got a lot of questions to answer, and I bet some of them go back to when he lived in the States.' She pulled her jacket tight around her waist. 'I'll pop back in the morning,' she said to Agnes. 'Will you be here?'

Agnes glanced at Helena, and nodded. 'Tell Sister Lucia that I promise it's my last night ever in Collyer House.'

* * *

She locked the door behind them all, then came back into the kitchen. 'More tea?' she said to Jared. 'Coffee?'

He shook his head.

She sat down opposite him. Outside a car passed, its tyres loud on the icy road.

'What will you do?' She pulled her mug towards her and took a sip of cold tea.

'I need to get back to the States, get on with my life out there.'

'And Leila?'

He glanced at her. 'I might have been wrong about Leila.'

'You mean, you'll leave her here?'

He stared at his hands as they rested on the blue formica.

'You think she's not yours,' Agnes said.

His head flicked up. 'Leila?'

Agnes nodded. 'For all your courage out there, you think she's Malcolm's child.'

He held her gaze, unblinking. Across the river came the chimes of distant bells, marking the hours of the night. Agnes thought of Alice, sitting in this very place, hearing the traffic on the river, the bells of the city churches.

'Nicolas Hawker,' she said. 'He lived here, three hundred years ago, with his wife and child. He believed that his child wasn't his, baby Jonjo, he was sure that Alice had conceived with someone else. He looked into the crystal, but the crystal showed him what he wanted to see. The crystal lied. So he had his wife declared insane. He had her locked up, he allowed his little boy to die of neglect, he took up with someone else. And all the time, Alice knew he was wrong. She was true to him, the baby was his.'

Jared closed his eyes, opened them again. 'What happened in the end?'

'After her child died, Alice died of grief. Her husband married again.'

'Did he get away with it?' Jared's eyes were still on hers.

'It's not quite murder,' Agnes said. 'What Nicolas did.'

'No,' Jared agreed.

Agnes watched him. 'When you killed Tina-Marie—'

'She's not my baby,' he interrupted. 'Leila. Tina told me. That night. All those years I'd believed she was mine, I was waiting until I could get back to her, I wanted us to be a family.'

'Did Tina know that you intended to take Leila back to the States?'

He nodded.

'Is that why she did the DNA tests?'

'I asked her to. I made her do it. And then next thing I knew, she was waving this bit of paper at me, and she was saying all this stuff, she was mocking me, saying that Leila wasn't my baby.'

'When was that?'

'I came to find her. She was staying in that flat, with Troy, across the way there. They'd had a big fight, she looked bad, she was scared he'd come back, so we went out, we started walking.'

'And then you saw Malcolm?'

'He's such a twat,' Jared said. 'He was driving along, arguing with her about Leila. And I told him to fuck off.'

'And did he?'

'In the end, yeah. I think he got bored. He told Tina he'd

come back another time. And then after that, we was just walking, me and Tina, we came up this way. And I told her my plans, and that was when she took out the DNA papers, she had them in her bag. And then...' He put his hands over his face. 'I'd given her money to keep Leila. For years. I felt bad about leaving, so I'd been paying for her. And she was laughing, then, laughing at me. And so I...' His words stopped.

'Do you usually carry a knife?'

He took his hands away from his face. 'Depends where I'm going. Round there, round where Troy lives, then yeah, I do.'

'Did you chase her? Did you pursue her as far as my doorstep?'

His face was drained, taut. 'She ran. She must have thought you'd protect her.'

'She didn't make it.' Agnes watched him.

He shook his head. 'No. She didn't make it.'

She leaned into her bag and produced the papers that Philip had given her. She pushed them across the table to him. 'Tina was lying,' she said. 'Whatever papers she was waving at you, they weren't the real tests. These are the results.'

Jared stared at the lined, white form in front of him. He pulled it towards him. 'That's – that's my name.' He frowned at it, jabbing his finger at the page.

'Nicolas Hawker was wrong too.' Agnes looked at her fingers, her hands clasped together on the table.

'You just rescued your own child.'

Jared stared at her. 'I killed her,' he said. 'I killed the mother of my child.' He slumped forward, his head buried in his hands.

CHAPTER TWENTY-THREE

The morning sun streamed through the window panes into Julius's office. Julius listened, his head on one side. When Agnes had finished, he spoke. 'You look exhausted,' he said.

'I am.'

'Did you sleep there last night? At Collyer?'

'I'm not sure sleep is the word. But yes, I was in my room there.' She reached a hand across the desk towards him. 'I kept thinking, I shouldn't have let him go. After he said those words, "I killed her" – he just got up and left, he walked out into the night. I watched him go.'

'But you called the police?'

'Yes. Immediately.'

'So they know that he confessed to it?'

She nodded.

'Well, it's up to them, then, isn't it?'

'Yes,' she said. 'I suppose it is.'

He stood up and went over to the kettle.

'He might go back to the States,' Agnes said. 'He might escape.'

Julius took the jar of sugar down from the shelf. 'Do you want him to escape?'

'No,' she said. She noticed how the sunlight made tiny

rainbows at the edge of each window pane. 'I didn't want Nicolas to get away with it either,' she said.

'Nicolas?'

'Nicolas Hawker.'

Julius brought two mugs of tea over to the desk. He glanced up at the clock which stood in the corner of the room. 'I'll have to go in a minute. It's the eleven o'clock soon.'

She frowned at him. 'Is it Sunday?' she said.

'You've been a long way away,' he said.

She met his eyes. He said, 'Have they gone, then, the ghosts? Has all this laid them to rest?'

'It feels like it, yes.'

'And the final vows?'

She ran her finger around the rim of her mug. 'Perhaps it was all the same.'

Julius watched the circular movements of her hand. 'Thank you for coming back to me,' he said.

She raised her eyes to his. She stood up and went over to him, bent and kissed the top of his head.

'Aren't you coming to mass?' he said.

She shook her head. 'I have to say goodbye to Alice.'

He watched her cross the room, heard her footsteps on the old stone steps.

She walked back to Collyer House, through sunshine pealing with church bells. It was cold inside the house, but the damp smell had faded a little. She began to pace, aimlessly, wandering through the hall, up the stairs. On the landing she stopped and listened, for nothing in particular. She went back downstairs, and pushed open the library door.

The room was bright; the uneven tiles of the parquet floor tilted here and there. The empty shelves returned her gaze.

It seemed a long time ago, the ghosts. The footsteps on the landing; the black dog.

As if in answer to her thoughts, she heard a growling. Her heart tightened in her chest and she ran to the library door. She stood in the hall, hearing it still, a low rough whisper. It seemed to be outside. She flung open the front door, blinking in the sunlight.

There was barking, and a sharp caterwauling. The tabby cat was on the high wall by the clinic. Below her stood a dog, a black, mangy-looking mongrel, growling. The tabby hissed, arch-backed. The dog fled.

The cat watched him go, then jumped off the wall and sauntered away along the drive towards the clinic.

Agnes shut the door.

A real dog, then. No longer the dog of her imaginings.

She went up to the room that had been hers, and packed the last of her things into a bag, then left, locking the door behind her.

The house reverts, she thought. The house becomes Jonathan's; becomes Alice's again. She walked down the drive, her fingers in her pocket counting the beads of Alice's rosary.

Athena was propped up in bed reading a magazine. She seemed to be almost submerged in vases of flowers, bowls of fruit. She put the magazine down as she heard Agnes approach. 'Do you know,' she said, 'according to this, Posh Spice's bum has disappeared.'

Agnes looked at her blankly.

'But the good news is,' Athena went on, 'that it says here that wedges are terribly last year after all.'

'Oh dear. What a shame.'

'No, you don't understand. It means I'll just have to buy another pair of shoes when the plaster comes off. As it is they're offering me the ugliest shoe-thing you've ever seen, I've told them, I'd rather go barefoot.'

Agnes laughed. 'You look well,' she said.

'Do I? Amazing what a decent lipstick can do.'

Agnes sat down by the bed. 'Where are all your men?'

Athena surveyed her nails, which were bright red and smooth-shaped. 'I feel a fool,' she said. 'I don't know what I was thinking of. I mean, I know Nic was neglecting me, and he knows that too, but to think that I was really considering...' She sighed. She pulled a grape from the stalk and put it in her mouth. 'He's very sweet, of course, Jake is, but—' She finished eating the grape. 'What I'd forgotten, about those days when I first knew Jake, all those years ago, was that even then, when he was going out with Anita, he was terribly Piscean about it all. Even then.'

'Right.' Agnes looked at her. 'And being Piscean about things means what exactly?'

'Oh, you know. Wafty. Neither one thing nor the other. Being over here and thinking it might be nicer to be over there. It used to drive Anita up the wall too. No wonder she ended up in Cyprus.'

Agnes helped herself to a grape.

'By the way, sweetie—' Athena began to stack her magazines into a pile. 'Nic thinks you should have your family home back.'

Agnes swallowed the grape. 'But – but I can't. I'm not allowed to own anything.'

'Well, I'm sorry, but he's absolutely right, it's no good for him and me if he's away the whole time, and anyway, kitten, you can't condemn him to spend all this time in France just because of your silly vows.'

'They're not silly.' Agnes spoke quietly. 'And anyway, the house is held by you in trust, we agreed all this last year.'

Athena ate another grape. 'But what can I do with it? Nic's going to come back to London and sort out his private practice again. He's wondering about going more corporate, you can earn a fortune these days, apparently, going into huge businesses and helping them understand the psychodynamics of leadership. I think that's what he said. And it turns out that Ben, you know his son from his marriage all those years ago, anyway Ben's wife Julia is expecting a baby, and they're moving back to Europe from Melbourne, and Nic's hoping to see a lot more of them...' She stopped for breath.

'And what about his family tree?'

'Oh, that.' Athena waved her manicured hand. 'He'd got it all wrong. The woman that he'd traced to those posh rabbis turned out not be his great-grandmother, so he isn't Jewish after all. Although I'm not sure the appeal of being in a beleaguered minority has worn off. He'll probably try to be Belgian next.'

Agnes smiled at her. 'I'd better go,' she said.

'You've got an awful lot of luggage,' Athena said, as Agnes stood up and gathered up her bags.

'I've moved out of Collyer House. Finally.'

'Where will you go?' Athena shifted on her pillows. 'Are you really going to live in the convent?'

'I'm afraid so.'

'If they had any sense they'd let you have your flat back.'

'Well, yes,' Agnes said. 'But I have to do as I'm told now.'

'You could always pray for it,' Athena said. 'Put in a word up there that you'd really like to live on your own again.'

Agnes laughed. 'But – but it doesn't work like that.'

'Doesn't work like that? I thought He was supposed to be omnipotent. Well, I don't know—' Athena pursed her lips. 'There don't seem to be many perks in this religion business.'

Agnes leaned over and kissed her cheek. 'We're both incarcerated now.'

'At least I get time off for good behaviour,' Athena said.

Sunday, Agnes thought, emerging from the hospital into the late morning sunlight, hearing her phone's antique ring in her pocket.

'Hello?'

'Hi, it's WPC Yvette Newland here. I just thought you'd like to know, we've arrested Jared O'Connor.'

'Where was he?'

'After your report, we tracked him down to Dalston. It was his cousin's house, apparently. He made no attempt to evade arrest. Oh, and Malcolm Noble has been charged, but he's entered a plea of not guilty.'

'What are the charges?'

'Breaking and Entering, Abduction and Section Eighteen.'

'Where's Jared now?'

'He's in the cells, he'll appear in court tomorrow.'

Agnes sat on the embankment wall. The Thames glittered in the sunlight. A riverboat chugged past, packed with passengers, their laughter floating on the air.

'Are you still there?' Yvette was saying.

'Yes,' Agnes said. 'Thank you for telling me.'

She walked into the convent house and straight into Sister Lucia.

'Ah, Agnes,' she said. 'We missed you at chapel this morning.' She allowed her gaze to take in the bags that Agnes was carrying. 'Do I understand that you're here to stay, now?'

Agnes nodded. 'Yes, Sister. I am.'

Lucia looked at her watch. 'After lunch, perhaps we could discuss various matters arising. Such as, what is to become of the two guests currently upstairs? And some time in the next few days, I'd like you and Shirley to sort out the final resting place for those boxes of books currently in the library here.'

'Of course, Sister.' Agnes bent her head in acquiescence, then stepped past her and went up the stairs.

Helena and Josie were sitting by the window of Helena's room. Leila was curled up on the bed, surrounded by colouring books.

Helena looked up as she came in. 'We heard,' she said. 'About Jared. Yvette phoned.'

'We were waiting to say goodbye,' Josie said. 'We're going back up to Leeds, Leila and me.'

'Don't want to go.' Leila drew a pink crayon spiral across a picture of a hippopotamus.

'I'm sorry you haven't been treated in a truly Christian manner,' Agnes said.

Josie smiled. 'I think, in the circumstances, it's understandable.'

'Did Yvette tell you,' Helena said, 'Malcolm's pleading not guilty?'

'It means we'll all have to give evidence,' Josie said. 'It's not kind of him. Some of the witnesses are very vulnerable.' She indicated Leila with a tilt of her head. Leila looked up at her, waiting for an explanation, then, getting no answer, went back to her drawing.

'What will happen to Malcolm's church, I wonder.' Helena slipped her feet into her shoes.

'It'll fall apart.' Josie stood up. 'It turned out, it was all about him.'

Agnes walked with Josie down to the door. Helena lingered behind, chatting to Leila, promising to visit her in her new home.

On the doorstep, Josie hugged Agnes. 'Thanks,' she said. She glanced back towards Leila. 'It's her I want to cry for,' she said. 'Not me.' She shook her head, searching for the right words. 'Who's going to tell her? Who's going to tell her what happened with her mother? How's she going to acknowledge Jared as her father? She's going to go through life carrying the past like a burden.'

Agnes held Josie's hands in her own. 'We all carry the past,' she said. 'For some it weighs more heavily, that's all.'

'Come and see us soon.' Josie kissed her on each cheek. She gathered up her bag in one hand, and took Leila's hand in the other.

From the street, Leila waved back at them, her pink sleeves flapping, all the way to the corner until she was out of sight.

Helena turned to Agnes. 'Well, Sister—'

'Yes, Sister,' Agnes said.

'I gather it's shepherd's pie for lunch,' Helena said.

CHAPTER TWENTY-FOUR

'There are two things I regret,' Agnes said, putting her foot down as the engine of the Metro struggled into fourth gear.

'And what are they?' Helena sat in the passenger seat. The Essex countryside passed by, grey and flat. The windscreen wipers scraped away in the drizzly rain.

'One is not having stolen the Mercedes that Athena hired for me. And the other is allowing Malcolm to walk off with Alice's diary. Presumably he's got it even now, unless some fellow prisoner has nicked it off him.'

'I wonder what we're going to find,' Helena said. 'I wonder how his church has survived without him.'

'It's probably just the same.' Agnes turned off down the lane. 'It's only been a few weeks, after all.'

The gate was propped open. Agnes drove up to the house and parked. They sat in the car, in the silence.

'There's no one here.' Helena looked out of her window.

The white-fronted house wore a blank expression. The doors of the barn were shut. The fields were deserted.

They got out of the car. Agnes went up to the house and rang the bell. Helena wandered away from her, down the path.

There was no answer at the house. Agnes followed Helena

to the barn. 'It gives me the creeps,' Helena said. 'It was some kind of madness, I think. Something took hold of me. I needed to escape, and so I ran. But I ran in the wrong direction...'

There was a shout in the distance, and they both turned. A woman on horseback was trotting towards them across the field. She was red-faced, breathless and smiling. 'I thought it was you,' she said to Helena.

'Lizzie—' Helena smiled up at her, as the horse came to a halt, blowing and tossing its tail.

'And Agnes, isn't it?' Lizzie patted the chestnut's neck.

'We came to see how it was here,' Helena said.

'It's all over.' Lizzie dismounted, and gathered up the reins, nuzzling her horse's face. 'Come on baby,' she murmured, 'you can go home now.' She turned to Helena and Agnes. 'I'll just put my baby away and then I'll tell you what happened.'

They followed her round to the stable block. There were two stalls, and in one stood a tall bay horse, whinnying and weaving its head as Lizzie approached. She led the chestnut into the empty stall and arranged some hay and water for it.

'Right,' she said. 'I'm with you now.'

'There weren't horses here before,' Helena said, gazing at the stable block. 'We used to stack chairs in there.'

'The Lord's been kind to me,' Lizzie said, then chewed her lip, staring at the ground. 'When I say Lord... Anyway—' she began to walk up towards the barn and they followed. 'Malcolm wasn't with us much in the last few weeks, as I'm sure you know. People were getting restless, the ones who lived here, and the ones from round and about stopped coming. The barn was empty some Sundays, the services deserted, just those of us who were still in the house. Marina tried to keep it all going, but without Malcolm...'

She pushed open the door of the barn and they went inside.

'Marina?' Helena said. She looked around in the dim light.

'Yes. She and Malcolm...she became his...'

'One of his "wives"?'

'By the end, the only one. She's suffered for it too. She's still around somewhere.'

There was a damp smell in the still air. An upturned chair lay across the stage. The microphones had gone, their stands bare and black like branches in winter.

'It's over,' Helena said, looking around her.

Lizzie nodded. 'It was like a flood. It's like we all ran into the tidal waves, willingly. And then the water receded, and here we are, left high and dry in the wreckage.'

'And the horses?' Agnes asked.

'I've been really lucky. All this is going to be sold, Malcolm's got terrible debts, you see. Anyway, a friend of mine in the village, she's got a riding school, and she's been paying me to keep a couple of the horses for her while she expands her business, and in a week or so, I'm going to move down there and work for her. I've always ridden,' she said. 'It was my first love.'

'And the church?' Helena asked. Lizzie met her eyes. They were like two survivors, veterans of war, shared horrors in their mutual gaze.

'I don't know,' Lizzie said. 'What I think is, Malcolm made a mistake and we all believed him. His mistake was to think that he'd do – instead of God, instead of Jesus.' She glanced at Agnes. 'I'm glad he's locked away.' She righted an upturned chair and leaned against it. 'Apart from all the things he did out there, he did a lot of damage here.'

Helena murmured in agreement.

'The horses have saved me,' Lizzie went on. 'But it drove some people mad, Malcolm's church. Do you remember Julian, that boy who worked in the workshop? He's back with his parents, someone told me. He doesn't speak, he doesn't go out, he stares at the wall...' She looked at Helena. 'People really loved Malcolm. And they're the ones who—'

The barn door creaked open. A thin figure stood, silhouetted in the doorway. 'Oh,' she said. 'It's you. I wondered who was here.' She took a few steps towards them, and Agnes recognised her as the young woman who was hoovering when she'd visited before. 'I thought perhaps he had come back.' Her voice was frail.

'Marina—' Lizzie went towards her, took her arm. Marina shrank from her touch. 'You remember Helena, don't you? And Agnes?'

Marina glanced up at them through her eyelashes. 'He promised he would come back,' she said. 'And little Leila, we were going to be a family, me and him and Leila, after poor Tina died. It was what Jesus wanted, Malcolm said, that Leila should have a home with us, and it was what we wanted too. I've prayed so much, I've prayed until I can't pray anymore. He will come back, won't he?' The words tumbled from her. She stood still, staring at the flagstone floor.

Lizzie put her arm around her. 'Go back to the house, Marina. Go and rest. I'll make us some supper later – you might eat today, perhaps. I'll make something nice, something you like.' She steered her towards the door. They watched as she made her way up to the house.

'As I was saying,' Lizzie said. 'For the people who really loved Malcolm, it's been very hard.'

They left the barn and came out into the soft rain. 'All this,' Lizzie waved her arm at the buildings, the fields around them, 'it's all been seized as assets. Malcolm had borrowed a fortune, it turns out. The banks will sell it all off.' She shut the barn door, and they walked up the path.

'And Marina?' Helena spoke quietly.

Lizzie looked at the toes of her muddy boots. 'She'll have to go somewhere. She's got a mother she doesn't talk to, and a father she hates. There's a half-sister in Liverpool who might take her in. Marina's not keen, but I've been trying to make her see she hasn't much choice. It's either that or floating around the ruins of this place like a ghost.'

Agnes opened the car door. Lizzie and Helena hugged each other. 'You and me,' Lizzie said to her, 'we're the lucky ones. We escaped. It's the people who give everything up, and then find that their beliefs are wrong, or dangerous even...they're the ones who suffer.' She turned to Agnes and shook her hand. 'Thanks,' she said.

'For what?'

'That day you came to visit...' She let go of Agnes's hand. 'I watched Malcolm with you, that day, and I began to think that perhaps he was lying. To you. To us.'

'You'd have got there in the end,' Agnes said.

'But it was because you were a nun. I expected you to treat him as we did, not to question anything he said. But you behaved as if he was just a man, nothing special – it changed the way I saw him.'

* * *

They drove out through the gate. Helena waved at Lizzie, as they turned out into the lane and headed back to London.

Helena broke the silence. 'She's right, isn't she?'

'About what?'

'About it being dangerous to give everything up to a belief.'

Agnes checked her mirror as they approached a roundabout. 'I suppose so.'

'But that's what you and I are doing isn't it? We'll go back tonight, and there'll be chapel, and supper, and more chapel...'

'I've got to go to the clinic after this,' Agnes said. 'I'm helping Philip clear the paperwork.'

'But everything we do, it's all in the service of God.'

'I suppose it is.'

'That's what I mean. It's submission. We're brides of Christ.'

'Oh, heavens, are we?'

Helena smiled.

The rain had cleared, and the clouds were tinted watery pink. Agnes thought about Marina, haunting the deserted barn. 'The difference is,' she said, 'that Malcolm's God was like Malcolm. Malcolm's God wanted power, and money, and women, and a Mercedes SL.'

'And our God?'

'I haven't the faintest idea about our God. I have an inkling that God is love. That's the closest I get.' Agnes pushed her foot hard on to the accelerator, and the Metro groaned and grumbled as they joined the dual carriageway. 'But I suppose if our God felt like giving me a Mercedes SL, I wouldn't complain.'

* * *

It was almost dark when she walked up the drive to the clinic, but there was a scent of spring in the evening air. The reception area was deserted, and almost empty of furniture. Philip's office was locked.

Agnes sat on one of the few remaining chairs to wait for him. She heard crisp footsteps, and turned to see Serena approaching along the corridor.

'Hello,' Agnes said.

Serena sat down on the chair next to her. 'He said you'd be here, so I made sure to get here first.' She smiled at Agnes. 'I'm not mad. He'll think I'm mad, he'll think I'm making it up, that's why I came here. I thought, I'll tell you first, and then you can tell Philip.' She leaned back on the chair.

'You can try, but I'm not sure Philip will believe anything I tell him,' Agnes said.

'Oh, he's bound to listen to you. He says you'd make a very good atheist.'

'Oh.'

'It's a compliment.' Serena looked at her to check. 'So, when you tell him I'm pregnant he'll believe you. Won't he?'

Agnes stared at her.

'Look,' Serena was saying. 'I went to the doctor. My doctor. I went today.' She produced a thin white wand. 'Blue line,' she said. 'Look. So when Philip comes you can say—'

The clinic doors opened and they both turned.

'What will she say?' Philip walked into the foyer. He glanced around him at the curled floorboards and sparse furniture. 'It's just as well we're out of here,' he said.

'Serena's pregnant,' Agnes said.

'No, she isn't.' Philip looked down at her, his hands in his pockets.

'Told you,' Agnes said to Serena.

'I am,' Serena said. 'Look.' She waved the white stick at Philip who stared at it without comprehension.

'Pregnancy test,' Agnes said.

'I suppose nuns know all about such things.' He took it from Serena and frowned at the blue line. 'That's a positive, is it?'

'I thought you were a doctor,' Agnes said.

'Of the mind. Which, of course, all this is about.'

'Not this time.' Agnes was aware her voice sounded loud in the echoing space.

'I went to Dr McCullen,' Serena said. 'He confirmed it. He said he'd phone you.'

'He left me a message,' Philip said. 'He didn't say what it was about. I haven't called him back yet.'

Both women had their eyes upon him, waiting. He looked at them, sighed, fished in his pocket for his phone, clicked on a number. 'Roy McCullen please,' he said. He waited, standing sullen like a child. 'Roy,' he said. 'Hi. You called me.'

Agnes and Serena watched his expression change as he listened. They glanced at each other, then both looked at the floor.

'Right,' Philip said into his phone. 'OK. Yes, you're telling me it's very unusual. Bloody miraculous if you ask me.' He listened for a moment, then he spoke again. 'Me?' He sounded gruff. 'Yes. Yes, I suppose I am. I'll – I'll be in touch. Oh, and Roy – thanks.' He put his phone back in his pocket and turned to the women. 'He said – how did I feel about becoming a father?'

'And what did you say?' Serena perched on her chair, her head on one side.

'You heard.' Philip sat down next to her. He picked up her hand in his own and looked at it. 'Well, well,' he said.

Agnes stood up. 'I'm going to take a last look next door,' she said.

'Yes,' Philip said. He held Serena's fingers in his own. 'Good.'

'I knew you'd believe it if Agnes told you,' Serena said.

'Well, actually –' Philip smiled '– I think you'll find I only believed it when a doctor told me.'

'You mean,' Agnes said, 'that as far as you're concerned, the conception of a baby is explicable by a biological process rather than by an act of God.'

'Bloody hell,' he said. 'It's miraculous enough it's been conceived at all, let's not go hoping for the next Messiah too.'

Agnes unlocked the door of Collyer House and found her way to the light switch. She stood in the dim shadows of the hall. She wondered where Alice had gone. She wondered whether she was ever here.

She made her way to the library and switched on the light. The windows were blank squares of darkness. The cabinet and desks had gone, the shelves were bare lines against the walls.

Agnes brought out Alice's rosary from her pocket. It swung in her hand, casting long shadows across the floor. She wondered who owned it now; she'd offered it to Jonathan, but he'd refused.

Perhaps Alice had given it to her, a gift across the centuries.

Agnes looked at it as it lay across her fingers; then she looked beyond it. Something lay on the floor, something left behind. A book, Agnes realised, as she took a step towards it. She picked it up, feeling the soft leather, the thin, worn pages.

Alice's diary. She must want me to have it after all.

She put the diary in one pocket, the rosary in the other. She switched off all the lights and left the house in darkness.

CHAPTER TWENTY-FIVE

The chapel bell broke the soft silence of the dawn. The sisters filed out of Lauds.

Agnes yawned, wondered about the chores rota, wondered about breakfast, wondered whether she could face cornflakes again, let alone cheap sliced bread and thin cut marmalade.

Sister Lucia found her sitting in the corner of the dining room. She frowned at Agnes's bowl of dry porridge oats, then said, 'Shirley's coming in at nine to clear the last of the books away. Would you help her? And then after that, I need to have a meeting with you.' Lucia swept along the row of sisters, and began to talk to Helena about this month's cat food bill and whether it might be reduced next month…'They're only strays, after all,' she heard, 'surely they can manage on leftovers?'

Agnes ate a mouthful of oats. She thought about her flat. In a parallel universe, she thought, I am still there, sitting at my lovely oak table, spread with my mother's old linen tablecloth, eating a proper croissant from the French bakery on the corner, and maybe some apricot jam.

Perhaps Helena's right, she thought. Maybe this is what it means to take final vows: to give up everything. Maybe a yearning for decent jam is just the beginning of it all going wrong, a slippery slope which ends in power, and money, and a Mercedes SL, and a false God made in the image of man.

She pushed the bowl of oats away from her, and went to help in the laundry.

Shirley looked smart and brisk and Agnes realised that she'd got a new haircut. They sat in the sunny lounge and smiled at each other.

'So,' Shirley said. 'Everyone locked up, then.'

It was an odd way to talk about the convent, Agnes thought. But then Shirley added, 'Jared. And Malcolm.'

'Oh. Yes. I spoke to Josie yesterday. Jared's on remand in Belmarsh prison, but they'll move him eventually. She's worried that he'll plead diminished responsibility on grounds of provocation, which means that his brief will try and blame Tina's behaviour.'

'And Malcolm?'

'He's awaiting trial too. They've moved him to Norfolk somewhere. Helena spoke to Lizzie who'd spoken to Marina, she's his only visitor. From what we can gather he's in complete denial and is waiting for the Lord to rescue him.'

'Just as well the Lord has sense, then.' Shirley smiled at her. 'With any luck, we can rely on him to keep Malcolm behind bars for some time to come.'

'And Troy was released. Philip saw him the other day, hanging around with Ryan and Luke. Now the clinic building's empty, they'll probably set fire to it.'

Shirley sighed in agreement. There was a small silence.

'How's your mother?' Agnes said.

'Mother?' Shirley looked as if Agnes had asked after a

holiday now become a distant memory. 'Oh, she's fine, thank you.'

'And her legs?'

'Well—' Shirley leaned forward. 'It turned out that we were entitled to home visits to help with Mother's care. You know Jonathan's young cousin, Matthew? Well, his girlfriend works for social services, and not only that, but we got an electric wheelchair, and now Mother can wheel herself down to the shops on her own, she's rather limited about which shops she can actually get into, Marks's is fine, but the fishmonger, she has to park outside and shout through the door. But it does mean that on the days when I'm working in the shop, Mother can pretty well look after herself.' She smiled, breathless.

Agnes felt as if she was reading a book and had missed some pages. 'Which shop?'

'Oh, didn't I say? Jonathan's, of course. He's moved premises, the old shop was in a terrible location. We're out on the High Street now, and business has picked up, particularly since I introduced the greetings card side of things.'

Agnes wondered how Shirley had come to look so much younger. 'I thought he was waiting for the sale of Alice's house?' she said.

'Oh, well, it would help, of course, he's still in hock to the bank. He's going to stake his claim, but as he said, he doesn't want it to get all Jarndyce and Jarndyce.' She laughed a girlish laugh. 'And he's dropped all that magic side of things, now he's decided to give the Hawker collection to the museum in Oxford after all. As I said to him, Jennifer's in a much better position to look after it than we are.'

The sunlight filtered through the pale curtains. Agnes

could hear the sounds of the rest of the house; hoovering, notes of music from the chapel as Sister Brigitte practised a new arrangement of a psalm. 'And the crystal?' she asked Shirley.

Shirley looked at her hands, clasped on her lap. 'He seems to have lost interest in it. The other day, he said, perhaps it ceased to exist. Perhaps it was smashed into bits years ago.'

'Perhaps it was.' Agnes smiled back at her.

Shirley stood up. 'It was fun working with you,' she said.

Fun, Agnes wondered, as she helped Shirley out to her car with the last box of books. Fun, she thought, as she watched her drive away. She turned back to the convent house, and went slowly up the stairs to the front door.

This is my home, she said to herself. The thought was a dead weight, sending the sun behind the clouds, dulling the polished floor of the hall. She went to the study to wait for Sister Lucia.

'Agnes. Well, well—' Sister Lucia came in and took up her position behind her desk, settling herself into her chair. 'You may be wondering why I've called you here.'

Agnes was aware of her mind sifting through the possibilities, most of which involved various breaches of her vow of obedience.

'As you know,' Lucia was saying, touching the wisps of hair at her temples, 'Madeleine is off to teach in the school in Yorkshire for a year or so, which means that we need someone to work in the hostel for the homeless again, with dear Father Julius and his team. Now, given that our sisters are so stretched as we are, what with Brigitte having to spend more time in France, the only person I could spare to cover Madeleine's work – was you.'

The last two words were barely audible. Agnes stared at Lucia's thin fingers tightly intertwined. 'Yes, Sister,' she managed to say.

'And, obviously...' Lucia's voice had shrunk to a mumble '...it's more convenient, given the location of the hostel, and the fact that dear Abbot Jean-Yves has to go back to Normandy, that we install you in the flat in Bermondsey again.'

Agnes bowed her head. She heard herself say, 'Of course, Sister. Whatever you wish.'

'Well, sweetie, frankly, it was bound to happen.' Athena signalled to the waiter for champagne. Her leg was still in plaster. It stuck out across a second chair, bare-footed, with red-painted toenails.

'What was bound to happen?'

It was a warm evening, and the restaurant windows were open to the street. Agnes listened to the passing traffic, the fragments of conversation from passers-by.

'You getting your flat back.' Athena leaned to one side, as the waiter poured two flutes of sparkling bubbles.

'Why?'

'Because—' Athena raised her glass, 'because I prayed for it.'

'You – you prayed for it?' Agnes stared at her.

Athena nodded, beaming at her.

'But you don't even believe.' Agnes held her glass between her fingers.

'Yes, but kitten, I thought, well it's worth a try. I thought, in your view, whether I believe in God or not has no bearing on whether he exists, right?'

'Right.' Agnes sipped her champagne.

'So, if I pray to him, and he does exist, it makes no difference whether I believe he's there or not, right?'

'Mmm.' Agnes frowned. 'Go on.'

'And then I thought, your God isn't going to be petty or small-minded, is he? I mean, if he gets a prayer from some hopeless non-believer like me, he's still going to be charitable about it, isn't he?'

'I suppose so.'

'So, I said to him, please give Agnes back her flat. And, obviously, everything I've just said must be true, because it's worked. Hasn't it. Cheers.' She raised her glass.

Agnes clinked her glass with Athena's. 'Well,' she said, 'if I had half your hopeless non-believer's faith I'd be a much better nun.' It was growing dark outside, and the candles flickered on the tables. 'And how's Nic?' she said.

Athena seemed to glow. 'Nic,' she said. 'Mmmm.'

'So, everything's all right, then?'

'He's determined to move back here, he blames himself for it all going wrong. And he's made contact with Janis, she's a healer he knew from ages ago, she's got a very successful practice in Primrose Hill. Anyway, she says he can join her, she says there's a great demand round there from people who want to find out who they were before they were born, and he says, all his family tree skills will come in useful because then people can find out who they were related to before they were born too.'

'So the house in Provence will be empty again.'

'Apart from Chantal, who it turns out is fifty-five and Marie's niece.'

'I thought so.' Agnes stared into her glass. 'What are we going to do? It's technically yours to dispose of.'

'Poppet, it's up to you.'

'I gave it to you, as a trust. I'm not supposed to own anything.'

'It's still yours, though. No one would deny your right to it.'

Agnes took a large mouthful of champagne.

'What's the matter?' Athena rested her chin on her hand.

Agnes sighed. 'I resisted it for so long,' she said. 'Final vows. I fought and fought. And now it turns out, it's rather a relief. Getting rid of that house, shedding my past...it's been really good for me.'

Athena shook her head. 'No, sweetie, you need the past. Everyone does. You can't just float around being adrift in the present. You'd be like that poor ghost, Alice. It's only because you respected the past that you were able to lay her to rest.'

'But I don't want to be chained to my parents' house.'

'It's not a chain. It's a connection. Nic says it's like the earth wire in a plug. Typical boy way of looking at things but I know what he means.'

'I could just be a good nun and give it to the order, that's what I was going to do before you took it off me.'

'You'll do no such thing. Look at you—' Athena pointed at her, 'look how glad you are to get your flat back. You like having your own things, your lovely linen, that Leeds-ware dish you've got there. Think what it would be like if you really just had to sit in your convent with nothing to call your own.'

Agnes had an image in her mind of a bowl of dry porridge oats.

'I have an idea,' Athena said. 'Jake and Justin have been talking about expanding the sculpture work, they need a bigger foundry, and Justin's got rather a following in Europe. I was thinking of suggesting your house to them. That way, I still have it in trust, but it's occupied. And to be honest, poppet, I could do with putting some ocean between me and Jake, even if it is just the English Channel.'

Agnes smiled at her. 'Did you pray for all this too?'

'I wish I could say yes, it would support my theory. But no, sweetie, it was just me this time. On my own.'

'Well, it's a great idea.'

Athena made a little bow of her head. 'Thank you. So, it's all sorted. And you can move back into your flat and live in peace, praise the Lord. I just hope the Abbot of Flanders hasn't made off with all your family silver, that's all.'

Agnes laughed.

Athena raised her glass, again. 'To someone I don't believe in.'

Agnes raised her glass. 'To someone I do.'

Bells, again, waking her up. She opened her eyes to darkness, and remembered it was Sunday. Then she remembered it was her last day here, in the convent house. Tomorrow, she'd move back to her flat. She stumbled out of bed, pulled on clothes, filed into chapel with the others.

She recited the Psalms, joining her voice to the soft chanting of the sisters, allowing her gaze to scan the choir stalls. There was Madeleine, and Brigitte, and Anna, and Lucia and all the others, all living out their path with varying degrees of humility and obedience, and rebellion and stubbornness.

She resolved to be here more, to spend more time in the chapel here, even when she was living alone.

'...In the name of the Father, and of the Son...'

The first rays of the sun touched the stained glass, and the chapel was flecked with blue and red and gold.

Later, there were hugs in the kitchen and the dining room. Phyllida had kept to her room with 'a bit of a cold', so Agnes ventured up the stairs and knocked on her door.

'I've come to say goodbye,' she said.

Phyllida was swathed in scarves and an ancient-looking pink bedjacket which gave her the appearance of a Hollywood star in her days of fading glory. 'Poor you,' she said. 'Being exiled to solitude.'

Agnes sat next to her by her tiny desk. 'I'll be all right,' she said.

'Well, we all serve our time.' Phyllida spoke cheerfully.

She had made her room her own, and Agnes looked at the photographs on the mantelpiece; a glamorous young woman smiling, a couple of babies; a handsome man in naval uniform. There was a bad painting of a vase of flowers on the wall; an embroidered cushion on the other chair; some high-quality notepaper stacked on the desk underneath a paperweight. The paperweight was a heavy, odd-shaped, round, clear crystal. Agnes picked it up. Underneath she saw two symbols: alpha and omega. 'Where did you get this?' She tried to keep a conversational tone, but her voice seemed to have gone shaky.

'Oh, that old thing. Funny isn't it? Terribly useful.' Phyllida took it from her and weighed it in her frail hand. 'It used to be knocking about when we had the house in South London, you know, Collyer House, the one you stayed in. Of course, I lived there when the order was thriving, such a gaggle of us in those days, always busy. Happy days. Such a shame we had to let it go.'

'But this—' Agnes took it back from her, holding it in the palm of her hand.

'I needed a paperweight. It was shut away in the old pantry, for some reason, and the Sister in charge said I could have it.'

'Could I...' Agnes glanced down at the crystal. It seemed to condense the sunlight into a single bright ray that cut across her wrist.

'Could I borrow it?'

'Of course. Keep it, if you like. I can always use my nephew's ashtray, heaven knows why he thought I'd need it. As if they'd let me smoke in here. Mind you, it must be getting on for sixty years since I last had a puff on a cigarette, and I still miss it.'

The mass had finished when Agnes crept into Julius's church later that morning. She sat at the back, aware of him to-ing and fro-ing as he extinguished the candles and cleared away the incense.

She held the crystal in her lap.

She heard his footsteps approach. 'You've managed to escape, then?'

'For ever. They're giving me my flat back.'

Julius raised an eyebrow. 'How did you manage that?'

'Athena prayed for it, it turned out.'

Julius exhaled, sharply. 'The workings of the Lord are truly a mystery. I must get her on to some of the trickier problems of my parishioners. And what's that you've got there?'

'This is it, Julius. This is the crystal that everyone was after, that Malcolm was prepared to kill for.'

He sat down next to her and she handed it to him. He held it out in front of his face. The space around it seemed to grow dark and the crystal glowed with light, as if it was drawing all the sunlight into itself. For a long moment, Julius stared into it. A hush settled on the church.

He sighed, and shook his head.

'Nothing?'

'Didn't see a thing,' he said. He handed it back to her.

'No,' she said. 'I tried earlier on. Nothing.'

'I mean, it could have showed me who they're going to choose as the Bishop here, the appointment's next month and it would help me a lot to know in advance.'

'I know,' Agnes said. 'I wanted to know whether the euro will weaken any more against the pound, it will help me decide what rent Athena should charge to the new tenants in Provence.'

Julius stood up, and took her arm. They walked up the central aisle of the church, towards the sunlit doors. 'Perhaps we're asking the wrong questions,' he said. 'Maybe we're too worldly. Perhaps if we were more spiritual it would grant us its wisdom.'

'It's supposed to show paternity,' Agnes said. 'That's what caused all the trouble.'

'Oh, well...' Julius shook his head. 'No good me looking

then. Unless it's really going to surprise me.' He glanced at her. 'Are you going to keep it?'

'No,' Agnes said. 'I've been seeing too many ghosts lately, I don't want to see any more. I know what I've got to do with it.' They came out into the sunshine of the churchyard. Daffodils were visible between the gravestones, and even the patchy grass looked lush and green.

'What ho!' came a voice.

'Jonathan,' Agnes said.

'I got your message.' He ambled through the churchyard towards them. 'You said you had something to give me.'

'Julius, this is Jonathan Harris. Jonathan, this is Father Julius.'

Jonathan took Julius's hand and made a little bow of greeting.

Agnes held out the crystal to him. It shone with milky white light.

He stared at it. He took it from her hand and lifted it up to see the symbols at its base. He weighed it in his fingers, then held it up close to gaze into it.

'Where...?' He was too breathless to speak.

'Let's just say, it's found its owner now.'

'You mean—' he met her eyes. 'You mean, I can have it?'

'Yes,' Agnes said. 'It's yours.'

He held it in both hands and stared into it.

'We didn't see anything,' Julius said. 'When we tried.'

Jonathan looked up at him, unsure if he was being teased. Then he smiled. 'It's a very subtle magic,' he said. 'It's probably not the sort of thing you need.' He nodded goodbye towards Agnes. 'I said I'd meet Shirley for lunch,' he said. 'Here—' he fished in his pocket and drew out a business card.

'—She insisted we print these. It's the new shop address. Do pop in when you're passing.'

He put the crystal into his jacket pocket. They watched him walk down the path, lopsided with the weight at his side. As he reached the pavement, a black dog appeared, mongrelly and square-jawed. Jonathan bent and patted it, then set off round the corner. The dog followed, trotting behind him.

'Magic,' Julius said. 'Perhaps he's right, that we don't need it.' He looked at his watch. 'I should get back inside,' he said. 'I've got the midday mass to prepare.'

'I'll come with you,' Agnes said.

She sat in the cool shadows of the church. She thought about Jonathan's magic, and Malcolm's God. She thought about Philip's Godless universe and Serena's prayed-for baby. In her mind she saw Marina, lost without her certainties; and Alice, abandoned by her God to drift through time. And Tina, worst of all, destroyed by Jared's lack of faith.

She heard Julius recite the eucharistic prayer. Around her people stood up to go forward to the altar to take communion. She joined the straggly line, aware of flickering candles, of incense smoke cut through with the sun's rays; of the chalice raised heavenwards.

The body and the blood, she thought. And there's Jonathan saying that we don't need magic.

Afterwards Julius stood by the church door, shaking hands, wishing his parishioners a good Sunday. Agnes waited with him.

'Lunch?' he said, when everyone had gone.

'That would be lovely,' she said.

'It'll be Easter soon.' His tone was conversational, as he locked the church door and offered her his arm.

'More magic,' she said, as they began to walk along the path towards the main road.

'Magic?'

'The Son of God—' she began.

'Oh, no,' he said. 'Not magic. People who believe in magic,' Julius said, 'they're expecting answers. Poor old Malcolm, for example – his so-called God was just a wizard doing tricks in the end.'

'Whereas us—' Agnes looked up at him as he opened the gate out to the street.

'We're different,' he said. 'We know there are no answers. We're ahead of the game. Tell you what,' he said, as they went out into the traffic's noise, 'I know it's Lent but I really fancy a Sunday roast at that pub on the embankment. Yorkshire pud and all the trimmings. What do you say?'

They rounded the corner towards the river, which sparkled in the sunlight. The beeping of the traffic lights was loud as they crossed the road.